Eagles of the Damned

By David Black

Published on Amazon by David Black Books 2012

Published in Paperback by CreateSpace 2012

ISBN-13: 978-1477500156

ISBN-10: 1477500154

Cover design: David Black Books

Although based on historical fact, this book is a work of fiction. Names, characters and incidents are either the product of the author's imagination or are used fictitiously. Any resemblance to actual persons living or dead or actual events are entirely coincidental.

Dedication:

'To dear little Ellie; but never forgetting Tracy and Malcolm

who have been quite wonderful in challenging times.'

******

With sincere and grateful thanks to Trevor Hall

for a job well done during his excellent work at

the critical proofreading stage of production.

Other great books by David Black:

The Great Satan

Playing for England

Siege of Faith

For more information see:

http://www.david-black.co.uk

Organisation of the Roman Legion –AD 9

Each Roman *Legion* was a self-contained battle group, with its own components of heavy infantry, cavalry and stone throwing and bolt firing artillery. Numbering five and a half thousand men, the Legions' highly organised ranks also included organic units of engineers, signallers, medical personnel and clerks.

At the core of the legion was the basic infantry unit - the *century*. It comprised eighty legionaries broken down into ten eight-man sections. Each century was led by a battle hardened and highly experienced *Centurion*, with an *Optio* serving as his second in command. Centurions were handpicked for their courage and willingness to die, fighting beside the men under their command.

The Centurion's legionaries signed on for twenty five years of military service. Only Roman citizens were permitted to serve within the Legion's ranks in 9AD. If they survived their term a small army pension awaited, granted by the Senate.

At full strength, six centuries made up a *cohort,* and ten cohorts made up the legion. The first cohort was double sized. Under the command of the Legion's chief Centurion, the first cohort was charged with the protection of the legion's precious *Eagle* in battle and at all other times.

Each legion had a strong cavalry component of four squadrons totalling one hundred and twenty men. The cavalry squadrons' horsemen often served in smaller groups as scouts and messengers, but their main task was to provide a highly mobile screen to protect the exposed flanks of their infantry comrades during both transit and battle. The squadrons were led by Decurions, who in turn were under the overall command of the Legion's senior cavalry Decurion, equivalent to that of *Cavalry Prefect.* Many but not all squadrons were formed from locally recruited auxiliaries, drawn from the conquered provinces, as were many of the Legion's attached light infantry cohorts.

A Legion was commanded by a Legate drawn from the Roman aristocracy. After serving for at least five years, some Legates looked towards a new political career in the Senate of Rome, having built a sound reputation during service with the Imperial army.

The Legate's second in command was the *Camp Prefect.* He was a long serving veteran; a true professional soldier who had served previously as 1st cohort Centurion.

Among the headquarters element of each Legion were numerous administration and staff officers, including *quartermasters, engineers* and *tribunes*. Tribunes were young men drawn from rich or noble families. They would serve in the army for a relatively short time to gain valuable administrative experience before returning to civilian life, and a more prosperous and peaceful future.

FORWARD

Rome's Legions appeared invincible. For hundreds of years in distant lands across countless battlefields, the fighting Legions won victory after victory, often against seemingly overwhelming odds. The armies of Rome conquered as they marched, gradually carving out a huge Empire. Few in the known world could stand against the superbly trained and equipped soldiers of the Legions. They were rightly feared and respected by any who dared stand against them.

*****

During one dark chapter however, the aura of Roman supremacy was shattered forever when three of its most powerful and experienced Legions, totalling over twenty thousand men were systematically and ruthlessly annihilated during seventy-two hours of unimaginable terror and unrelenting butchery. They were mercilessly slaughtered within a vast tract of dark and foreboding forest called the Teutoburg Wald on the northern rim of the Empire. Little could they have imagined that their fate had been irrevocably sealed by their own Roman system of provincial governance, and one man's overwhelming thirst for vengeance, and his ruthless craving for his people's freedom from the heartless tyranny of Imperial Rome.

When the massacre was over, the silent Teutoburg in Germania Inferior became a sombre graveyard filled with scattered bones. In the long months that followed, as thousands of legionaries' remains bleached and weathered on lonely paths deep in the forest, the lost Legions became an enduring symbol of Roman arrogance, overconfidence and critically misplaced trust.

This is their story....

Chapter 1

Part One

8 BC – Germania

Freezing winds blew from the east, tightening winter's icy grip on the shattered Cherusci settlement. Flurries of snow carried on howling winds spiralled and swirled through the charred frameworks and drifted slowly across the lonely heath which surrounded them. Icicles hung from jagged timbers; a mantle of shining ice glistened on the blackened remains.

Paraded in a square around the remains of the settlement, their warm breath turning instantly to clouds of steam, four cohorts of Roman infantry stood at attention. Protected within the vast hollow square by the 1st Cohort was the physical and spiritual heart of the 19th Legion. Their golden Eagle; touched by the Emperor's divine hand was proudly displayed before them by the standard bearer. It was the unique symbol of the Legion, representing the honour, courage and character of the 19th. The Eagle was adored and revered by the men who had sworn to protect it with their lives. Where the Imperial talisman went, the Legion followed.

Beneath leaded skies inside the ring of Roman steel, fresh snowflakes settled silently on the charred huts, fired when the settlement had been overrun seven weeks earlier. Not all were destroyed in the chaos and killing which ensued, but many had felt the burning kiss of the pillaging legionaries' torches as the Cherusci community was sacked.

Inside the settlement's blackened remains the helmets and cloaks of the General's mounted escort, arranged into a wide arc around their commander were also turning white under the fresh fall of snow. The menace of the spears gripped by the armoured horsemen was stark; their deadly threat clear in the hooded eyes of the prisoners who stood shivering before them.

Separated and shoved roughly to his knees by grinning auxiliaries, the defeated leader of the Cherusci people hung his head in resignation and despair. Scowling armoured soldiers flanked him; long cavalry swords gripped firmly in their hands.

Fighting against the bitter cold the chieftain tried desperately not to shiver. What little pride remained demanded that the Romans not think him afraid when the end came. Like his face, the animal skins he wore were soiled with grime and filth. His long hair hung lank and matted around his cold pinched face. He closed his eyes and mumbled a short prayer; begging forgiveness from the cruel Gods of the forest for his failure in battle against the Romans.

Vanquished by the invaders, the Cherusci king had lost everything; position, lands and his most treasured prize of all, the freedom of his people. Many of his bravest warriors were dead; their corpses already picked clean where they fell weeks earlier by hungry bears and wolves. Others were Roman prisoners, torn from the land of their ancestors, driven far away into a life of slavery.

Surrounded by the same freezing winds, his wife and children huddled miserably behind him, manacled in cold iron chains like their humbled chieftain.

Now it was time to pay for his failure. It was time for him to die.

It had taken two long and bloody years of brutal campaigning to bring the wild Cherusci tribe to heel. Roman casualties had been heavy during their guerrilla warfare of hit and run fighting. Each new encounter had been more savage and deadly than the last.

In the beginning when defiance burned bright, the chieftain's warriors had been successful. Once, tactics of mass attack and unexpected ambush had thrust them to the cusp of final victory. The ferocious Cherusci warriors had wrong footed the invading army as they marched through a narrow and heavily wooded defile in their thousands. Unprepared for the sudden onslaught the Romans couldn't manoeuvre into battle formation. There was panic in the tightly packed ranks and heavy casualties as the screaming Cherusci crashed into the Roman's extended line and cut them down. At the last moment, through brilliant leadership General Drusus managed to extricate his trapped army, but the Roman war machine had been badly mauled.

Fearing further catastrophe, the wily Roman General withdrew his men from the Cherusci homelands until reinforcements arrived.

Smarting from near disaster, Drusus planned his next move more carefully. Having chosen his killing ground well, the General returned and lured Segimer and his barbarian horde into a well bated trap. During the savage fighting that ensued Segimer their king was captured and the highly trained and disciplined Roman legionaries, now with the opportunity to deploy properly, annihilated his fighting elite. The tribe's rout in open battle had been final and decisive. Wounded Cherusci were executed where they lay on the blood-soaked battlefield. Captured warriors and their families became Roman spoils of war.

In the gruelling weeks that followed, the prisoners were taken by land and sea to the Imperial capital, where they were herded through the streets manacled in chains, to the delight of the cheering crowds of Rome.

All uncivilised tribes lacking a written language were regarded by Rome as barbarians. As a result of their lowly status, the captives were classified within Imperial circles not as human, but simply a valuable commodity like cattle; and absolute property of the State. Once humiliated by public display the prisoners were stripped of their last vestiges of dignity. They were sold off piecemeal to the highest bidder in the slave markets.

Profits to the Imperial treasury swelled as barbarian warriors and their wretched families were torn apart forever. A few of the strongest were bought by the feared Gladiator schools, where they would be trained to fight for the entertainment of the common people. Violent death awaited on the bloody sands of gladiatorial arenas scattered throughout the vast Roman Imperium.

When bidding was done and coin was paid, flesh was seared with hot iron to display the brand of their new owners. Those deemed unworthy of the schools were taken in chains to a life of exhaustion and thirst, toiling from dawn to dusk in the hot shimmering fields of the Roman countryside. Others were bought to replace unfortunates killed while labouring as beasts of burden, beneath the whips of heartless guards in the hell hole of the stone quarries. The unluckiest of all went to a soulless existence of claustrophobic backbreaking work, digging by flickering torchlight in the deepest bowels of the many mines which honeycombed Rome's seven hills.

Some of the young and more attractive Cherusci women were bought and marked by rich masters as playthings or body slaves. Older women were bought for a life of drudgery and menial servitude in large and noble houses. Others were even less fortunate. The women's path would take them to a life of servitude of another kind, in the disease ridden brothels which abounded every litter strewn street corner, often nestling beside rowdy taverns in the poorer quarters of Rome. The children were sold off piecemeal to those who wanted them...

Huddled against the freezing wind, commander of auxiliary cavalry Decurion Vitellius settled himself firmly in his saddle beside General Drusus. Staring down at the shackled prisoner with thinly veiled contempt, he reached inside his thick winter cloak, removing the sealed parchment scroll concealed beneath it.

The moaning of the wind eased slightly as Decurion Vitellius turned and nodded to one of his armoured troopers. Holding his oval shield tightly at his side, the auxiliary trooper tapped sandaled heals against his horses' flanks. The trooper broke ranks with his comrades and walked his horse forward until he was positioned between his General and the Decurion.

Recruited as an auxiliary from a neighbouring German tribe, whose king had seen the wisdom against war and thrown in his lot with Rome several years earlier, the mounted trooper acknowledged his role with a curt salute to his commanders. His tribe were sworn enemies of the Cherusci. He had lost many of his own kin to the never ending raids and blood feuding between the two warring tribes, and now, like the rest of the mounted escort he was savouring the bitterness of the Cherusci defeat and their abject and hopeless misery.

Vitellius handed the scroll to his General who broke the hard wax of the Imperial seal. He slowly began to unroll it. His cold face betrayed the arrogance of the victor. Why not General Drusus thought to himself? These filthy animals were not citizens but mere chattels of Rome, beaten and subjugated to the will of his Emperor and the Imperial Senate.

The Cavalry officer stared for a moment at his trooper then he said.

'You will translate the words of the General.'

The auxiliary nodded.

General Drusus flicked his eyes at the kneeling king before returning his gaze to the opened parchment. Raising his voice above the wind, he cleared his throat and began to read.

'On behalf of the Imperial Empire, hear now the illustrious words of our beloved Emperor Gaius Julius Caesar Augustus.'

Running his tongue over chapped lips he continued.

'We are always deeply saddened by the strife of war, and in particular the recent necessity of crushing the resistance of the Cherusci people. We want only peace within our Empire and desire to build strong bonds of friendship with the peoples of our northern lands. We wish to demonstrate the truth of it on this occasion by showing generosity and mercy to those of you who have foolishly raised your hand against us in the past.'

The General waited as the trooper translated then continued with the Emperor's message.

'We have decided that the Cherusci chieftain known as Segimer is to be spared the disgrace of public execution. We grant him his life and return to his homeland where we wish him to become a loyal and trusted friend of Rome... and continue as client king of his people.'

As the trooper translated, Segimer's head snapped up in surprise. He had awaited his end after languishing in a Roman jail for almost two moons. The last thing he expected when he was dragged from his stinking cell that morning was to be pardoned by the Emperor and returned to his people as their king.

The mounted escort muttered amongst themselves in incredulous disbelief. How could this be? They had all expected that the Cherusci rebel would be executed by their hands. A growing murmur of outrage and disgust rippled through the surrounding cavalrymen.

Decurion Vitellius scowled and stared them all to silence. The Roman General noted with pleasure the confusion on the Cherusci chieftain's face. He also saw the bitter disappointment on the faces of the translator and the Bructeri auxiliaries'. After a few moments he continued.

'Naturally, there are terms attached to this generous and merciful offer of treaty with the Emperor and Rome.'

Waiting again for the translator to finish, he continued.

'Firstly, you will give your sacred covenant that you will never again raise an army against Rome, on pain of immediate forfeiture of your life and lands and the enslavement of your entire tribe.'

As the wind moaned anew, blowing fresh swirls of snow around him Segimer listened intently to the trooper's translation. With a deep sigh of relief he locked eyes with Rome's most senior officer in the Northern provinces. His prayer had been answered. The Gods' favour had returned.

Still regarding his prisoner with a cold Imperial stare the General continued.

'Second... Suitable tithes at a rate set annually will be paid by your people to our tax collectors soon after your harvest has been gathered in, every year.'

His head bowed again, the Cherusci's leader nodded.

'Thirdly, men will be released from your tribe into the service of the Roman army as auxiliaries.'

With shoulders slumped there came another sigh followed by another reluctant nod.

'You will accept the occupation of your lands by the soldiers of Rome and obey the edicts of the appointed Governor of your province, and those officers and administrators under his command.'

The General began to roll the parchment scroll closed. There was one more clause to the agreement. Drusus knew that for the proud man kneeling before him it would be cruel; perhaps the harshest condition of all. He didn't need to read from the scroll any more, he had read the last clause in similar treaties before; he knew its words by heart.

Decurion Vitellius and the General's horses snorted suddenly as their ears pricked up. Both trampled the frozen ground nervously. Vitellius' skittish horse reared, startled by the mournful howl of a wolf, carried on the winds from the distant snow covered hills which circled the Cherusci settlement. Vitellius leaned forward and talking softly stroked his animal's neck, gradually calming it. As he straightened, he wondered for a moment if the superstitious barbarians would hear the lone wolf's cry as an omen of good fortune or future evil. No matter he thought to himself with a smirk, his men knew what to do if his General gave the signal. The barbarian king would accept the treaty, or die where he knelt.

Staring at the chained Cherusci before him, with a sly self-satisfied grin General Drusus delivered the final and most damning part of the agreement.

'These terms are of course offered subject to immediate agreement....But there is one more clause which is the final and most binding condition to seal this agreement between us.'

Segimer lowered his head once more. The treaty that Rome offered was harsh, but his life would be spared and his remaining people would survive if he agreed to honour it.

'Finally, to ensure you loyal co-operation in the future, your firstborn son will be taken as Imperial hostage, and sent immediately to Rome.'

Segimer's head snapped up once again, this time his face reflected a mixture of loathing and heartbreak. His woman suddenly cried out behind him as she wailed her pain and anguish.

Irritated by the interruption of the woman's hysterical cries Vitellius held up his hand to give warning, and still the boy's mother from further displays of grief.

Nodding his thanks to the cavalry officer, the General returned to explaining the detail of the final clause.

'While the boy is hostage, as long as you adhere to the terms of this treaty your son will be kept in safety and educated as if he were a true Roman nobleman.' With a slight condescending nod towards the shackled chieftain he added.

'And of course be treated with the respect his father's noble birth deserves.'

Segimer shuddered. He thought desperately. What could he do? If he refused to accept the terms, execution and no doubt the death of his entire family would be swift and final. He would not even live to see the breakup and enslavement of his people. If he accepted the conditions he would lose his beloved son. The heir to his throne would be taken away by the hated Roman conquerors.

Struggling to rise, Segimer shrugged off the rough hands of his guards. The General raised his hand to stay further restraint by his men. Segimer shook his hair back from his face and doing his best to restore some dignity squared himself before the mounted Romans. Segimer stared directly at the trooper sitting on his horse next to the commander of the Roman army. Being King was sometimes a terrible burden but only one course of action made any sense to him if the Cherusci people were to continue and survive. He had no alternative but to agree. With a contemptuous sneer he said.

'Translate my words carefully, Bructeri dog.'

The General and the Decurion glared at the trooper. Both knew the hatred which existed between the wild Germanic tribes. Neither man reacted to the insult.

In a voice which pierced the winds Segimer's words rang across the ruined settlement.

'I agree to your terms Roman, but not while I am on my knees... I speak for my people when I give you my word bond to obey this treaty between the Cherusci and the Emperor of Rome.'

He turned to the huddle of his family behind him and said softly 'Herman, come here to me, my son.'

A small nervous boy dressed from head to toe in warm skins reluctantly pulled himself from his mother's arms and walked obediently towards his father. He shivered; his face was pale and hot tears ran down his burning cheeks.

The boy's thin reed like voice pleaded and cut through Segimer like a knife.

'Please father, I don't want to go away, I want to stay here with you and Mama.'

Segimer shook his head. 'No Herman, as my son it is your duty to go with them. One day you will understand...you will return to our lands and be king... It is my command that you will serve your people.' Segimer knelt down beside his crying son and hugged him gently. He whispered. 'You will keep us all alive by going with these men.'

Before releasing him, Segimer fixed the boy with a kindly stare and still in a whisper he said. 'Go with your father's love my son, and never forget who you really are.

Remember too what I have taught you of our war against the Romans.'

There was something in his father's eyes that shook the weeping boy. The message was unclear but something was certainly hidden in his father's words. With the back of his sleeve Herman wiped away the tears as his father looked back at the two Roman officers.

General Drusus' patience was at an end. Agreement was reached; there was no point in further discussion. Coldly he growled.

'Enough of this!' Angrily he snapped his fingers. 'Bring the boy here.'

One of the auxiliaries grabbed the boy's shoulder and pushed him roughly away from his father towards the General. Unprepared and off balance, Herman slipped on the ice hidden beneath the powdered snow and with a startled cry fell heavily. For a moment the auxiliaries laughed loudly at the child's distress but stopped abruptly as Herman's pet wolfhound leapt forward, snarling and straining against its rope leash.

Until now it had laid un-noticed, part covered with snow, silently watching from inside a darkened doorway. It was tied firmly to the door's stout wooden frame. Suddenly alert, with fangs bared it desperately tried to wrench itself free and protect its young master. The beast struggled frantically against its leather collar, snarling and snapping as it tried to launch itself at the nearest dismounted cavalrymen.

Vitellius had seen enough. He had what he came for; the Treaty was sealed and the General and perhaps even the Emperor would be pleased with him. The Cherusci would stay on their lands and each year they would pay the high taxes demanded by Rome. Despite his thick cloak he was cold and wanted to start the long ride back to the Legion's base quickly. Angrily turning in his saddle he motioned to one of the mounted auxiliaries behind him, then pointed directly at the snarling dog.

With a savage grin, the auxiliary understood. He lent forward and withdrew his powerful bow. In a quick practiced movement he notched an iron barbed arrow. Drawing back the bowstring he took careful aim. Herman yelled a warning but it was futile. With a twang the arrow was released and in a heartbeat flew across the frozen courtyard, plunging through shaggy grey fur into the hound's heaving chest. With an agonised yelp the huge dog fell to the ground.

Seeing it fall, with a nod from his commander, one of the legionaries guarding Segimer swaggered with a spreading grin and the ringing laughter of the escort towards the wounded animal. Despite the pooling blood which ran from its mouth and the arrow embedded in its chest the dying hound bared blood-stained teeth and growled weakly at the approaching auxiliary. Almost with contempt the soldier returned the animal's snarl. Laughing, he drew back his muscular arm and drove his long cavalry blade into the dog's exposed throat.

The boy screamed. The dog was his oldest friend, and now these terrifying men who served the Romans had killed it.

On a signal from General Drusus, Decurion Vitellius walked his horse forward and leaning down snatched up the sobbing boy and dropped him over his horse's broad neck. Holding the boy firmly, he turned his head back towards the General.

With a nod of approval the General's face changed abruptly. He roared.

'Let that be a sound lesson Segimer, king of the Cherusci. Death is the only reward for defiance of Rome.'

Chapter 2

Rome – 4 years later

"The teacher must decide how to deal with his pupil. Some boys are lazy, unless forced to work; others do not like being controlled; some respond to fear but all respond to the discipline of my vine cane."

Quintilian, a teacher in the 1st Century AD.

Rome shimmered in the unrelenting heat of another hot and airless summer afternoon. Both citizens and branded slaves endured the burning sun, seeking temporary respite during their journey, beside the cool waters which hissed and sprayed from ornately carved fountains built on many of the city's broader streets. Linked to the great masonry aqueducts outside the city, to the eternal relief of the sweating population, the fountains brought rainbows of cool sparkling water cascading down from the distant snow-capped mountains and were rightly considered a blessing and an engineering marvel of the Roman world.

Despite the open windows the temperature inside the airless classroom was oppressive. Sitting behind his small wooden desk, one of the boys' thoughts began to wander again from the problem etched on the clay tablet in front of him. His dark eyes stole away to the bustling street below where merchants cried out beneath shaded stalls, extolling the virtues of their rapidly wilting produce. Groups of straining slaves passed by carrying heavy bundles across aching backs towards the grand houses of their masters, surrounded by the echoing rumble of iron shod cartwheels and the sharp clatter of horses' hooves.

Absently, the boy sighed. Dressed like the others in open sandals and short cotton tunic, he still carried inside a dreadful sense of loss and loneliness, which his teachers had failed to notice or beat out of him. His heavy heart still yearned to return to his homeland.

The true torment of being a hostage of Rome had quickly become apparent when he arrived at the school where he was to be educated. They immediately ripped everything from his young life when he arrived in the Empire's capital four years previously. His hair was shorn and his clothes had been stripped away and burnt before him on his first day. They had even forced him to bathe after he stood naked before the bonfire of his furs. His parents, his home and even his name had been stolen from him.

Since his first day in Rome, on the orders of his principal teacher he no longer cleaved to the name Herman, but instead he was addressed and allowed only to answer to the Roman name of Arminius.

The food, customs and rules of the bustling city were all equally foreign in the confusion of the months that followed. He had suffered the pain and humiliation of his teacher's punishment more times than he could remember, as he began to grope his way forward and learn the strange language of his new masters. He wasn't singled out; a classroom mistake by any unfortunate hostage of Rome was always punished with a painful beating. The young boys hailed from across the empire; among them were Nubians from Africa, Gaul's from the west and swarthy boys from the desert lands of Palestine and Syria. In the eyes of their teachers, such punishment deterred the lazy, toughened their charges and made them much more attentive and willing to learn. Reading and writing in Latin came hard at first, but as Arminius began to understand the words of his teachers, the beatings diminished just a little.

Arminius hated everything about his new life. He desperately wanted to go back to his people but knew that escape was unthinkable. The repercussions of running away had been repeatedly beaten into him. He understood that his family would be executed long before he somehow found his way back to his homeland. Shunning the offered friendship of the other boys, the anger and hatred he felt towards his captors smouldered inside him. Wisely for a boy of tender age he learned to hold his tongue and keep his loathing hidden.

Arminius had discovered quickly that open defiance led to the most severe of punishments. He had learned that to his cost when a teacher had him forced down on a bench, and held prostrate by two slaves. The teacher thrashed him mercilessly with a leather belt after he made the gross mistake of defiantly arguing when the teacher had casually cursed all barbarians during one lesson. Despite his lack of years, Arminius knew his only choice was to remember his father's advice, remember who he really was, and quietly bide his time.

He was torn from further bitter reflection by the sudden entrance of his school's principal Cepheus. The tall Greek ran his hand through his white hair then clapped his hands to get the boys' attention.

'Listen to me boys. I have an important announcement for you all.'

The room's young occupants sat straighter and all eyes turned towards him.

'A public holiday has been declared tomorrow in honour of the Emperor's birthday. As a result, school will be closed for the day.'

The boys' faces lit up at the thought of a day away from their repetitive lessons and the inevitable punishments. From dawn to dusk, seven days a week they laboured in the cramped classroom learning everything by rote, and any religious festival or special occasion was a welcome break from the same grey monotony.

'We have been invited by the House of Varus to join in the birthday celebrations. We shall watch the gladiatorial games being held tomorrow in the Emperor's honour.'

An excited murmur broke out in the stifling classroom. With chariot racing, the games were considered the highest and most exciting entertainment Rome had to offer. Gladiators locked in combat often fought to the death in the arena. A few had become household names and wagers were often placed in dark corners on the outcome of the biggest fights. Sometimes, specially trained gladiators were even pitted against wild beasts for the further entertainment and enthrallment of the people.

None of the boys had ever been allowed to view the spectacle of combat in the arena before and their shinning eyes and excitement at the prospect was clearly evident to the elderly Greek.

Cepheus raised his hand to quieten the excited murmur of his students. Smiling for once he said.

'The House of Varus is linked closely to that of the Emperor himself. As guests of the Empire and a further part of your education it has been decided that it is time for you to witness the greatest spectacle of all. Tomorrow, you will experience the arena, and the martial power of mighty Rome.'

Beneath gaudy fluttering banners, to the echoing fanfare of the great arena's trumpets Patrician Publius Quinctilius Varus stepped into the bright sunlight and entered the cushioned luxury of his private box. Grey haired and in his early sixties, dressed in a finely cut toga of pure white edged with the purple of the Senate of Rome, he waved benignly towards the cheering crowds who filled the stadium to capacity. As the roar of the throng began to subside, satisfied that the eager populace had seen him make his grand entrance, Senator Varus took his seat, surrounded by members of his high ranking family, privileged friends and honoured guests.

Sitting close to the Senator's box, but higher in the arena Cepheus lent across to his students and said above the surrounding clammer.

'That is Senator Varus. He served the Empire as a Legion commander in his younger years and has dedicated himself to public service ever since.' Knowingly he added. 'He is related to Emperor Augustus through marriage and has become one of the most powerful men in Rome. Soon, he is to leave Rome and become Governor of Syria.'

Impressed, Arminius and the other boys nodded eagerly. Cepheus continued.

'He has paid for these games from his own purse as a tribute to the Emperor and we are here at his specific invitation. Senator Varus is our school's greatest benefactor. Through his office in the Senate he is responsible for the lives of those of you who have been taken as hostages of Rome.'

Arminius' eyes narrowed as he whistled softly to himself. He stared at the white haired man sitting below him. Casting his gaze around the crowd he estimated there must be as many as ten thousand people in the audience. How could one man have enough gold to pay for so many, he wondered?

Further questions were stifled by another loud peal of the arena's trumpets, which heralded the Pompa; the grand opening parade of the Gladiators.

Released from their cells beneath the arena, led by their Lenistas' who owned, fed and paid for their training, flanked by whip carrying Lorarius who maintained discipline in the gladiator schools, two rows of powerfully muscled men began to emerge from one of the iron gates below. Some entered the arena bare chested, others wore half armour and carried metal rimmed wooden shields. Every man held a murderous looking weapon. A few were armed with wickedly curved Thracian swords; others carried the short Roman style gladius sword. Several wore greaves on one or both shins depending on their fighting style while two helmeted Retiarii marched in procession with nets cast over their broad shoulders, carrying long three pronged tridents tipped with lethal barbs. Many gladiators wore helmets of different design but a few paraded bare-headed, wearing only loin cloth and sandals. They were armed with long spears whose iron heads glinted menacingly in the bright sunshine.

To the roaring approval of the crowds, the gladiators marched in file, swaggering confidently around the arena. Many of these men were known and adored by the crowds but despite their prowess with the deadly weapons they carried, they were still slaves, whose lives were worthy only while they lived to entertain the cheering audience in the stands.

The crowd hushed as the marching column finished its parade and halted before the Senator's box. Turning towards him they raised up their weapons in a display of respect for the noble Patrician. When the Senator nodded his acceptance of their salute, with their weapons still held aloft, together they roared as one.

'We who are about to die salute you!'

A sudden and eerie silence descended on the arena for just a few seconds, and then the crowd erupted. A cacophony of whistling and stamping feet filled the arena as the people cheered the courage of the men below, and chanted the name of the Senator who had paid so generously for their coming entertainment.

Senator Varus stood beaming with pleasure and raised one hand slowly in grateful acknowledgement of their applause. Eager to continue, the roar and chanting of the crowd quickly subsided as they noticed the elderly Patrician had risen to his feet.

Delighted with the splendour and pomp of the opening ceremony, still grinning broadly he gave the order all had waited for.

'In the name of our beloved Emperor... Let the games begin!'

Senator Varus sipped thoughtfully from a chilled goblet of wine as he watched the two men standing in salute before him in the arena. It was the last event and the sand beneath their feet was stained with the blood of the fallen from bouts which had already been fought. They had been mere warm up fights, and he thought like many of the cheering crowd, had only added to the wonderful spectacle and rich atmosphere of the final event. Relaxed and happy that his money had been well spent and the day had thus far enthralled the crowds who filled the arena, Varus chatted amiably with those around him.

'This last bout promises to be the best fight of all.' He said knowingly. 'I have it on good authority that the net man has fought well in previous fights. One day it is said that the Gaul might well become a champion and perhaps even earn his Rudis.'

The Rudis was a wooden sword which was the ultimate prize dreamt of by every man who entered the deadly arena. The wooden sword was a ticket to freedom. It was presented only rarely to the very best gladiators who had entertained the crowds for years and fought well enough to be considered worthy of release from slavery, and the arena.

'But what of his opponent I ask?' One of the Senator's guests enquired. 'He looks a powerful beast that may well make your future champion's victory elusive.'

Varus was dismissive. Imperiously he waved away the idea and laughed.

'A last minute replacement I am told, hardly worthy of consideration.'

The merchant rose to the bait. 'I don't know so much, he looks suspiciously like he has known combat before.'

Senator Varus grinned slyly at his guest.

'Do I sense disagreement and perhaps even a small wager on your mind Lootus?'

The slave merchant smiled.

'Far be it for me to take the money of our much loved Patrician.' He shrugged with mock sadness as he added. 'But in my world coin is coin...wherever you find it?'

Those sitting around the two men on their silken cushions leaned forward and smiled to each other. This might prove an interesting sideshow to the main entertainment.

Senator Varus nodded. 'True...true, Lootus my friend. Would perhaps a hundred gold denariiy be too much for an impertinent trader in flesh, who thinks he knows more about the arena than me?'

Appalled by such a large amount, the merchant's face palled. He had expected at most to risk a small purse of silver. In an ill-considered moment having freely imbibed of the Senator's excellent wine during the morning he had trapped himself, surrounded as he was by his peers. He could not lose face in front of so many wealthy and highly placed members of Roman society who often bought slaves from him. To do so would certainly make him appear a fool in their eyes and certainly cost him valuable future trade by refusing the bet. He had no choice but to look as if it were a small thing.

Lootus shrugged and spoke dismissively, cementing the lie that it was a trivial matter. Suppressing a sudden hiccup he grandly declared.

'I gladly accept your wager Publius Quinctilius Varus. I place one hundred gold denariiy on the mystery man with the sword!'

Keeping his trident thrust forward, the Gaul swung his net above his head as he slowly circled, looking for the slightest sign of weakness in his opponent. When the gladiator's eyes strayed or betrayed the slightest sign of fear that would be the instant he would launch his first attack. But for now, he must continue to be patient, circle his enemy...and watch him closely.

A survivor of many savage bouts in the arena, he had spilt the blood of men to survive. It gave him no pleasure to slaughter strangers, who were also fighting for their lives, but the Gaul wanted to live and only one man would take the adoring applause of the crowd and walk from the arena to live another day.

The Gaul's practiced eye knew instantly the man circling him was no novice. He had faced untrained criminals and terrified slaves in the ring before as he climbed the rankings, but this was no wretched prisoner sentenced by a

Magistrate to die on the sand. Beneath his helmet, only the man's dark unwavering eyes were visible and they were locked with his. Worn cross belts of brown leather adorned the unknown gladiator's chest. His physique was heavy yet for a big man he moved almost gracefully. To the Gaul's growing consternation his powerfully built opponent held his curved Thracian sword balanced perfectly in his hand like a true professional.

Suddenly flinging his open net like a fisherman of the seas the Gaul pounced. With no sign of weakness, he decided at that moment surprise would be a useful weapon in his opening move. He followed the spinning net by lunging forward with his trident, but it was a bad mistake.

Lightly sidestepping the flying net, the gladiator parried away the prongs of the trident, to the delight of the cheering crowd and horror of Senator Varus. The unknown gladiator spun a full circle on one well balanced foot and slashed down at the overbalanced net man as he blundered past.

The razor sharp blade sliced unto the Gaul's shoulder but the speed of his momentum and his other armoured shoulder saved him from serious injury. The Gaul roared with pain and surprise as his opponent danced lightly away to access the bleeding wound.

In the Senator's box Lootus the slave merchant watched the match with glee. His voice was beginning to slur as he crowed triumphantly.

'I think I have backed the dark horse of the day Senator. I'm sure if you wish to call off the wager I will hold no ill feelings.'

For a moment Varus glared at the slave merchant then quickly returned his attention to the arena.

Below them, the two fighters had returned to the deadly ballet of cautiously circling. The Gaul winced as he flexed his injured shoulder. The pain was bearable but he knew he was losing blood. He had seen the effect on men he had toyed with before killing in the past. As their blood ran freely his wounded opponents had become weaker and slower, making them easier to finish when he judged the crowd and the moment to be ready. If he was to survive, he knew he must strike fast and end this quickly.

Above the Senator's box, Arminius and the other boys watched the men's movements intently. Obligatory military service loomed at the end of their education and swordplay was already part of their training. They had all suffered many a purple bruise while practicing against each other with heavy wooden swords. So far the boys had treated their combat lessons as little more than a painful game, but now they could clearly see blood running down the net man's back. The game of swords had suddenly lost its childhood status and became very real to them all.

Arminius enjoyed an advantage over some of his classmates. Several of the hostages came from foreign Royal Courts. Before being taken, they had enjoyed privileged backgrounds where slaves catered for their every whim, whereas even as a young boy, through the necessity of survival in the wild forests of his homeland, his father and closest kinsmen had taught him the basics of hunting and the use of both sword and dagger.

The Gaul Arminius judged to be nothing more than a mindless brute. Slow and clumsy, the man relied on his physical power whereas the other man....There was something oddly comforting and familiar about his lithe movements. With the crowds roaring and clapping around him, he shrugged off the feeling and went back to watching the fight.

In the heat and stink of the arena, the two men were now sweating freely. After several unsuccessful attacks by both combatants the Gaul knew he was in trouble. Try as he might, he could not get close enough to land a killing blow. As blood ran down his legs and dripped onto the sand behind him he was beginning to feel lightheaded. He had taken wounds before in combat and knew his opponent was waiting, as he had done, for the moment to close and kill him. In desperation he lunged forward. Feinting towards his opponent's groin with a sudden and powerful thrust he changed direction a moment before impact, thrusting up at the gladiator's throat. The trick almost worked but a split second before he plunged the razor sharp prongs into his opponent's neck, the gladiator pulled his head to one side. One of the prongs nicked the man's neck as it sliced through the leather strap securing the helmet under his chin. Momentarily blinded as the heavy helmet flew from his head, the gladiator couldn't see the Gaul closing on him. As both men crashed together, the Gaul landed a savage punch to the back of the gladiator's neck.

Stunned by the powerful impact of the illegal blow, the gladiator's sword flew from his hand as he dropped to his knees. With a triumphant roar the Gaul reached down, scooping up a handful of dry sand. In one fluid movement he hurled it in an explosion of dust and grit into the gladiator's eyes.

In a deafening mixture of cheering and catcalls, the crowd were on their feet. Not everyone had seen the rabbit punch. Most thought simply that the Gaul had got the upper hand, but some sharper eyed spectators loudly whistled their disapproval. There weren't many rules governing mortal combat bouts, but the Gaul had broken one of the most sacred which stated that gladiators must always fight to the death with honour.

Still raging, the Gaul kicked the blinded gladiator onto his back. As the sweating Gaul planted a sandaled foot on the Gladiator's chest, he held the prongs of his trident to his fallen opponent's throat. Turning his head away he looked up expectantly towards the ageing Patrician's box.

Senator Varus was on his feet, smiling and clapping delightedly at the outcome of the fight. To add to his pleasure, he had publically won his wager with the drunken flesh pedlar who was sitting sour faced and sullen close beside him.

Lootus silently fumed. The Gaul had won illegally but what was the point of complaining? No one else in the box seemed to have noticed how the Gaul had won his victory and a fuss would look like an attack of sour grapes and forever tarnish his all-important reputation as a bad loser in the eyes of the others.

In fact, all had seen the blow, but they were the Patrician's guests and had no desire to upset such a powerful ally, especially over the death of a common slave in the arena.

The crowd hushed expectantly for the coming moment of truth. Still standing, Senator Varus held his right arm horizontally towards the centre of the arena. His fist was clenched. If he raised his thumb, the fallen gladiator lived, but he thought there might be contention behind his back afterwards as to whether his Gaul had actually won fairly if he was merciful. No, he thought to himself, there could only be one satisfactory decision, which apart from Lootus would keep everyone happy. Staring haughtily to his left and right he slowly cast his gaze across the hushed and expectant crowd. Suddenly, his mind made up, he plunged his extended thumb down to show his decision. *Death!*

The crowd erupted once again as the Gaul rammed the trident into his opponent's neck, killing him instantly.

Amongst the cheering delighted crowd, apart from Lootus, only one other spectator looked on with anguish. Arminius had known the truth in a blinding instant when the gladiator's helmet had fallen from his head. Memories of happier times of sunlight and laughter had flashed back in that moment, when he first gazed upon his noble Uncle Attilus lying dazed and blinded on the arena floor.

It was well after midnight, the ravages of the previous day's heat were consigned to memory. It was much cooler now in the dormitory where the boys slept. Some snored softly in the darkness, others made odd sounds as they slumbered fitfully beneath their blankets. Sleep continued to elude Arminius; only he remained awake, breathing softly in his despair as he stared in silence at the plaster ceiling above. His troubled mind picked over the stark and hideous images of his uncle's last moments on the blood-stained sand of the arena floor.

Laying silently on his pallet other memories long since buried began to churn back into his mind. Arminius shut his eyes, rubbing his tired eyelids with gentle fingers to expunge the powerful images which kept forming so vividly before him. But all attempts to wipe away his memories failed. His crying mother's face flooded his mind, quickly replaced with the cruel expression of the teacher who most often beat him so cruelly. He saw his dog being butchered without reason and the face of the laughing legionary who held his bloody sword aloft over his beloved pet's body. But most of all, he pictured the grinning face of Senator Varus as he gave the signal to finish uncle Attilus.

Arminius struggled to find a single culprit for the gnawing misery and hatred that was consuming him. Was there an individual to blame, guilty of everything which made him so very angry and unhappy?

The answer he knew was certainly no.

For over four years the Romans had turned his existence into abject and almost unbearable misery, filled with pain, heartache and homesickness. The arena had been the defining moment which made everything suddenly converge into sharp focus in the young boy's troubled mind as he lay still on his bed in the dead of night. No individual or incident was the focal point of the overwhelming hatred which had suddenly ignited inside him. It burned white hot, fanned by the flawed concept of empire which surrounded him, a belief system devoid of humanity, a corrupt and decaedent society where life was held worthless. The blood of his ancestors seemed one moment to boil and rage inside him, and then as suddenly run cold as ice through his veins. A merciless desire fell upon him to strike out and avenge himself against his true enemy... Imperial Rome.

But how could he, just a boy make such a powerful Empire tremble and pay for their cruelty and arrogance? Arminius's mind churned as it sought answers.

In the stillness of the dormitory he found the strength to overcome his despair. Something came to him. He must take his time and think things through carefully. To survive the future and the ordeal of his childhood he must appear to become one of them. He suddenly remembered his father's face on that cold winter's morning, and something his father had said to him during their last moments together. Memories tickled at him as they faded in and out of his mind. Somewhere he thought, somehow there had to be a way.

Chapter 3

Months became years as Arminius continued his life as a prisoner of Rome. Time passed slowly, but he grew tall and strong as his adolescence slipped away.

Arminius had chosen to fight them in his own way; every day became another hidden victory as they failed to discover the secret flame of hatred which burned inside him. He became ever more adept at fooling Roman society and those who crossed the path of his life. Arminius began to feel nothing but contempt towards his captors. The fools believed him to be a shining example of Romanisation. He often smiled inside at his cunning, when held up as a paragon among his peers by Cepheus and the other teachers of his school.

The basics learnt, now they taught the senior boys' more complex subjects. Oratory, mathematics and philosophy filled their days in the schoolroom hidden in a drab suburb of Rome. He hungered for their knowledge; anything he could learn might one day become a powerful weapon when his chance for revenge came.

There was one light in his life which sometimes lifted the young man's spirits and set Arminius free. He had become a skilful horseman, learning the equestrian art under the able tutelage of a retired cavalry officer, who supplemented his army pension by teaching the boys in his school to ride.

Held in such high and esteemed regard, trusted Arminius had been granted the unusual privilege of riding alone outside Rome's high walls when not in lessons. His heart soared free like the birds above as he galloped across the open fields beyond the walls of the city. It was only temporary freedom, but every moment was precious to him. While he rode alone, unshackled from their strict discipline and petty rules he found something akin to happiness.

Gripping the reins with practiced hands and leaning forward on the horse's neck Arminius listened with pleasure to the snorting breath of his galloping horse, synchronised perfectly with the rhythmic pounding of its flying hooves. Dust swirled behind man and beast as they thundered along the deserted track which led down from the hill behind them. The sun had reached its zenith in the cloudless sky. It was time to return to the city. To be late for afternoon lessons would cause upset and might damage his untarnished reputation. Reluctantly he allowed his mount to slow. The drumbeat of the beast's hooves eased until the sweating horse had finally slowed its pace to a mere walk. He patted its neck affectionately, pleased with its energy and spirit.

Arminius's route back to the city led through vast fields of green vines, growing in neat rows that stretched off as far as he could see on both sides of the track. Tired slaves tended the vines, pruning and weeding their charges under the burning sun, and the ever watchful eyes of their whip carrying stewards.

Lost in his pleasure of the moment, Arminius came upon a large circular treadmill close to one side of the track. Inside the creaking wooden wheel which had been erected years before by the landowner, two slaves walked for hours in never-ending revolution to raise life-giving water for the vines. The contraption drew from an underground spring buried deep beneath the exhausted slaves who were locked inside the wheel. More slaves lifted clear water from the brimming troughs filled by the slowly turning waterwheel. They dipped their buckets, which hung from heavy wooden yokes chained across raw, sunburnt shoulders. Once both buckets were full they turned and trudged wearily up the slopes on their unending dawn to dusk duty of irrigating their master's precious grape bearing vines.

At last, still flanked by lines of nurtured green vines Arminius came to the end of the track, where it joined the cobbled Appian Way. The ancient road would lead him straight to the gates of Rome.

Ahead, a small crowd had gathered on the roadside beside a wooded olive grove. From the structures erected among the trees, Arminius realised instantly what he was approaching. He had seen the tall wooden crosses too many times before. This was a permanent place of death where condemned slaves and the worst dregs of the criminal underworld were publically executed. Deliberately situated beside the main highway, it was clearly visible to rich and poor, freemen and slaves alike. It was a warning of what awaited those who dared break strict Roman law, or defy the word of their Emperor.

They were long gone now of course, but Arminius remembered during one history lesson his teacher had told the class of six thousand escaped slaves, followers of Spartacus, the Capuan gladiator had lined the very same road he was now riding on. Each rebel had been crucified and left to die as punishment for joining the gladiator's slave revolt against their legal masters. The Legions eventually defeated Spartacus and his army of beaten and half-starved slaves. Revenge had been cruel and Roman mercy non-existent. Prospering in a society based on slavery, an example the Senate decided must be made. It was agreed in the Forum that surviving slaves guilty of rebellion had lost the right to live. As a black hearted warning against similar rebellion in the future they were left to rot where they hung along the Appian Way, which led to the very heart of the Roman Empire.

Arminius shuddered. He considered for a moment turning his mount and finding another way into the city. Time was against him however; he had no choice but to pass the grove, and the ghastly spectacle it contained.

Crucifixion was considered a most shameful and disgraceful way to die. All but the worst condemned Roman citizens were exempted from such execution. The manner and process of crucifixion was unspeakably brutal. The criminal, after sentence had been pronounced, carried their cross to this place of execution outside the city. Often, the condemned's backs were scourged to the bone by their guards as the prisoner dragged the heavy timber towards the place where they would die. The damned criminal was forced down and nailed through wrists and ankles to the wooden cross by soldiers specially trained as executioners. A medicated cup of vinegar mixed with gall and myrrh was sometimes given, for the purpose of deadening the pangs of the sufferer, providing sufficient coin was slipped to the guards by the condemned's grieving family.

As Arminius drew near he saw that two men and a woman had been recently crucified. One of the men was white haired and ancient, the other young. The woman was also young, perhaps even attractive once, but not anymore. Their clothes were rags, all three dirt streaked and filthy. They were still alive and moaned pitifully as they struggled through the agonising pain to take their next breath. Nailed to the cross, they suffered massive strain on their wrists, arms and shoulders which all too often resulted in the further agony of dislocation of the shoulder and elbow joints. The rib cage was constrained by their body's weight, which made it extremely difficult to exhale, and impossible to take a full breath. As life slowly ebbed away, the prisoners would continually try to draw themselves up by their feet to allow inflation of their lungs, while enduring terrible pain in both feet and legs. Soon, the pain would become unbearable and the condemned would be forced to trade breathing for pain. Sometimes it took days for the release of death to come. It was a terrible, slow and excruciating way to die.

Arminius slowed his horse and stopped beside a water trough. As his horse drank he looked across the narrow clearing. He called out to the Centurion in charge of the execution detail, who had his back turned and was talking casually to one of his men.

'What was their crime Centurion?'

The Centurion turned with a scowl on his face. Suspiciously eyeing the young man on the fine horse he snapped.

'Who wants to know?'

Arminius drew himself up in his saddle. Station in Roman society was everything, and he had learned that even a name could be used as a weapon.

'My name is Arminius. I am Prince and heir to the Cherusci throne; an Imperial hostage of Rome under the patronage of Senator Varus.'

Most of his Legion service had been spent marching across in the parched wastes of Syria and Judea. The Centurion had never heard of the Cherusci, but since he'd returned to Rome, he'd certainly heard the name of Senator Varus. Anyone under the powerful Senator's protection was worthy of respect. The Centurion's attitude towards the young man changed in a heartbeat. He nodded and came to attention.

'Ah, they're slaves Sir. Escaped slaves, that is. All owned by the House of Crastus. They were caught about twenty miles north of here, hiding in an old outhouse by these men a few days ago. One got away but these three were brought back this morning to their owner's villa... to face his judgement.'

Arminius nodded as he glanced at the rough looking group of men nearby. He noted the weapons and manacles each of them carried on their belts before returning his gaze to the Centurion.

'And?'

'Well Sir, their owner has been having trouble with escaped slaves recently. Being merciful and just giving them bread and water for a month, and a good flogging of course hasn't worked so he called us in and told us to make an example of all three of these scum...' The Centurion jerked his thumb towards the dying slaves and shrugged. 'Can't just have them cutting off their slave collars and skipping when they feel like it, can we Sir? They work...' A smile at his own slip drifted across the Centurion's face. 'Or rather they used to work in the vine fields behind us. That is, 'till they made the mistake of doing a runner.'

Arminius nodded. At least they had the option to try, he thought sadly. Arminius turned to the group of men who stared back at him.

'And who exactly are you?' He enquired.

One of the surely group, their leader stepped forward.

'We're slave catchers, professionals.' With a sharp warning glance from the Centurion he added reluctantly 'Sir.'

'And that's what you do is it? Spend your days hunting down runaways?'

The leader of the group nodded.

'Yes, that's exactly what we do.' He shrugged. 'There's nothing wrong with it. All perfectly legal and it pays well...' He glanced up at the woman hanging on the cross. She had screamed shrilly when the iron nails bit into her flesh as the soldiers nailed her up. Now she just rolled her head and moaned in her agony. With a sly grin and a wink he added.

'And there are plenty of perks for the taking... if you know what I mean sir?'

The other men leered and sniggered knowingly to each other.

Arminius nodded tight lipped. He didn't recognise any of the slaves, but he did feel both empathy and pity for them. There was nothing he could do for them but understood their suicidal hunger for freedom. In one sense he knew himself to be the lucky one. One day soon he would leave the confines of Rome to begin his officers' training. Eventually perhaps, even be allowed to return to his homeland. Staring one by one into the agonised faces of the prisoners, he understood why they had run. They would never see their home or loved ones again if they didn't try, doomed as they were forever to a life of misery and hopeless bondage.

Still disturbed and somehow deeply moved by the agonising fate of the slaves he had seen outside the city, Arminius handed the reins of his horse to the groom.

'I watered him once he'd cooled down, but he needs feeding. See to it, will you?'

The groom bowed slightly. Patting the horse's neck he said.

'Yes Sir, I'll see to it right away.'

Suddenly, there was a commotion outside and the school's clerk rushed into the stable sweating profusely.

'Ah, there you are Arminius.' Breathing heavily, he spoke with obvious relief. 'I thought this is where I'd find you.' Leaning against a support pillar for a moment to catch his breath, he gasped. 'I have a message for you from Cepheus. He sent me over to find you. We have received word from Senator Varus' office and Cepheus says you are to report to the school office immediately.'

Surprised by the urgency of the clerk's tone Arminius left the stable without another word and strode through the bustling cobbled street towards his nearby school.

Arminius rubbed his hands through his hair and did his best to wipe down his dusty tunic. Satisfied that he had done what he could, he knocked smartly on the principal's door. A familiar voice from inside called.

'Come in!'

Arminius grasped the latch and entered. Cepheus was sitting behind his desk, talking to a senior army officer. Resting on the desk next to a half empty cup of wine was the officer's helmet. It bore the plume of a Legate, the commander of an Imperial Legion.

Cepheus rose when he saw who it was.

'Ah, well done Arminius. You've made good time.' Looking towards his guest who wore a white cape marked with a broad purple stripe over his uniform, he said. 'I'd like to introduce you to Legate Quintus Gaius Ovarious, Commander of the 7th Claudia Legion.'

Arminius did his best to hide his surprise. Legate's held Senatorial rank in Roman society. He had never been introduced to anyone so senior or important.

Noticing the shock in the young man's eyes the Legate smiled. 'Ah, so you're Arminius. I've been hearing nothing but good about you from your Principal and others who know of you. I also hear since you arrived you've become a true friend of Rome.'

Arminius nodded. Without hesitation he lied. 'Yes...Of course Sir.'

Legate Ovarious beamed. 'That's excellent, excellent. I also believe you have become a damned fine horseman.'

Arminius quickly recovered himself. Truthfully this time he said.

'Yes Sir, I do love riding.'

The Legate nodded. 'Good...good. Now, I expect you are wondering why I have asked to meet you.'

His curiosity aroused, Arminius nodded politely.

'Well, we are currently recruiting replacement officers for my Legion. I don't usually get involved with such mundane matters, but my friend Senator Varus suggested I take a personal interest in you. Your Principal sends regular reports to the Senator's office and it appears your record here has been exemplary. You have consistently shown yourself to be loyal, hardworking and respectful. Most important of all young man, you have shown yourself willing to learn.' The Legate paused and sipped from his cup and then continued. 'As you may know, Senator Varus is keen for his charges to serve Rome through military service, so it has been decided you will join my 7th Claudia. You leave here tonight, and will begin your military training tomorrow.'

Arminius' mouth dropped open with genuine surprise.

'But I'm not a Roman citizen Sir, I can't...

The Legate held up his hand for silence. He reached under the richly decorated helmet lying on the desk and removed a scroll concealed beneath it. He smiled.

'We are nothing if not efficient Arminius. I have here a formal document bearing the Seal of the Senate which grants you citizenship with immediate effect.' His face softened as he shook his head and added. 'Now I can't have a mere citizen serving in my Legion as an officer...The document also confirms your elevation to the noble Equestrian Order. From now on you may own your own horse and wear a toga adorned with the Order's thin purple stripe, to publicly display your new enhanced status into Roman nobility.'

Legate Ovarious reached under his tunic and handed a gold signet ring to the astonished young man standing before him.

'Wear this with pride. It bears the mark of the Order...and confirms your position.'

The Legate advanced smiling and slapped Arminius on the back.

'On behalf of Rome and the Imperial Senate I offer you my sincere congratulations.'

As Arminius stared at his new ring, and tried to absorb the magnitude of the last few minutes the Legate turned away and looked out of the window. He stared down thoughtfully at the busy street below.

Suddenly he turned around.

'Tell me Arminius' he enquired. 'What do you know of Pannonia?'

To his relief, Arminius remembered his lessons.

'Err; it's a Roman province to the Northeast Sir. It's famous for its hunting dogs, forests and a strange drink called beer.'

The Legate slapped his thigh, threw back his head and roared with laughter. Because his guest laughed, Cepheus laughed too.

'Yes, that's it. It's an awful place by all accounts. Full of flies, marshes and mountains.'

Suddenly, the Legate's earlier warmth disappeared. His face turned grim.

'Rome received urgent dispatches from our Governor in Pannonia several days ago. He has declared a state of emergency out there and is facing full scale rebellion by a large part of its population. General Tiberius has been ordered by the Emperor to take the 7th Claudia and four other Legions to quell the revolt.' The Legate's face was grave. 'There's no question in my mind. It's going to be a long, tough, campaign. When you complete your military training at the officers' academy, you will immediately join my Legion in Pannonia, where you will serve as a junior officer in one of my auxiliary cavalry squadrons.'

Chapter 4

Loaded down with grain and medical supplies, the supply vessel's oars dipped rhythmically into the water, splashing softly as they propelled the wooden ship through the deep waters of the River Lippe. The skies were darkening. Cold damp swirls of mist hung silently above its rippling surface as the ship made headway into the growing gloom, against the river's gentle current. At the stern of the ship the steersman lent against the long wooden tiller, watching his Captain for the slightest indication of a course correction.

As the trader's civilian master peered into the mist beyond the prow, the Roman officer beside him asked.

'How much further up the river before we reach the supply depot at Anreppen, Captain Drusilla?'

Drusilla rubbed his chin, trying to decide if truth was the best option.

'It's difficult to say exactly.' He quickly added. 'What with this damned mist and all.' He didn't mention that he was sure he had missed the last way point that he usually used to judge the remaining distance to the Legion's main supply dump upstream, nestled on the banks of the Lippe.

The missing way point was a prominent hill on the right bank, but try as he might, the mist he thought had hidden it from his gaze. He wasn't overly worried however; he had made the same journey countless times during the past two years.

Keeping 25,000 men fed and supplied in the field was never an easy task for him and the other supply ship captain's. The logistics were incredible. The three Legions consumed grain, fodder and other supplies at an alarming rate of 40 tons per day and the Lippe was their key supply artery from distant Gaul. Every stockpiled grain of wheat and barley was carried overland by pack mule and cart from the main Anreppen depot on the Lippe, through a chain of smaller supply dumps to the soldiers of the Eagles, stationed deep inside the wild Germania interior. While the river remained free of ice from spring to autumn, it was the only route that worked efficiently, ensuring no interruption to the constant stream of vital supplies to the men on summer campaign.

Absently scratching a mosquito bite on the back of his neck the Captain said.

'We'll probably arrive just after dark. They always keep the torches burning on the riverbank outside the Depot to help guide us in, and I reckon we'll see them shortly.' He smiled reassuringly at the tall auxiliary cavalry officer standing beside him. 'Don't worry though Decurion,' he said. 'We'll be there soon enough.'

Excitement pounding in his chest, Arminius smiled. For him, it couldn't come soon enough.

'Raise Oars!'

The crewmen lifted their oars clear of the water on the command of their Captain. Swinging them vertically above their heads the sailors held them steady as the supply ship coasted the last few feet and bumped gently alongside the wooden jetty. Crewmen in the bow and stern threw mooring ropes into the hands of the waiting legionaries, who quickly secured them fast to anchor points on the jetty side. Laying down the oars inside the open rowing deck, the remaining crewmen set about their duties in preparation to begin unloading the numerous hemp bags of grain, medical supplies and other stores the ship was carrying.

Wearing the full uniform of a cavalry Decurion, with his personal belongings wrapped in a flax bag slung over his shoulder, Arminius was first to step heavily onto the wooden jetty when the narrow gangplank was lowered. In the early evening's darkness the wide landing stage was illuminated with burning torches which threw long shadows into the surrounding mist, which still hung silently above the dark rippled water. Somewhere in the darkness a bird screeched suddenly.

More torches lit the Anreppen depot's tall palisade walls beside the river's edge. Sentries patrolled behind the wall, their helmets and spearheads glinted in the flickering torchlight. At the end of the jetty, two wooden towers straddled the tall wall of vertical logs, and were also patrolled by alert sentries. They kept watch on the main jetty gate, which had been unbolted and swung open as the supply ship arrived. His hobnailed sandals clattering on the landing stage planks, Arminius hurried through the gates.

Inside the huge depot, it was a hive of activity. Lines of men dressed in local garb carried sacks across their shoulders, hefting their dusty burdens onto wooden carts and wicker panniers strapped to the backs of mules. Local drovers stood beside their teams of docile oxen, waiting for the order to hitch their animals to the next fully loaded wagon. When the signal to move came, they pulled the laden wagon clear of the loading point and joined the waiting supply convoy forming on the other side of the busy depot. Beside the open doors of the nearest grain store, Arminius watched as an ageing clerk wearing the uniform of the supply corps carefully marked off the procession of sacks on a clay tablet, as each one was carried from the stone building behind him.

Arminius walked past the line of waiting animals towards the main headquarters building. Two sentries drew their spears close to their chests and snapped to attention as he approached. Arminius stopped beside one of them.

'I have orders to report to Prefect Verillian.'

The legionary was used to officers in transit, intent on making their way to their new Legion stationed in the interior.

With a jerk of his head the guard replied crisply.

'Yes sir. You'll want the second door inside on the right. See the clerk if the Prefect isn't there and he'll sort you out.'

Arminius nodded and stepped inside. The corridor was empty. He counted off the second door and knocking lightly opened it and went in. Sitting behind a desk was a portly officer studying a manifest. Assuming he had found his man, Arminius saluted and said.

'Decurion Arminius reporting Sir. I have orders to report the General Varus' summer headquarters.'

The Camp Prefect looked up from his supply list, his brow furrowed. Staring up at the tall cavalry officer he mouthed Arminius' name slowly, as if trying to remember.

'You have your orders with you?'

Arminius nodded and reached beneath his tunic. He handed a scroll to the Prefect, who unrolled it and read.

'Ah yes, I remember now. You were due yesterday, why are you late?'

Arminius was ready for the question.

'Bad weather delayed my last connection Sir. There was a savage storm and the coastal ship I was travelling on put into port until it blew itself out.'

Satisfied with the answer, rolling up the scroll the Prefect sniffed absently. Sudden storms along the treacherous coast of Gaul were always delaying his tight schedules.

'Hmm, very well. You will join the next supply convoy leaving at dawn.' He handed the scroll back to Arminius. 'Go and get something to eat at the officer's mess and report at first light to the escort commander at the east gate.'

Arminius saluted again. With a curt 'Thank you Sir.' He turned and went in search of a hot meal.

'Sir, wake up. It's almost dawn.'

Arminius snapped into wakefulness. After serving for two years with the 7th Claudia Legion in Pannonia, he was well versed in the early morning routine of the Roman army.

The legionary who had woken him saluted and left the tent where Arminius had slept away the night. Sitting up on his wooden cot, Arminius stretched the tiredness from his body, threw off his blanket and shivering in the chill pre-dawn air stood up and reached for his armour.

The supply train was fully formed. Long rows of carts pulled by oxen and heavily laden and loudly braying mules lined up inside the compound beside the east gate. At their head, the cavalry section forming the escort was waiting for the final order to depart. Arminius was eager to find the mount he had arranged the previous evening and make his report to the escort's commander. A legionary was standing near the closed gate, holding the reins of two horses. Arminius walked up to the legionary and asked.

'I am Decurion Arminius. Is one of these my mount?'

The legionary snapped to attention and nodded. 'Yes Sir. I've brought them over for you on the order of the Decurion in charge of the depot's stables.'

Arminius nodded as the legionary handed him the reins of the horse he had chosen. As he began to walk the animal forward, he saw the escort commander talking to one of his men. The commander was a junior Decurion dressed in the tunic and chainmail armour of a German auxiliary.

Clearing his throat, Arminius spoke to him.

'My name is Decurion Arminius. I am ordered to join you and proceed to General Varus' new summer headquarters.'

The junior cavalry officer saluted Arminius and said.

'Yes sir, I was told to expect you... Have you served in Germania before Sir?' Although his Latin was passable, his heavy accent betrayed the young officer had been recruited from one of the local tribes in the pacified interior. His accent was strangely familiar.

Arminius allowed himself the luxury of a wry smile.

'You could say that. I was taken from my tribe as a child to Rome as an Imperial hostage.'

Arminius saw genuine surprise in the junior officer's eyes. But there was something else; there was a hint of suspicion too. As he climbed into his saddle Arminius added.

'I am Herman...Son of Segimer, chief of the Cherusci tribe.'

His mouth fell open as the junior officer stepped back in surprise. For a moment, wide eyed he was routed to the spot before his wits returned. Struggling to recover from his surprise he said.

'Herman, Son of Segimer? No. Surely not...Can it really be true?'

Arminius looked sternly down at the dumfounded auxiliary and nodded. To reinforce his heritage he slipped back to his native Cherusci dialect he remembered from long ago.

'Oh it's true all right...now tell me, who exactly are you?'

The auxiliary beamed. Pointing his thumb to his chest he said in the native tongue. 'Don't you recognise me Herman? I am Rolf, your blood cousin, son of Attilus... Don't you remember me?'

Arminius nodded. He mind flashed back. He did remember a small sickly boy called Rolf who had come to his father's hut to be nursed by his mother, who was well versed in the use of the medicines found among the wild flowers and herbs of the forest. His mind also flashed back to the fate of Rolf's father in the arena.

This was not the time thought Arminius. Brightly he said. 'Yes of course... I do remember you. Cousin Rolf.' He smiled as he stared at the powerfully built young man before him. 'But you were so small and weak then?'

Rolf laughed with genuine pleasure. 'Your mother cured me of my sickness and nursed me back to full health.' His eyes glazed for a moment. Suddenly were they filled with bitterness.

'I still remember that freezing morning when they took you cousin. After you had gone your father and mother told the Romans I was their younger son.' The smiles fell away as he added sadly. 'So they didn't take me away like my own parents and my brothers and sisters.' With a sigh he said sadly. 'You know, I have never seen or heard from any of them since.'

Arminius nodded sympathetically. He knew their fate only too well.

'Yes Rolf, I remember it clearly. It was a dark day and a terrible time for us all...'

Suddenly, a horn blew a long baritone note from high on the depot's defensive wall. It echoed across the interior then faded towards the slowly brightening horizon. Rolf straightened. The huge bolts rumbled as they were withdrawn by the guards, and the heavy east gates swung open.

'That is the signal I have been waiting for cousin. I must lead the supply column from the depot and begin our journey to the summer camp of General Varus. It is a long slow journey but we must go quickly...'

As Rolf turned and raised his arm to signal those behind them to prepare to move, Arminius nodded silently to himself. He felt a strange stirring inside. In the halls of his mighty ancestors the uncertain wheels of fate had inexorably been set in motion. He knew he had taken the first step in a journey of destiny, to which there would be no going back.

For the time being though, he knew it wise to keep his own council, but this chance meeting had been a good omen and a worthy beginning. Casting aside the false deities of Rome, he was sure the ancient spirits who dwelt in the dark forests and lurked in the deep rivers of Germania had heard him... within hours of setting foot on the rich soil of his homeland the Gods had bestowed their first blessing.

He stared at the back of Rolf's helmet and kicked his own mount forward. Already he thought he had been graced with their bounty. It could be the invaluable gift of his first real ally. Never far from his thoughts, the flame of vengeance flared hot as its fire surged through his beating breast. One day he thought to himself...one day he would avenge his people and the hated Romans would pay. He would drown them in a sea of their own blood....

CHAPTER 5

Rolf had been right in his assessment. The journey towards General Varus' distant headquarters and the summer campaigning encampment of the Legion's Eagles seemed to go on forever. Constrained to the pace of the slowest carts, the supply column ground on at walking pace towards its final destination. The forest's canopy blossomed in the distance under the warm spring sunshine.

The path of the primary supply route followed the River Lippe upstream for many miles before eventually turning north. The going was flat and easy; Roman engineers had cleared and levelled the route several years earlier. Where needed, sturdy wooden bridges had been constructed over the deep and treacherous watercourses which occasionally rushed and foamed across the supply convoy's path. The engineers' hard work ensured no natural obstacle further slowed the convoy's already sluggish progress towards their final destination.

The supply convoy arrived at the first fortified way station close to dark on the first day.

After the animals were fed and the wagons put safely under guard the men looked to their own comfort. Arminius and his cousin sat alone beside their small cooking fire. Lost in his own thoughts, Rolf absently poked the fire with a stick, sending sparks dancing into the night.

'Is there ever trouble with local tribes Rolf?' Arminius asked.

His cousin shrugged. 'There is always trouble with someone Herman. The Romans impose their laws on us all, but they can't be everywhere at once.'

Arminius nodded. 'I noticed that you put plenty of men out on guard tonight. I thought we were in pacified territory?'

His cousin stared at him and then smiled grimly.

'There are many families out there who are hungry. The Romans increase the taxes every year and our people can only grow so much.' He shrugged. 'When the tax gathers depart from a settlement after the harvest has been gathered in, there is sometimes not enough to last out the winter and the people starve. Fully laden supply columns like this make tempting targets when the wolf growls in their children's empty bellies.'

Arminius stared into the burning coals before him. The glow reflected in his dark eyes as he asked.

'But what of the feuds between the tribes Rolf? Do they still raid and fight each other like in the old days?'

Rolf sniffed. 'No, not so much since the Romans came. Our new masters have forbidden it. It does still happen sometimes of course, but the punishments outweigh the gain of booty.' He grinned. 'There is no love lost between us even now, old feuds still smoulder but it's mostly quiet.'

Arminius was probing. There were still several days ahead of them before they reached General Varus so he asked just one more question.

'If punishment is due to a tribe, exactly who meters it out, you or the Romans?'

Rolf laughed. 'Unless they wish to question our loyalty, the Romans punish where they will, in their own way. They like to divide and conquer but they don't usually push us too far. After all, as auxiliaries we provide the majority of their cavalry and light infantry.' His voice dropped to a whisper. Knowingly he said, 'The last thing they want is a mutiny within their own ranks.'

After breaking camp at dawn next day, Arminius rode at the usual walking pace at the head of the supply train beside his cousin. Only a few of his men followed behind as bodyguards and standard bearers. The rest were out providing a mounted screening force, while one patrol checked that the route ahead was clear, another acted as the column's rear-guard.

Somewhere high above the winding column, a skylark sang its welcome to the spring.

The blue sky was cloudless and the wind blew gently, barely enough to create a ripple on the open grassland which surrounded them. The flat plain ahead rolled on towards the horizon, but the land to their left was becoming more undulating and wooded by the mile.

Arminius noticed movement on the tree line, some three hundred yards away. It was a magnificent stag in the prime of its life that had wandered from the cover of the forest. It was intent on grazing peacefully at the lush grasses growing on the tree line's edge. Suddenly it raised its antlered head and sniffing the air caught their scent. It stood defiantly watching them. Suddenly it turned and bounded back into the dense cover of the trees. Arminius pointed at the disappearing animal.

'Fancy some fresh meat tonight?'

Rolf shook his head. 'No. We are forbidden to enter. That is the beginning of the Teutoburg Wald.'

Arminius sniffed. To him it was just another of many vast woodland tracts he remembered from his youngest days.

'So?'

'The headquarters of General Varus is perhaps only thirty miles across from it on the far side of the Wald, roughly in that direction.' His cousin raised his arm and pointed towards the heart of the immense forest. He continued. 'Our standing orders are to always go round, never through because, well, you understand the fighting doctrine of the Legions better than do I.'

Arminius nodded. After two solid years of waging war against the rebels in Pannonia, he knew exactly what Rolf was getting at. The Legions were practically invincible when they could deploy in the open in their large scale set piece formations. Fighting hand to hand in dense tightly packed formations they had defeated the wild charges of less disciplined enemies for centuries, even faced by seemingly overwhelming numbers. Open ground was the key, it allowed cavalry to deploy on the flanks and range freely across the battlefield. Even bolt and stone throwing artillery could be used if there was sufficient room to use them.

Rolf continued. His tone for once was almost sombre.

'I hunted in there for a wager once, against my better judgement. The Teutoburg Wald is dense and gloomy inside. It has a dank eerie atmosphere where the trees fold over the skies and keep much of it shaded in semi-darkness, even on the brightest of summer days. It is the realm of demons and the dark spirits of the dead.' The junior Decurion shuddered at the memory. 'There are countless ridges and gullies in there too. Break a leg in its depths and believe me cousin, you're finished. Many ponds of standing water seem to appear from nowhere as you ride through the forest and beside them are great areas of badly drained marshland. They can swallow a man and his horse without trace. You know soaking ground is a nightmare to travel across.'

Arminius held up his hand and laughed. 'Very well Rolf, you have convinced me. No meat tonight. Slower is safer.'

His cousin looked suddenly apologetic. 'Forgive me Herman. I fear no man, but I fear getting lost in there above all things. It is a place that reeks of evil, where the soul could be trapped forever.'

Arminius smiled his understanding. 'I suppose there must be hidden hunting tracks running through the Wald somewhere? The forest must be full of game and no doubt someone lives in there and uses them?'

Rolf nodded. 'Yes, I suppose there are, but they would be fools if they didn't guard such secret and precious routes like hidden gold.'

The two men rode on in silence for a while.

Arminius had something else to occupy his mind. Like Rolf, he was preoccupied with the dark expanse of the Wald. As he remembered his father's almost forgotten tales of war against the Romans, his mind was following a very different path as they rode together. Once again he thought the gods of the great forests were smiling on their newly returned Cherusci prince.

CHAPTER 6

The rest of the journey was dull and uneventful. The column had wound its way past several settlements along the route but with explicit orders to make no contact with their sour faced inhabitants, the auxiliaries and drovers ignored them. A few had approached, dishevelled and dirty to beg for food, but had been quickly turned away empty handed by Rolf's men. With the implicit threat of half drawn swords the hungry locals scampered back to the safety of their huts. They stood in their doorways scowling and cursing Rome and its lackeys as the supply train rumbled on and passed them by.

At last, days later, Arminius' horse breasted a final ridge. The huge encampment they sought finally came into view. It was always an impressive site, even to the most experienced of soldiers. In the broad valley below, laid out in their thousands, in a precise grid pattern were the tents of the three Legions. Each Legion had been designated its own area on the valley plain, but the layout was identical in all three encampments. Each cohort had the same section of ground allocated to it each time a campaign camp was built. The headquarters, hospital and even the latrines were also always uniformly placed in the same spot so the men could easily find anything they sought, even at night.

Surrounding each legion's encampment, a high palisade twice the height of a man had been constructed from locally felled trees of uniform girth and height. Outside the wall, a deep ditch had been excavated by the legionaries as another barrier, and beyond that the ground was liberally sown with a carpet of sharpened wooden stakes and metal caltrops. Each caltrop was a small iron obstacle only inches high. They were manufactured in their thousands within each Legion's forges. When sown by hand the caltrop was designed to always land with one of its sharp points facing upwards. Cheap to manufacture, the effect on horses' hooves, light sandals or the naked feet of anyone foolish enough to attack the defensive walls was agonising, especially if the attack came in the darkness of night.

Rolf had already been alerted to the close proximity of the encampment by one of his mounted patrols. Arminius turned to his cousin and said.

'I will report our family tie to the Romans. They see conspiracy everywhere and it would not be good if we were suspected of disloyalty.'

Rolf nodded. Germanic auxiliaries' were given a high degree of respect as fighting men and were generally trusted within the Empire, but it would be foolish to omit the family connection and raise the slightest hint or suspicion of treachery. Arminius grasped his cousin's forearm. Rolf returned the grip.

'I must report to the General's headquarters while you hand over the column and make your own report. When I have been assigned a position, I will seek you out.'

Arminius kicked his horses' flanks and cantered away from the supply train towards the gate of the nearest Legion. As he approached the temporary camp, a Centurion and an eight man guard of legionaries doubled from the foot of the tower beside the gate and stood in his path.

Hands on hips the Centurion waited as the mounted figure approached. Seeing the uniform and armour of a senior Decurion the Centurion ordered his men to attention and saluted.

'I'm looking for the headquarters of General Varus.' Arminius returned the salute and waited for directions.

The Centurion pointed towards an adjacent encampment.

'Yes Sir. You'll find it next to the 18th Legion's headquarters, over there Sir.'

Nodding his thanks Arminius turned his horse and cantered off towards the HQ. With his eyes still fixed on the disappearing back of the Decurion, the Centurion, to the amusement of his men spat onto the ground and muttered.

'Bloody auxiliaries!'

Remembering he had thought it might be some important Roman officer and called out the guard, the Centurion spun round. Angrily he snapped at them.

'Right you men. Stop that sniggering and get yourself back into the guardroom sharpish...quick now...before you feel my sandal studs up your arse.'

Arminius handed his reins to one of the grooms who waited outside the headquarters. The tented HQ complex was even bigger than the 18th's. Decked throughout with wooden slats to provide mud free walkways, it housed the sleeping quarters of the General, briefing rooms, offices and even a banqueting suite where the old General could wine and dine high ranking guests. Behind the banqueting section stood another tented structure, where sweating cooks prepared meals for the General, his small army of staff officers, clerks and when necessary, visiting dignitaries.

Used to the bustle of General Tiberius' campaign HQ in Pannonia, Arminius calmly reported to the Prefect who ran the day to day administration of General Varus' headquarters.

Jabbing his arm forward with his fingers extended, Arminius saluted in the prescribed manner.

'Senior Decurion Arminius reporting Sir, ordered to report from Legate Ovarious' 7th Claudia Legion, currently stationed in Pannonia serving under General Tiberius.'

Arminius handed the scroll which contained his movement orders and details to the Prefect. A clerk entered the Prefect's office carrying a bundle of clay tablets.

'I found those records you wanted Sir.'

The Prefect looked up from the transit orders he was studying. Irritated by the interruption he snapped.

'Not now Tribius, I'm busy and will deal with them in a moment.' Dismissing the clerk from further thought he went back to reviewing the scroll. When he finished reading he looked up at the tall Decurion still standing silently to attention before him.

'Your record is impressive Arminius. Legate Ovarious speaks highly of your quick wits and valour. Promoted to Senior Decurion after the siege of Andetrium I see?' Suddenly his eyes narrowed. 'Were you aware that the General personally requested your transfer?'

Arminius was startled by the news. 'No Sir, I wasn't aware..'

The Prefect waved Arminius to silence.

'Well, no matter.'

He turned his eyes to the Decurion's dirt streaked uniform.

'Well, it's getting late and you're certainly not going to meet the General in that condition.' He turned his attention to his personal clerk who was still awkwardly holding the bundle of tablets.

'Put those down and go and find somewhere for this officer to sleep... And while you are at it get his uniform cleaned and his armour polished.'

As the clerk carefully placed the tablets on an adjacent desk the Prefect turned back to Arminius.

'I want you here at dawn tomorrow. The General is a busy man but I'll try to get you an audience when I can. I know he is keen to talk to you.' He rested his hand on the scroll. 'I'll keep this; the general will want to review it.' With a flick of his hand he added. 'That is all for now Decurion. You are dismissed.'

Arminius saluted and left the office, closely followed by the Prefect's clerk.

Standing alone in his tent, Arminius washed himself in the bucket of warmed water. It had arrived shortly after Tribius had shown him to his bed space in the temporary accommodation plot beside the 18th Legion's officer's mess. Free of interruption, he considered his next move carefully. First, he decided not to mention his uncle's death in the arena to Rolf. As it had been Varus who had passed the death sentence, the last thing Arminius wanted was to ignite a fresh blood feud. It was too easy to imagine Rolf trying to settle what he would see as a debt of family honour by attacking the General with his sword. Arminius knew he needed Rolf and his tough squadron of German auxiliaries as allies. There was no question that their future assistance would be absolutely vital to the plan that was beginning to come together in his mind.

Secondly, he considered the unexpected circumstances of the General requesting his transfer from the 7th Claudia. His Legate had initially opposed the move, but he had been overruled. As he had never met Varus, what did the old man want, and why him? It was true that he had distinguished himself during the breaking of the siege of Andetrium but so had many other officers. It would certainly have reinforced his credentials and loyalty in the eyes of the Roman high command of course, but that was not enough to be called halfway across the Empire. What did a German officer of auxiliaries have to offer he wondered? There was only one answer. It had to be something to do with his heritage.

Drying himself, Arminius decided the only way to play Varus was to wait and see what the old man wanted with him, when his audience was granted next day.

CHAPTER 7

Arminius had expected a long wait when he presented himself to the Prefect next morning, before the sun broke on the horizon. To his surprise the Prefect had immediately ushered him into an anti-room and said.

'The General always rises before his men. He is currently at his breakfast and has ordered that you join him...wait here.'

With that, the Prefect turned and entered another flap within the small room's tented walls. Arminius heard muffled voices and the Prefect suddenly returned. Sternly he said.

'Enter as soon as I announce you. Salute but don't speak until spoken to and keep your answers short and to the point...do you understand?'

Arminius nodded.

The Prefect disappeared again through the hanging flap. Moments later he heard him say.

'Senior Decurion Arminius Sir; recently transferred to your command from the 7th Claudia Legion.'

Taking a deep breath, Arminius threw back the flap and marched in. He recognised Varus instantly. The General was lying comfortably on a cushioned couch, biting into a piece of bread he had taken from one of the bowls of food which lay on a low table before him. He looked older than Arminius remembered him. The room was furnished with silk wall hangings depicting scenes from Rome. The floor was covered with a rich gold carpet; around its edge was a broad purple strip. There was the faintest smell of incense hanging in the air. On a small table was a jumble of small oblong blocks with magical symbols painted one on each side.

Arminius halted smartly several feet from the food laden table and saluted. He remained at attention with his eyes fixed firmly above the General's head.

Varus put down the bread and swallowed the piece in his mouth. With a smile of welcome he said.

'Ah yes, Arminius, I am delighted to meet you at last. Please, sit down and relax, you don't need to worry, we are all friends here.' He turned his gaze away and said 'Isn't that right Dalious?'

The Prefect had remained at attention. In a clipped tone he replied.

'Yes Sir, quite correct Sir. All friends here.'

Varus nodded and smiled. 'That will be all, thank you Dalious.'

The Prefect saluted, turned smartly and left the room.

General Varus returned his gaze to his guest.

'Have you eaten?'

Arminius shook his head. 'No Sir.'

Varus swept his hand towards the food. 'Then sit down, relax and join me in breakfast Decurion. I have a busy schedule today so let's talk while we eat.' He stared down at the table. 'The bread is still hot and excellent. I recommend the garum. It is simply superb...my own stock you know from the waters off Alexandria.'

Arminius nodded, sat down awkwardly on the couch opposite the General and helped himself to one of the warm hulks of bread. Like most who served in the Legions, he had developed a great liking for garum. Eagerly he spread the pungent fish paste over his bread and bit into it. The General was right, it was delicious.

Arminius nodded his appreciation and said.

'Thank you Sir. I've never tasted better.'

General Varus grinned conspiratorially and laughed.

'Yes, don't let on but good garum is one of the perks of being in charge when on campaign.' Casting his hand towards the small side table Varus enquired. 'Tell me, have you seen those things before?'

Arminius nodded. 'Yes sir. They are runes, sometimes used by haruspex; the diviners of mystery and truths who can interpret the omens in the entrails of animals, and sometimes foretell the future.'

Renowned throughout the Empire for his superstition, the general beamed.

'Yes, and I have a most gifted haruspex who divines daily for me. He was here earlier when he cast the runes in my morning reading. He foretold me that the future seemed somewhat clouded but divined that great success awaits those with the courage to grasp it...Tell me Decurion, what say you of such things?'

Arminius shook his head slowly. He knew he must not cause offence to a man of the General's stature who believed. Cautiously he said. 'I have not been blessed with the gift of divining the future Sir, but I know such men talk to the shades of the dead and do other things we cannot. Their power is a gift from the Gods and only a fool would scorn them or ignore their predictions.'

Varus nodded, delighted to hear that his guest was so enlightened. 'Quite right young man, well said.'

Having removed some formality, and, he hoped put his subordinate at ease, the General's grin faded. 'Now then

Arminius, son of Segimer, clan chief of the Cherusci, let's get down to business.'

General Varus clasped his hands together and rested his chin on his fingertips.

'I expect you are wondering why you are here? Have you worked it out for yourself?'

Arminius thought for a moment, the truth couldn't hurt him. He said.

'Well Sir, you command three Legions. You have many capable officers serving under your command, the majority with far greater experience than I.'

Arminius paused for a second to gauge the General's reaction. He had played this game before, and played it well.

The General smiled and nodded. 'Go on.' He said.

Taking his cue Arminius continued. 'I believe it must have something to do with my family background General.'

Varus slapped his thigh with delight.

'Excellent! You are absolutely right, that is exactly why I want you to serve me here in Germania.' Helping himself to another piece of bread he enquired. 'Tell me, what do you know of our mission here Decurion?'

Arminius considered this question carefully. If he spoke the truth he knew it would destroy him. It was safer to speak the words of a loyal Roman citizen and officer of the

Imperial army. He judged this meeting critical to his future and must at least for now do what he had done for many years. He must continue living the lie.

Clearing his throat softly, he began his answer.

'We are here on the orders of the Emperor to project Roman laws and civilization Sir. As our Empire constantly expands we discover new peoples who can only benefit from our society. Many lands like Germania were wild and lacked any trace of peace before we came. They worshiped false Gods who demanded human sacrifice and wasted their time constantly warring against each other. As barbarians they didn't have written records, roads, or a unified culture. To move forward they needed the balancing hand of Rome to guide them toward a better future.'

With the practiced face of a true believer he added. 'Clearly Sir, our efforts have brought the greatest prize of all to Germania...the gift of a peaceful and enlightened civilisation.'

Varus jumped to his feet with delight.

'Well put young man. I couldn't have said it better. That is exactly why Rome's soldiers are here.'

Suppressing a smile of satisfaction Arminius nodded modestly. The Prefect had warned him to keep his answers short and to the point.

Arminius had to move carefully. He had deliberately employed the same flowery rhetoric spoken in both the Senate and public places by powerful men. Their fine words cynically concealed the reality of Rome's insatiable greed.

In his last years of school Arminius had studied many eloquent speeches made by those who secretly coveted riches above all things. Their oratory carefully concealed the truth; justifying with high ideals invasion and conquest to those who still waivered in the Senate; invariably resulting in ringing cheers within the Forum, but also outside in the squares and market places from the ordinary people of Rome.

'Your opinion does you credit Arminius.' General Varus poured two cups of warmed watered wine and passed one to his guest. Arminius nodded, took the cup and smiled.

Naturally, Arminius had also wisely ignored the plight of the hundreds of thousands Rome enslaved, tortured and put to death each year in the provinces, or the gold which flowed daily into the Imperial Treasury. Some of course found its way into the pockets of corrupt provincial governors and their crooked officials. Rome prospered and a few Romans grew rich by false accounting; the riches were looted from Rome's ordinary people. The money flowed from the punitive taxation in the pacified lands, which the fighting men of the Legions had mercilessly subjugated, at the point of their blood-stained swords.

On the parade square outside, Centurion's orders rang out, calling men from warm tents to inspection and drill in the cold morning air. Hobnailed sandals pounded the ground and armour and weapons clinked as hundreds of legionaries hurried to their positions, hefting shields and straightening helmets beneath a flurry of barked orders.

Ignoring the noise and distraction outside Varus resumed his seat and continued the interview.

'Although I command three Legion here as a military General, I am also De Facto Governor of Germania. Sometimes I must remove the armoured helmet of a soldier and wear the soft cap of a politician.' He smiled. 'Of course, this is not my first Governorship you understand; I have served Rome as Governor before in both Africa and more recently in Syria too.'

Arminius nodded in silence. When he was still at school, one of his classmates taken from Jerusalem had shown him a secret pamphlet smuggled out of Syria. It had declared Governor Varus had arrived in rich Syria a poor man, but had left poor Syria a rich man.

Arminius kept his council, but was nevertheless listening carefully to every word.

Varus stared over Arminius' head, as if searching for his next words. Finding them he continued.

'Naturally, I gained great experience during the years I ruled distant provinces, on behalf of the Emperor. Those experiences have taught me that the key issue to successful control in a province is undoubtedly maintaining Pax Romana....the peace of Rome.

Arminius nodded again as the General's face looked far away for a moment, as he remembered.

'While I was stationed in Syria, shortly after the client king Herod of Judaea died, there was a serious and prolonged uprising by the Jews. There had been much infighting within Herod's extended family as different factions fought for the vacant throne. This civil unrest spread and escalated until it became open defiance of Rome, led by rebels who saw their chance for what they foolishly believed to be freedom.'

The ageing General sadly shook his head at the memory. 'Of course, I put the Legions in straight away and crushed the revolt, but then I was criticised in Rome afterwards for my leniency towards the captured rebels. It is usual to execute the ringleaders and enslave the rest but at most, I crucified no more than a mere two thousand malcontents. What Rome didn't seem to understand was that

I was trying something new. I wanted to create a stable country under Pax Romana, not simply a host of new martyrs for future insurrection.'

Arminius said gravely. 'Yes Sir, I see.'

General Varus sipped from his cup absently pausing for a moment as he savoured the wine's aromatic flavour, then he continued.

'Although with the help of the Legions I reinstated peace in the province, I was left afterwards with the profound feeling that if I had someone on the inside as it were, I would have been better forewarned of the uprising in the first place. I'm 72 and a firm believer now you see, that more politics and less force can achieve the same conclusion, and of course at the same time avoid dangerous criticism at home.' Sadly, he shook his head. 'I had to endure too much of it last time from my enemies within the Senate.'

The General stood up. With hands clasped behind his back, he paced back and forth as he continued explaining his situation and plans for the future development of Germania.

'I was called out of retirement for this new office by the Emperor. Naturally I enjoy his absolute trust. I plan to put my past experience to good use, and am intent on running a more enlightened Governorship, where the future development of Germania is, wherever possible, driven by the carrot, rather than the stick.'

Arminius nodded politely. Clearly this old man didn't understand the first thing about the people he was governing.

'Now, this is where you come into the picture.' Varus stopped his pacing and folding his arms, stared intently at Arminius. 'The Emperor decreed that trade must be increased within the province and I am to speed up the process of its Romanisation. Sadly, progress to date has been lamentably slow; there is still a great divide between plans and reality. I have of course given the matter a great deal of thought and decided while my Legions were still in winter quarters, that to assist me in this complicated and difficult task I needed help. I contacted my office in Rome and asked them to search out suitable candidates. Only one name came back which was ideally suitable... It was yours Arminius. I contacted General Tiberius' headquarters in Pannonia and requested your transfer to my command here in Germania.'

The ageing General returned to his couch. A hint of tiredness showed as he sat down with a grateful sigh.

'I want you to establish a new network of market places throughout the province while you act as my eyes and ears among the tribes. Make contact with each you understand, explain my rationale, and by that, earn their trust. When you make your reports to me, your advice will be invaluable and with the flow of intelligence you bring, I shall have an incalculable advantage against any who may wish to disrupt the Romanisation process or revolt in future against the will of Rome.'

His voice suddenly became softer. 'Your loyalty to Rome is well known and beyond reproach Arminius; your background makes you simply the ideal choice for such an important position on my staff.' He smiled broadly. 'To assist you in your mission it is my order that you will take command of the auxiliary cavalry squadrons of the 18th Legion as their senior Decurion. Choose your own staff, make contact with the different tribes and create your own network of spies in the process.'

Arminius' face reflected the shock which set his heart racing and churned inside his breast. If he understood correctly, the old fool had just offered him more than he could possibly have wished. Once again destiny beckoned, and the Gods smiled on him. He must seal this astounding news with his greatest lie since arriving in his beloved homeland. Arminius leapt to his feet and grinning broadly saluted.

'It will be an honour General. I shall be proud to serve you...the Emperor and the people of Rome.'

CHAPTER 8

Part Two

'*Stand still* you pathetic little man.'

Centurion Rufus glared angrily at one of the legionaries who were paraded in front of him. The man's appearance reflected a disrespectful lack of attention to detail. The unfortunate soldier had hoped he might get away with rising slightly later than the others but nothing missed his veteran commander's steely eyes when all eighty of his comrades paraded for their Centurion's daily morning inspection.

'You are a disgrace to the 18th sunshine. Just look at you, you're a fucking mess!'

The legionary palled. He knew Centurion Rufus set high standards in the premier century of the second cohort, but after a heavy night of secret drinking and dice with his comrades his appearance wasn't even close to what was expected by the tough veteran.

'You are a nightmare, you festering little maggot! Look at you! Your sandal straps are loose, your shield has got mud on it and look here, one of your shoulder straps is undone.'

Centurion Rufus stepped forward and flicked the errant armour strap with his vine cane. Suddenly, he stopped dead, only inches from the legionary's face. He sniffed.

'Is that booze I can smell on your breath soldier?'

The colour drained completely from the man's face.

'No Sir.' He lied.

Centurion Rufus stepped back and bellowed '*Optio Praxus!*'

Rufus's second in command doubled forward from his position in the front rank. He slammed his heels together beside his commander in the regulation manner and at attention bellowed back. '*Sir?*'

With a glare that would have melted lead, the Centurion roared.

'Take this miserable excuse for a legionary away and double him around the outside perimeter in full fighting kit until he pukes up the booze inside him. Don't stop until you're sure he learns that no-one comes onto my parade stinking of booze. Is that clear?'

His Optio nodded, doing his best to suppress a grin.

'Perfectly clear Sir!' he replied in his clipped parade ground voice. Turning towards the quaking legionary he said.

'Right then you little worm. At the double Legionary Trenious, follow me!'

As the two men jogged away Centurion Rufus spun round and glared at Trenious' grinning comrades. He bellowed at all of them.

'Oh! Think it's funny do you? Right then, let's see if an hour's close formation drill will curb your sense of humour.'

A groan went up within the paraded ranks of the Century. One of the legionaries standing several rows back whispered to his mate from the corner of his mouth.

'He's not a morning person is he?'

His mate hissed back. 'Shut up you idiot! If he hears you he'll have us all running round the fucking perimeter.'

Rufus had sharp ears and heard the two men's whispered conversation, but chose to ignore it. He had firmly disciplined one sloppy soldier and made his point to the rest of his men. Anyway he thought, they were good lads mostly, and didn't deserve too much stick for one man's dereliction. Drawing a deep breath from beneath his plumed helmet he roared.

'The parade will turn to the right in file...wait for it...*Right Turn!*'

Arminius found Rolf supervising his men who were busily grooming their squadron's horses. Several auxiliaries were taking canvas buckets of oats to their mounts while others carried bundles of fodder. Another auxiliary was emptying a bucket filled with fresh water into a wooden trough.

Rolf saw his cousin walking towards him. He turned and saluted. In his native tongue he said.

'Good morning cous.... I mean Sir.'

Arminius nodded. 'Good morning Rolf. I need to talk to you. Leave someone in charge and come with me.'

Rolf called to one of his men, then wrapping his cloak around him to ward off the morning's chill, he fell into step beside his cousin as they walked together towards one of the encampments four main gates. Arminius deliberately kept the conversation in the Cherusci dialect.

'For now Rolf, while we are in front of the men, you will follow Roman procedure when addressing me. You will call me sir at all times. Is that clear?'

Rolf nodded. He looked a little wounded by the sudden formality. Discipline was different in the auxiliaries and relied more on native rank than the strict protocols followed in the infantry Cohorts of the Legion. Clan sub-chiefs were usually promoted, as the Roman commanders were eager to exploit the existing rank structure of their mounted mercenaries.

Arminius saw the hurt look on his cousin's face and smiled. He said gently.

'Don't worry cousin; it is purely for appearance sake. General Varus has given me command of all four mounted squadrons of the 18th and for now anyway, I want them to feel that I am still loyal, and one of them.'

Shock quickly followed by confusion spread over Rolf's face.

'I...I don't understand?'

'Don't worry, you will.'

They were close to the gate now. Rolf sensed conspiracy in the air, but he didn't understand why. As they came within earshot of the Roman guards Arminius dropped his voice to a horse whisper,

'I'll explain everything to you when we are clear of the compound.'

As senior officer, Arminius returned the salute of the legionaries as the two men left the compound.

Ahead of them, a river wound its way slowly through the valley. Its banks were covered in tall reeds which wafted slowly in the light morning breeze.

When they reached the bank, Arminius found a deserted spot by a tall willow where they wouldn't be overheard. Picking up a stone, he bounced it in his hand several times then suddenly hurled in into the middle of the river. It hit the surface with a loud plop and disappeared. Ripples spread from the point where the stone had struck.

Arminius pointed to the expanding ripples.

'You see how the stone has made shockwaves in the water Rolf?'

His cousin nodded. Staring at the ripples he answered. 'Yes, of course.'

Arminius looked at Rolf until their eyes were locked. There was something odd about the look, a dark intensity in his cousin's eyes which unsettled the young auxiliary.

Arminius knew he had reached a crucial crossroads in his long journey from Rome. It was time for the next step. If he was wrong in his assessment of Rolf, the road he must now tread would lead to swift and brutal death of his kinsman or execution at the hands of his hated masters. If he was right, it would lead perhaps to great victory and freedom in the future. He realised it was a huge gamble to say what he must. The stakes were high but he had no choice but to press on. Death hung in the air. If he had chosen badly, the wrong man was standing beside him by the river. For the first time in many long years of sorrow, he would have to throw the dice and risk everything.

Taking a deep breath, Arminius pointed again towards the widening ripples on the river's surface.

'I need to talk to you about something of the utmost gravity Rolf.'

Arminius let out a sigh. There was no hiding behind a wall of lies any more. Now, the moment of ultimate truth was upon him.

'I believe beneath that uniform you wear your heart is loyal to your people....I have a plan which will cause ripples to spread throughout the Roman Empire. It is a plan so bold and immense that if it works the Romans will be gone from our lands forever.'

Rolf stood rooted to the spot. His mouth fell open. He looked at the man standing before him dressed in the uniform of a senior Roman officer. He was dumfounded, rendered utterly speechless.

Seeing his shock, bitterly Arminius continued.

'As you know, I was torn from my family when I was still a small boy, taken to Rome and trained to be their pet.'

Rolf nodded, still unsure that this wasn't a dream he would snap out of at any moment.

'I have never forgotten who I really am. I am the noble born son of my father, a German Cherusci king.'

Rolf closed his mouth and nodded. The confusion was gone from his face. Now it was replaced with raw suspicion. Ignoring the look Arminius drove himself on, the floodgates were open and he mustn't stop now.

'Before I left Rome several years ago, I was given a scroll which made me a citizen of the Empire, a fully-fledged Roman....'

His face clouding with a lifetime of humiliation and suppressed rage, Arminius spat into the dark water as long repressed emotion gripped him. Through clenched teeth he snarled.

'Did they really think a piece of parchment could change my blood? Change forever who I *really* am?'

This time, Rolf slowly shook his head; he was beginning to recover from his initial shock and confusion; there wasn't a torrent of comprehension, more like the faintest trickle, but he was slowly beginning to feel his cousin's pain, and understand his words.

'My plan involves you Rolf. I need someone I can trust implicitly, someone who will obey me without question and never betray me to the Romans or their lackeys' among the tribes.'

Arminius gently laid his hand on his cousin's shoulder.

'You are absolutely vital to me and to my plan to free our people, and destroy the Romans!'

Rolf stared unblinking at his cousin. Falteringly he replied.

'We are of the blood Herman, bound together by family bonds far stronger than Roman iron. I ride for the Romans only because I have to... but my word on it cousin, I give them no homage. They are, and always will be the invader!'

With fists clenched Rolf blew out his cheeks in a sigh. He felt a surge of overwhelming relief, at last to be unburdened from the guilt of his servitude to those he hated. He said.

'If time could run backwards I would stand beside our fathers and fight the Roman to my last breath, and the very last drop of my blood.'

He stared with his own intensity now. Chest heaving, his own anger was bubbling to the surface and his blood was beginning to burn in his veins.

'Like you Cousin Herman, I am Cherusci. I would never give you up to the Romans.

A sudden wave of relief washed over Arminius. He knew now he had chosen well and had the ally he so desperately needed. He dropped his hand from Rolf's shoulder and asked.

'Then you will follow me even unto death, to rid our land of the invaders?'

Rolf continued to stare unblinking into his cousins eyes as the war drums of his ancestors beat in his ears, to the rhythm of his pounding heart.

'My word Herman, to the last moment of my life...I give you my bond.'

Nodding, Arminius turned and stared towards the vast sprawl of the three Legion's encampments.

'For now we must appear obedient and continue our duties as we gather allies to our cause. It will be months before I can ignite the tribes in total rebellion. For now we will work silently until all is ready.'

As he stared at the patrolling sentries on the distant watchtowers, Arminius drew his dagger. Opening one hand he sliced across his open palm. Rolf understood and did the same. As blood flowed they clasped bleeding hands together to forge the unbreakable blood bond. With eyes flashing pure hatred, in turn they both spat the words which sealed the future.

'Death to Rome!'

CHAPTER 9

Walking from the senior officer's briefing, Camp Prefect Macros scowled. A grizzled veteran who for many years before promotion to the Legate's deputy had faithfully served his Legion as Chief Centurion, spoke softly to the Tribune who walked beside him.

'I don't like this at all Paulo. We know virtually nothing about this man Arminius, but the General has seen fit to give him command of our cavalry?"

Tribune Paulo nodded. Like Macros, his face was clouded with concern.

'The man's credentials are certainly impeccable but even if he is a citizen and member of the Equestrian Order, he's still a barbarian at heart.'

The Prefect sighed. 'This is the trouble with having a politician as our general. He's just doesn't think like a soldier anymore.' Marcos growled. 'You know how it works in the Legion Paulo. Promotion in the fighting cohorts and squadrons comes after years of experience. Men must first distinguish themselves in battle. They must be seen by their peers to be truly worthy.'

Tribune Paulo smiled at his friend.

'What, like you?'

Prefect Marcos returned the salute of a century which marched past them. He turned his attention back to his companion.

'Yes, exactly like me. Look, I'm a professional soldier who has gone as far as anyone promoted from the ranks can go. I've been with the 18th for more years than I care to remember. This is my home Paulo, and the cohorts are my family. I just don't like the idea of a complete stranger, and a barbarian to boot who none of us know suddenly promoted into such a senior position. '

Tribune Paulo nodded and replied.

'I understand how you feel. I'm sure there are plenty of other officers who feel the same way.'

Both men walked in silence before the Tribune enquired.

'What do you think the Legate will do?'

Marcos shrugged. 'Nothing probably. This has come directly from the General. His hands are tied.'

The 18th's Camp Prefect stopped suddenly and looked around to make sure he wouldn't be overheard.

'Keep this to yourself Paulo but personally, I think Varus is way past his prime. He's far too old for this job, and relies on his soothsayer a bit too much for my liking. You can't run a province on the cast of a handful of runes, can you? The barbarians out there need a firm hand, not a soft velvet glove. They're still savages and aren't even close to being tamed.'

The Prefect snorted. 'If he thinks they're even remotely pacified, he's wrong. I wouldn't trust them as far as I could throw them... I don't know about you, but I rue the day Drusus died. He knew the score all right. An iron fist, that's the way he would have dealt with them.'

Shaking his head sadly he continued. 'To lose such a brilliant General to something as stupid as falling off his bloody horse, and then dying from the infection of a broken leg is tragic enough, but to get an old fool like Varus as his replacement bodes ill for the future, you mark my words.'

Tribune Paulo nodded. Matching his companion's whisper he said. 'I hate to agree with you my old friend, but for once... I think you're absolutely right.'

The mounted column entered the sprawling Cherusci settlement slowly. The horses snorted and their bridles jingled as they walked their mounts towards the clan chief's hut. Behind Arminius and his cousin, his escort squadron of thirty mounted troopers were all dressed in the chainmail armour and uniforms of Roman cavalry. Each man had been carefully chosen from the reorganised 18th Legion's cavalry after Arminius had taken command. Listening carefully to Rolf's advice, every one of them had been handpicked for their loyalty to their clan. Every man in the squadron was a paid Roman auxiliary, but more importantly, every man was Cherusci.

Arminius pulled back gently on his reins and raising his arm, signalled the column to stop. There was movement ahead. An old man threw aside the blanket which covered the door of his thatched hut. Walking with the aid of a long staff he limped towards the officers at the head of the column.

The old man's voice was bitter. There was no hint of welcome in it. In a croaking voice he demanded.

'What do you want Roman? We have paid our taxes and my people have little enough left to eat. What is it then, will you take hostages again to ensure we pay your taxes?'

Arminius remained silent as he climbed down from his saddle. Beside him, Rolf dismounted. The two men walked towards the old man and stood before him.

For once, the pain of his past was gone from Arminius. It was replaced with something else; an emotion he hadn't felt for many, many years. There was a sudden surge in his armoured chest, an overwhelming flood of pride, and then pure unadulterated joy.

Despite his years and failing eyesight the chieftain remained unflinching and defiant.

'Well, what is it you want with my people now Roman, is it more tribute?'

Segimer squinted at the faces of the tall young men before him. He stepped forward and recognised his nephew instantly, but he didn't recognise the other man. And why was Rolf grinning so, he wondered?

There was a long silence between them. Arminius stared at the old man and swallowed the lump which had suddenly come into his throat. Removing his helmet, he spoke softly.

'Don't you recognise me father?...I am Herman...your eldest son.'

The ailing chieftain stumbled backwards. Arminius grabbed his father's elbow and steadied him before he fell. Segimer's chest heaved and tears weld in his eyes with sudden shock. Disbelief changed to recognition in his tired bloodshot eyes.

Segimer muttered between shallow gasps.

'Herman? Is it really you?'

Arminius beamed. 'Yes father. Truly...It is me!'

To the delighted cheers of his escort Segimer dropped his staff and threw back his arms before enveloping his long lost son in a bear hug.

There were tears now from both of them. His voice lost its frailty for a moment as Arminius's father roared.

'By the Gods Herman. *It is you!*'

Despite his initial protests, Arminius secretly welcomed the banquet his father ordered that night to celebrate the return of his son. The hunters sent into the forest returned triumphantly before dark. Their success was before them. A huge wild boar and two deer turned slowly on spits as they roasted slowly above smoking beds of glowing embers, which spat and sizzled as globules of fat dripped from the carcasses and splashed into the burning charcoal below.

Arminius and his men had gladly shed their uniforms and weapons. All were now dressed in the same linen trousers and smocks as the villagers who surrounded them and noisily shared their celebration. Arminius had chosen carefully. The troopers of his personal escort hailed from the settlement, or shared kin who lived there. All were trusted and welcomed.

Sitting at the high table, Segimer guzzled down another horn of mead. He belched loudly and smacked his lips with pure pleasure. Rivulets of honey coloured liquid dripped from his beard as he called for another horn from one of the boys who waited on his table. Beside him, reflected in the light of the cooking fires and burning torches which ringed the clearing Arminius watched the faces of his people. They seemed genuinely happy with his return. Word had spread like wildfire, and Cherusci families had drifted in from the surrounding settlements during the afternoon, as Arminius told his father of his childhood in Rome.

Many of the men were getting louder and louder as they talked and laughed with their friends in the flickering light. It was a sure sign that the potent mead was doing its work.

Arminius sipped from his own vessel. The mead was sweet and delicious. He turned to his father and said.

'If things are so bad father, I know the animals came from the forest, but where did you get so much to drink?'

Segimer turned to his son and tapped the side of his nose with his finger. His voice slurred as he answered.

'We have to play a dangerous game Herman. The Roman bastards always get what they demand, but they don't know our secret hiding places. They would see us starve, they couldn't care less.' He slammed his fist onto the wooden table. 'But I won't see my people suffer through the winter to feed those pigs.'

Taking a great gulp from his brimming horn Segimer grinned drunkenly.

'We have a few secret stores of grain and barrels of mead hidden throughout our land.' He shrugged. 'If they find one stash they think themselves clever, but they are stupid bastards because they will never find them all!'

The ageing chieftain hiccupped happily as the first platters of steaming meat were brought from the cooking fires and placed before him. He waved imperiously across the table.

'Ah! Now enough talk of sad times. Eat and drink your fill tonight Herman. Remember the joy you have brought to this old man's heart, and how your people celebrate the miracle of your return.'

Arminius smiled. Now was not the time to plan and plot. He would seek his father's wise council on war in the morning. Tonight, he could be his true self and drop the facade of lies and deception. Surrounded by laughter and his people's happiness he would give himself up to the celebration, and be who he truly was.

He surrendered gracefully to his father's wishes and gave himself over to the new and wonderful experience of being surrounded with family, true friends and allies. As he drained his horn and demanded another, he smiled to himself.

At last he thought, he had made it home. For once, he basked luxuriantly in the warmth of true happiness.

CHAPTER 10

Arminius stood before his General and a panel of senior officers. He had been gone for five days, and now he had returned safely to the Legions it was time to make his first report. There was an air of cold formality in the room which put him on his guard. He knew of the resentment and mistrust among the men sitting before him. He chose his words carefully.

'I rode into the homelands of my own tribe first General. I had to begin making contact somewhere, and I thought it best to inform my own people of my return, and earn their trust.'

General Varus rubbed his chin and nodded.

'Yes, that makes sense. What happened?'

Arminius smiled.

'My father Segimer was suspicious at first after he got over the shock of seeing me, but when I explained your plan to increase trade, after a lot of talking I managed to convince him. He did take some persuading but eventually my father saw the wisdom of it. Once he had warmed to the idea of improving the life of the Cherusci through trade he gave his agreement and said he would call a council of the tribal elders. He promised me he would personally see to it that the Cherusci people welcomed our merchants into his settlements. I suggested that as his forests abound with game, he might begin by bartering fresh meat and furs.' Arminius smiled. 'I know that meat would be welcomed by our men, and pelts are prized among the merchants who have joined us here.'

The old General beamed with pleasure.

'Well done Arminius. That is exactly what I wanted to hear. You appear to have made an excellent beginning.'

Arminius bowed his head in recognition of the praise he had received.

'What else did he agree to?' enquired Varus.

'My father has also given his permission for us to start building a road through Cherusci territory. This will facilitate us easy access and make trade easier.'

The Legate of the 17th Legion interrupted.

'And make it easier to move troops in there quickly if they are needed.'

Arminius nodded. 'Yes Sir, of course, but I didn't labour that point.'

Most of the commanders and staff officers smiled. Only one remained stony faced.

The officer sitting furthest from General Varus enquired.

'Permit me General; I have a question if I may?'

Varus nodded. 'Of course Prefect, feel free to ask your question.'

Marcos turned his head and stared coldly at Arminius.

'My Legate is away on leave at the moment but he'll want to know why you have reorganised the 18th's cavalry in such a manner to surround yourself only with members of your own tribe?'

Arminius felt the cold hand of the Prefect's suspicion on his shoulder. To hesitate would suggest hidden purpose, and could spell disaster.

Keeping his face relaxed, Arminius smiled and answered quickly.

'A good question Sir. The General gave me permission to recruit my own staff when I accepted the post. As you know, I must travel into dangerous territories in the coming months. We showed a friendly face out there in the last few days but there is always resentment of the uniform I wear and Roman rule in general among the tribes. Some hold my Cherusci blood suitable to be spilt on their sacrificial alters. I thought about it carefully and decided I would be best served by auxiliaries whose blood might also be deemed equally worthy of boiling in their fires or splashing on their sacrificial stones. The men I have chosen as my personal escort are all loyal to Rome of course, but such an incentive of common blood just might motivate them to fight that little bit harder and help cut us out of an ambush.'

There were nodding heads around the General. Having men in a fight that you could trust your back too, made sense to the professional soldiers who sat around the general's table.

Prefect Marcos scowled, then reluctantly accepted the answer and nodded as well.

General Varus smiled towards the Prefect.

'Thank you for clearing up that point for us Prefect.' Turning his attention back to Arminius he asked.

'Where will you go next?'

Arminius appeared to consider the question for a moment.

'Well Sir, I thought it wise to suggest sending the merchants into Cherusci territory in the next few days with a limited escort from one of my other squadrons, while I plan my next patrol deep into the Angrivarii and Bructeri homelands. They both border the Cherusci and are probably friendlier to Rome than the other tribes are. I want to create an expanding network for trade Sir. Word will naturally spread throughout Germania of the prosperity and advantages involved, and I'm hoping that will make my job easier with the others as the months go by.'

There was a look of satisfaction on the old general's face. He had the right man for the job, there was no question about it.

'Good! Well done Arminius. Plan your next patrol and bring back more good news. Dismissed!'

Arminius saluted and left the briefing room.

Outside, Rolf was waiting.

'Well, how did it go in there?' He asked once they were out of earshot and walking back towards the squadron stables.

Arminius smiled. 'They swallowed every word. I convinced Varus and the other fools that all was well and that trade in our homeland could start in days. My father suggested it thrive for now at least, to allay suspicion by the Romans that anything is even slightly amiss. He has already sent runners to the Angrivarii and Bructeri requesting a meeting with their leaders on neutral ground in the deep forest between our lands.'

'When?' asked his cousin.

'We meet them in three nights when the moon is full.' Arminius was silent for a few moments, and then he said.

'We have perhaps eight thousand men who will take up arms if my father orders it, but between them the Angrivarii and Bructeri can field perhaps another fifteen thousand.

Rolf's face darkened at the numbers.

'But that will only give us equal numbers against three Legions cousin. Since the Romans came, training for war has been strictly forbidden on pain of death, except for the auxiliaries of course and very few of our people out there still possess proper weapons.'

Arminius nodded. 'Yes, you are right of course. To meet the Romans in open battle with equal numbers would mean certain annihilation. Even with proper weapons, with just three tribes we couldn't hope to be victorious.' He shook his head. 'We couldn't possibly match them, even with the Angrivarii and Bructeri's help.

Rolf's face betrayed his confusion.

'Then how are we to prevail?'

Arminius's eyes flashed for a moment. 'I have given great thought to just that question Rolf, and I think, with the help of the Gods I have discovered a way...'

'Why us, that's what I want to know?' Grumbled one of the Legionaries as the Century marched towards the distant hills.

'Because its orders stupid' snapped Optio Praxus, who was hurrying past towards the carts at the front of the rear-guard. 'And the General heard you were handy with a shovel.'

The legionary remained silent until Praxus was gone.

'Bollocks to that!' He snapped when it was safe. 'My back's killing me and we've been lumbered with two weeks of guard duty and digging bloody road foundations. I thought that's what our engineers are for?'

His friend marching beside him laughed. 'No, we're the muscle when it comes to building, you know that Sextus. Join the Legion and see the world.... If you can't take a joke mate, you shouldn't have joined.'

Sextus spat. 'I'm getting blisters on my feet already, and for the next fourteen days I'm going to have them all over my hands digging bloody great holes...I should have listened to mother and taken that job in the bakery when I had the chance. I bloody hate the army!'

His mate sniffed. 'Yeah mate, same as the rest of us.'

In front of the rear-guard, three wagons pulled by oxen rumbled forward, loaded down with shovels, picks and all the other engineering implements necessary for road construction. The drovers cracked whips above their docile animals, encouraging them to keep pulling the wagons forward. An Engineer Centurion sat beside the drover in the lead wagon. Walking beside him was Centurion Rufus.

'So we start work from the next ford then?'

The engineering officer nodded.

'Yes, the ground needs improving from there on. My lads have already surveyed and marked out the route with posts driven into the ground. While your men dig and gather rocks for the foundations, my lads will be surveying the next section. We keep leapfrogging until we reach the river. We'll stop there, and then get cracking building the bridge.'

Rufus nodded. 'Fair enough.'

He looked back towards the rear-guard and said. 'My lads were getting lazy with nothing to do. I had them training hard every day but they needed a change of scenery and some fresh air, so I volunteered them for this little duty.'

The engineer chuckled. 'Did you tell them you put them up for it?'

Rufus grinned, his eyes wide with mock horror.

'Not likely. I have enough trouble with them as it is. You know what they say...Never volunteer.'

A veteran of many campaigns across the Empire the engineer laughed. Winking at Rufus he whispered. 'Absolutely!'

Optio Praxus doubled up beside his Centurion.

'Rear-guard closed up Sir. No injuries or stragglers and no sign of any trouble behind us.'

Rufus nodded. 'Thanks Praxus. How are the men doing?'

The Optio grinned. 'Oh, grumbling about everything Sir, same as always.'

By the flickering light of the oil lamps arranged about the room, in the eerie semidarkness, Varus licked his tongue over his lips expectantly. He lent forward in anticipation, eager to hear what the future held for him. The answers were hidden in the riddle of the black stones. The omens had been good lately and he was delighted with his master plan for Germania; it was already starting to bear green shoots. His entourage of civilian merchants reported the beginnings of good trade with the barbarians. Bartering cheap pottery and trinkets for valuable pelts and furs had made them very pleased with their bargains, and eager to quietly pay Varus his own percentage. The barbarians had wanted iron to forge more farming tools but for now they must make do with the merchandise that was offered in trade. Varus had no doubt that the faceless Imperial spies within his camp would report back favourably to Augustus in Rome that all in the north was well under his steady hand.

His special envoy Arminius had departed that very morning on the next phase of his mission to expand the trading network, and now that Arminius had secured his barbarian father's agreement, building work was due to begin on the first proper road through the province.

At last he thought, after coming out of retirement and two years of hard work it seemed finally worthwhile to have journeyed to this awful place, peopled by wild savages that even the Gods shunned.

'What do you see Ignatius, what do the stones tell you?'

Varus watched intently as the haruspex stared down and cast his hands magically over the fallen runes. He threw powder into a burning brazier which erupted into a cloud of foul smelling smoke. The soothsayer's coal black skin glistened in the flickering light. His eyes rolled back into his head as he intoned something in a strange tongue that Varus had never understood. The Nubian groaned and shuddered as if making contact with the spirits; they whispered to him from the Underworld and helped him understand the scattered black stones beneath his shaking hands.

Ignatius knew the faith his master put in his predictions. It gave him the comfortable life of a slave without beatings or manual labour. The law of averages said that he must sometimes get a prediction right. If things went wrong, he'd shrug and explain it away as advice from a demon who had tricked him.

It paid to put on a particularly good show of dark spirits and unexplained mystery occasionally, when his master least expected it.

Suddenly, Ignatius froze. Gasping he cried out.

'A demon is coming master!'

He rolled his head again. There was terror on his face and dread echoed in the deep baritone of his voice. His practiced stare looked beyond the sight of mortal man as he gasped.

'A great wind from the Underworld...Fear the wind and save yourself master.'

The Haruspex moaned again and slumped forward across the table smothering further sight of the jumbled runes. He lay panting and emitting groans filled with fear of something dark and terrible. Whatever it was, it was nearby thought Varus, risen from the underworld and lurking in the shadows unseen. He glanced fearfully into the shadows about him.

Varus looked on pale and horrified. What was the man talking about; a wind, what wind? What portal to the afterlife had been accidentally opened? This couldn't be right. He sensed great danger.

'Sit up Ignatius. Explain yourself.' Varus commanded in a trembling voice.

The Nubian had his master exactly where he wanted him. Displaying the perils of meddling with those beyond the veil always worked on the gullible old fool.

The whites of his eyes stood out starkly as Ignatius cast his head left and right, searching into the shadows with growing terror.

'We must make sacrifice to the Gods master.' His eyes rolled again. 'We must beg for help and seal the rift before it is too late.'

Varus shuddered. He knew his soothsayer sometimes got too close to the demons of the Underworld. It was both enthralling and terrifying to be so near to him when it happened. The General knew that Ignatius crossed into the afterlife during a trance. There he made contact with the dark ones who helped him interpret the meaning of the runes. On rare occasions, the very foulest of underworld shades duped and tricked their way past the Nubian's defensive charms and his many years of experience. Ignatius' great power was sometimes twisted by their cunning and only the shedding of blood through animal sacrifice would close the rift and force the demons back to the darkest corners of Hades.

His mouth suddenly dry Varus stammered.

'Quickly then man, get outside and make an offering to the Gods.'

Varus knew, as a devout believer in the power of the magical runes, he paid a heavy price for exposing himself to such dangers. But what else could he do? To govern successfully, he needed all his experience as both politician and soldier. His trump card though made the risks acceptable. Unknown to his political enemies in Rome, and the savage barbarians who roamed his province, he had one special advantage over all of them.

With his Nubian's help, he could see into the future...

CHAPTER 11

The narrow path between the trees was only just visible in the light from the torches his men carried. Arminius, Rolf and a handful of his escort stayed close to each other as they threaded their way in single file along the secret trail. They had removed their uniforms and left them with their horses and the rest of the escort almost a mile behind them. Now all wore the linen and plaid of the Cherusci. High above, the bright moon's disc scattered a lattice of silver moonbeams into the depths of the black forest which surrounded them. An owl hooted somewhere behind them, but all else was still except the leaf litter beneath their feet, which rustled softly with every step they took.

At the front of the party, the guide watched the ground carefully in the flickering light for the tell-tale marks which led the way. An untrained eye would miss them, but the man leading Arminius and the others was a skilled hunter, trained by a lifetime of living in the deep forests. He could see sign around him which others could not. The guide stopped suddenly and whispered towards Arminius.

'There! Do you see it?'

Arminius looked past the hunter. There was a faint glow in the trees beyond the torches' spill of light.

'It is the meeting place' the guide declared softly. 'Walk straight into the hollow with your sword sheathed. The others are there already. They are waiting for you.'

Arminius nodded. He whispered to his men.

'Stay here quietly with our guide and wait for me. This will be a delicate meeting. Do not enter the light ahead unless you hear my shout, or the ring of steel on steel.'

His men muttered their understanding. Arminius turned to his cousin.

'Rolf, you will come with me. We will enter with hands empty and outstretched to show peaceful intent. A slip or misunderstanding now will ruin everything and cost us our lives.'

Rolf nodded and said quietly. 'I understand.'

Relations between the three tribes were usually peaceful. Clear-cut geographical boundaries, intermarriage and regular trade helped to keep all-out war at bay. Arminius knew that the Angrivarii and Bructeri would by now have heard he and his men rode for the Romans; their suspicions would be roused, but this meeting was vital to gain their trust. He also realised that only the respect neighbouring chieftains shared for his father's name had brought them here. There would be only one chance; he simply had to make it work.

Arminius turned and began to walk slowly towards the hidden hollow. As he moved softly between the tall trees the glow grew brighter until finally he stood on the lip of the natural depression. It was bright down there, illuminated by a dozen flaring torches and a fire which burned in the centre of the sunken dell. A group of men stood around the fire, their shadows crisscrossing the clearing and radiating out into the darkness beyond.

Arminius reached down and picked up a dead branch by his feet. He began to bend it until it snapped with a loud crack. The men huddled together close to the fire spun round and drawing their swords looked up towards the sudden noise. Dropping the two pieces of wood Arminius called out.

'Peace and greeting chieftains of the Angrivarii and Bructeri. It is I Herman, son of Segimer, Lord of the Cherusci.'

There was silence for a moment and then a gruff voice from below called out.

'Step forward Herman, son of Segimer, join us in the light that we may see you clearly.'

Arminius whispered to Rolf. 'Follow me down when I call you cousin. Now listen very carefully. I want you to trip and tumble when you are halfway down.'

In the reflected light Rolf's face was confused.

'I don't understand?'

Arminius hissed. '*Just do it!*'

He turned and slid down the steep bank until he reached the bottom. Keeping his hands clear of his body, he approached the silent group standing in front of him. Their blades glittered menacingly in the torchlight. He stopped the length of a man before them.

'I am Herman.' He turned with exaggerated slowness and pointed back up the slope. 'My cousin Rolf, who is known to most of you stands above us. With your permission I will call him down to vouch for me.'

One of the men stepped forward. There was suspicion in his voice.

'Yes, call him down.'

Arminius heard the tension. They were all taking a terrible risk by meeting here together in secret. The Romans had forbidden inter-tribal councils. They feared clandestine meetings were a precursor to revolt; all communication and arbitration between tribes must be made through General Varus' office. Tension among the assembled group was palpable. This was a critical moment and must go as Arminius planned it. He called softly to his cousin.

'Rolf, come down now.'

His cousin began to slide down the slope. Close to the bottom, with a sudden curse he tumbled head over heels, landing flat on his back with a thump and another even louder curse.

The effect on the group was immediate. Laughter echoed around the darkened clearing as the tension evaporated as suddenly as Rolf's clumsy entrance.

Joining in, Arminius turned to the laughing chieftains. Shaking his head, he said sadly.

'Rolf rides better than he slides.'

Wiping a tear from his eye one of the bearded men sheathed his sword. Reaching out his empty hand he growled.

'Welcome Herman, son of Segimer. An ambush might begin with a shower of arrows from the darkness, but not by throwing a young Cherusci at us.'

Arminius laughed again and shook the offered hand. The men's tension was gone, the danger had passed. In the secret meeting place he felt a huge surge of relief. His plan had worked.

Rolf limped up to the group scowling and still busily dusting himself down. Pulling a twig from his hair, with an embarrassed smile he offered his hand to the assembled Angrivarii and Bructeri leaders, as a token of his own friendship.

The meeting of the chieftain's broke up as dawn's light crept into the hollow. Plans had been explained and promises made. The Angrivarii and Bructeri peoples were with Arminius. Their leaders were eager to rid their lands of the Romans. One in particular wanted action straight away. His wife and daughters had been raped in the middle of his settlement by laughing Roman legionaries on the orders of their officer. It was the tribe's punishment for failing to meet their quota of grain when it was due, and a cruel lesson for the future. The fires of revenge burned in the chieftain's eyes. He was ready to attack them and take their heads tomorrow if they let him. Arminius pacified the man with promises of retribution to come. Calm was only restored when a solemn oath was given that he could spill all the Roman blood he wanted, and burn his prisoners alive when the time was right.

To encourage the lie of peace in the invaders eyes, it was agreed that Roman merchants would be allowed to enter and trade with both tribes.

Training of their fighting men must begin in secret, Arminius cautioned. The art of war was remembered, but the skills of the tribesmen needed honing back to the days before the Romans came. New swords, spears and arrowheads would be forged in their blacksmith's fires but it would take time to equip so many men. Arminius agreed to send part of his trusted escort to each tribe in turn to help them train. Those the auxiliaries taught would become trainers themselves and lead their young men into secret glades deep in the forest where they could practice close quarter fighting between them without fear of discovery.

Iron was a rare and valuable thing in the wilds of Germania. Arminius counselled the chieftains to be careful when asking for it in return for their valuable pelts and furs. The Romans would quickly become suspicious if too much was demanded too soon.

Some important questions remained unanswered as the meeting ended. What of the other tribes Arminius had enquired? Could they be trusted when he had asked them to join him in rebellion? To be sure of victory, Arminius needed them all, but any one might betray him to the Romans.

There was no way to know the answers for certain without first making contact. Arminius planned to kill Varus and destroy his Legions in the autumn. He needed the summer months ahead to recruit new allies and train them. During the council meeting he had been warned about one particular tribe, the Ampsivarii. Their leader, Segestes was regarded with suspicion by the men around the fire. He was an opportunist without honour they said. His men numbered in their thousands and they were good fighters, but as to which side Segestes would choose when rebellion began they had no answer.

Riding back to the Roman's summer camp Arminius was deep in thought when Rolf asked.

'Do you think we will have enough men when the time comes Herman?'

Arminius turned his head towards his cousin and replied.

'I don't know yet Rolf, but something occurred to me during the council last night when we spoke of it. We should be able to destroy the Legions if at least some of the others will join us. What we need to do, to be certain of victory is thin out the Roman's numbers beforehand. If we can do that, they will be a weaker enemy and therefore easier to kill.'

Rolf nodded then asked.

'But how can we do it Herman? You said we cannot defeat them in open combat, they are too strong.'

Arminius smiled reassuringly. 'That's right Rolf, but I think I've thought of a way...'

CHAPTER 12

'Come on you lazy bastards. I said *Pull!*'

Centurion Rufus stood on the edge of the steep riverbank, urging his men to haul harder on the ropes, and lift the last upright into position on the partly constructed wooden bridge. Beside him, the engineering Centurion looked on anxiously as the heavy beam was manoeuvred into position.

'That's it lads. Steady now....Slowly...I said *slowly!*'

Their road building phase was complete. They had reached the river and were now busy spanning it. The Cohort's sixth Century was due to relieve them at daybreak next day and Rufus was keen to finish building the bridge's framework before they arrived.

The long wooden pole cut down from the surrounding forest hung suspended in the air under an intricate web of blocks and tackle. As the men held the rope and pulled on it, the long beam swung slowly into position, guided by two of his men who balanced precariously mid-stream on one of the supports, which had been driven into the soft gravel of the riverbed by Rufus's sweating men the previous day.

Centurion Rufus had followed standard procedure when organising the work detail that morning. Half the Century were stripped to the waist and involved in building the bridge, while the other forty men were fully dressed for a fight; fully armed, wearing armour and protected by their shields. Their sole task was to act as perimeter guards against surprise attack by renegade bands of marauding barbarians. Rufus would swop his men around after the midday meal of bread and olive oil had been eaten to provide a fresh workforce for the afternoon's labours.

The heavy beam was almost in place when there was suddenly an ominous cracking noise above it. One of the upper support beams was bending under the weight of its burden.

Rufus yelled at his nearest men.

'Quick lads, get something braced under that beam to support it before it snaps!'

As the legionaries ran to comply, concentrating on averting catastrophe Rufus stepped forward as he drew breath to yell more instruction to the men controlling the beam.

Without warning, the sandy riverbank beneath him suddenly collapsed, pitching him forward into the fast flowing river in a shower of stones and sand. Dressed in full armour, with a mighty splash Rufus immediately disappeared from view as he was sucked beneath the dark surface of the water.

In the darkness below the surface Rufus frantically struggled to return to the life-giving air above, but he was trapped. The deadly combination of heavy armour and strong current held him firmly pinned among the rocks and weed on the riverbed. His struggles were rapidly weakening. Lungs burning, despite his desperate struggles, cold darkness began to overwhelm him.

Most of the men were engrossed in trying to save the cracking beam and hadn't noticed their Centurion fall from the bank. One of the legionaries perched on the support in the middle of the river had a clear view and saw him fall. He shouted a warning and dived headfirst into the turgid water below. Swimming powerfully against the current, the legionary dived under the surface close to where Rufus had disappeared. By now, the work party had the beam under control. As several tied if off, the rest, alerted by the shouted warning ran to the edge of the collapsed bank and waited for sight of their comrade.

He suddenly appeared further downstream in a spray of foam and water. Frantically, he tried to pull his Centurion's head clear of the water as he yelled for help.

Men ran along the bank. Several who could swim jumped into the water to help the legionary pull their leader to the safety of the bank.

Lifting and dragging him onto solid ground Praxus and some of the others knelt down around Rufus's body.

'Roll him over and give him some air!' Ordered Praxus urgently.

Luckily Rufus had been pulled from the water just in time. There was still a spark of life left in the veteran Centurion. His sopping body was suddenly racked with a paroxysm of coughing as he brought up several pints of muddy river water. As the worst of the coughing subsided, slowly Rufus opened his eyes.

'By the Gods, that was too close.' He mumbled. Focusing on his second in command Rufus asked. 'Who was it that pulled me out?'

Relieved that his Centurion was alive his Optio replied.

'Legionary Severus Sir. None of the rest of us saw you fall in. He didn't wait for orders, just dived straight in and grabbed you from the bottom.' The Optio shook his head gravely. He looked almost guilty. 'Truth is Sir, if it hadn't been for his swift action I doubt we could have got you out in time.'

Sitting up, Rufus coughed and spat out more water. Taking off his helmet he looked up at Severus. Scowling he said.

'I suppose you think this will get you off guard duties back at camp laddie?'

Severus remained silent. There hadn't been time to think of reward.

Rufus smiled at the dripping legionary then slowly shook his head.

'Can't show favouritism I'm afraid, it's against regulations so it ain't going to happen' Rufus wiped the droplets of water from his scarred face. 'But don't you worry; I won't forget what you did for me.' He looked back at the fast flowing river. 'I hate to admit this to anyone...' He sighed 'but I'm in your debt son, and I owe you one.'

Arminius lay in his tent and considered his next moves carefully. To weaken the Legions before he attacked them, he must devise a plan to thin out the huge numbers of Centuries and Cohorts they contained. To act now he thought, would be counterproductive. His own men were still training deep in the forests and not yet ready to fight.

All three Legions were busily engaged in patrolling, building duties and guarding the summer camp. In an emergency, he knew that gallopers could be sent, and those units deep inside the province would be recalled within days. The Legions would quickly reform and be back to their full fighting strength.

No he thought, what he needed was an excuse to scatter full cohorts, each containing hundreds of soldiers throughout the province, and keep them there permanently. They must for some reason have orders to stay in the temporary camps throughout the winter. His men could then attack the numerically weakened remainder as they marched west to the safety of their winter quarters on the other side of the Rhine, just before winter's first snows began to fall. The small garrisons dotted around the province were at present planned to be temporary, and would only be manned until the Legion's winter withdrawal.

Varus had decided that the presence of his soldiers guarding the settlements where his new trading markets were being established would reinforce the authority of Rome and deter rogue bands from attacking and sacking unguarded settlements for plunder.

Rolf had wanted to know how the mighty Romans could be defeated by a loose alliance of many tribes. Arminius hadn't answered at the time because his plan wasn't fully formed in his mind, but now, in the darkness which surrounded him, it was beginning to come together.

Hit and run was the key. The wild tribes of Germania were masters of bursting from the dense cover of the forests to ambush their enemies. Arminius had questioned his father closely on the near success of his own war against the invaders years before. He had listened very carefully and learned much from the old man's council. His tactics were now clear to him. Despite the awesome fighting power of the Legions, his conversation with his father and his own knowledge of Roman formations had highlighted a glaring weakness, where the Roman's huge numbers could be turned against them.

When they moved back towards the other side of the Rhine in early September, he would trap them in close and heavily forested country. The Romans wouldn't be able to communicate with each other or deploy. Victory, he was certain would be his.

For now, what Arminius needed was a non-pacified tribe who would harass the Romans and put them on their guard. If there was a clear danger to the stability of his Germanic province, Varus wouldn't dare leave it alone and unguarded. He would have no choice but to leave strong garrisons behind when the winter's snows came to protect greater Germania.

Satisfied with the evolution of his plans, Arminius rolled over and pulled the course blankets over his shoulders.

In the morning he would begin planning another patrol to the farthest reaches of the province, on the very northernmost border of the Empire. He must somehow go beyond the edge of the known world and make contact with the distant Ampsivarii, and their highly volatile and dangerous leader, Segestes.

How far he had come, he thought sleepily, from that night so long ago when he had lain brooding in the darkness after the death of his kinsman in the arena.

Soon now, he thought as sleep overcame him, the moment would be at hand when Attila and the lost Cherusci people would be avenged.

'Column Halt!'

Surrounded by early morning mist, close to the broad Alara River, Arminius walked his horse forward and called up to the sentry standing in one of the two towers guarding the small frontier fort's gate.

'I am Senior Decurion Arminius, commander of the 18th Legion's auxiliary cavalry. I am here on the orders of General Varus. Where is your Centurion?'

Still surprised at the end of his long night vigil by the sudden appearance of thirty armoured horsemen through the clinging mist, the legionary called down.

'He's probably still in his bed asleep Sir.'

Irritated, Arminius shouted back at the sentry.

'Well send someone to wake him up, damn you.'

Startled, the sentry stammered 'Yes...yes Sir!'

There was a muffled conversation behind the palisade. Arminius heard iron shod sandals rapidly descending the steps on the inside of the tower. As they waited, Arminius sniffed the cold damp air. He looked around him at the native huts erected outside the fort which appeared and disappeared in the swirling mist then said.

'Things seem a little relaxed here. Perhaps it will work in our favour before we make our return?'

Suddenly, the gate swung open and a bleary eyed and portly soldier, dressed in a creased tunic and sandals stepped outside. He stared sleepily at the line of horsemen, and then turned his attention to the two officers sitting on their mounts at the front of the column.

As commander of a Legion's cavalry, Arminius outranked the Centurion. Seeming confused by the detachment's sudden appearance the Centurion said.

'I'm sorry you didn't receive a better welcome Sir; I had no warning of your arrival.'

Arminius stared at the Centurion for a moment. Coldly he said.

'Just get the damned gate open Centurion. We have ridden all night and my men are tired and need warmth and food.'

The Centurion nodded and snapped at one of his guards.

'You heard the Decurion. Get the gate open and see the squadron to the stables.'

Arminius and Rolf sat in the Centurion's office gratefully warming themselves by the glowing brazier which threw welcome heat into the small room. Like their men, they had been provided with a simple breakfast of bread and water. Both men ate in silence.

Sitting behind his desk, the Centurion noticed the Equestrian Order's ring on the stern faced Decurion's finger. It was a mark of nobility and made him feel even more confused and uncomfortable. Both his guests wore their hair long in the usual auxiliary style, and had conversed freely in the barbarian's tongue. And yet the Decurion was of a noble Roman caste? He decided to try and break the icy atmosphere which he felt, despite the warmth of the brazier.

'What are the General's orders concerning my missing men Sir?'

Arminius pursed his lips.

'I don't know what you are talking about. I am not here about missing legionaries; I came to gather information Centurion, and to further project Rome's influence on the outer rim. I also have orders from General Varus to reconnoitre the area. He is disappointed with your progress and instructed me to encourage more trade with the Ampsivarii.'

The Centurion's eyes widened with shock.

'The Ampsivarii Sir?' The Centurion held up his hands as if to ward off the very idea. 'But...but they're untamed savages.' He shook his head slowly. 'Headquarters doesn't understand what it's like up here or the difficulties I face on the frontier. I have followed orders and tried to make better contact with them several times but my last messenger's head was left spiked on a stick outside the gates two weeks ago. I've no idea what happened to the three men I sent as his escort?'

'You made no attempt to find out?' Arminius snapped.

'No sir, I couldn't. Without reinforcements I simply don't have the manpower to enter Ampsivarii territory and launch a punitive mission to rescue them. I thought that's why you had come. I have only half a century to guard the fortress and protect the trading settlement outside. My other men are spread out, stationed in two smaller forts which control the only other roads into Ampsivarii territory.' The portly Centurion wrung his hand with growing anguish. It wasn't fair; he hadn't asked to be sent here, none of this was his fault but he was sure he would be blamed.

'I did make a full report on the incident to headquarters, but haven't received a reply, or any fresh orders.'

Arminius nodded and sighed impatiently.

'Very well Centurion.' Arminius drummed his finger on the desk between them as he thought. He fixed the Roman with a cold stare and said.

'I'll let headquarters deal with your lack of action over your missing men in their own good time... But now, I need information. How do you suggest I contact the Ampsivarii's leader, Segestes?'

The Centurion shook his head.

'I'm not sure anymore Sir. Like most of the barbarians in this province, the Ampsivarii like to take the heads of their victims. They believe that the power of the dead is transferred into the warrior who killed them...or some such nonsense. I think they only relinquished their trophy and left my Optio's head outside the gate as a warning of what would happen to anyone else who dared enter their land. As for their leader Segestes, well Sir, it's said that he's mad at the best of times, others whisper he's just plain evil.'

Arminius raised an eyebrow. 'How so, Centurion?'

The Centurion shuddered. 'There's an animal Sir.'

Arminius sniffed. 'Go on.'

'He feeds prisoners to the bear he keeps in a pit, or at least that's the latest rumour to come out of the village. Apparently he believes it inhabited by his god.'

Arminius had heard this story before. He held up his hand and nodded. 'All right, thank you Centurion.'

He turned to Rolf, who had been listening wide eyed.

'I could take the entire squadron into their territory, but without a guide I'd never find him. We'd probably be ambushed before we even got close.' He turned back to the Centurion. 'Do any of your men know exactly where his village is?'

The Centurion shook his head. No Sir, I'm afraid not. I've tried going in blind already.' He sighed. 'And you know what happened.'

'What about the locals who live here, some must be Ampsivarii?'

'Yes Sir, there are Ampsivarii living in the settlement but they're here to trade, not be friendly with us. I tried to question them for information but even the whip got nothing from them except stubborn silence.'

Arminius stared at his cousin again. 'Perhaps a more subtle approach is called for Rolf. We might have more luck.' He gripped his tunic between his fingers. 'Without the fanfare of being caught wearing Roman uniforms.'

CHAPTER 13

They had been riding for almost an hour. The mist hung white and clinging around them as Arminius and Rolf followed the winding track into Ampsivarii territory. It was cold, very cold. The sort of cold which seeps into a man's body and chills his very soul.

The sound of the horses' hooves was deadened in the swirling stillness of the atmosphere which pressed heavily down on them both. The dense canopy of trees overhead made the path seem as though they were riding through a dark and unending tunnel, ever deeper into the dank and dripping forest.

Both riders cast their heads left and right as they strained to see or hear movement. There were no distant animal cries or birdsong. Neither man detected anything but eerie silence beyond the tightly packed trees which grew up to the very edge of the track. The ground mist constantly swirled as its tendrils enveloped them in its chilling embrace.

Rolf pulled his plaid Cherusci cloak tighter around his shoulders to ward off the creeping cold. His eyes constantly scanned the mist as he watched for any sign of life. His voice was a whisper.

'I don't like this. We ride in a land of evil Herman; it is the place where the darkest spirits dwell.' He looked anxiously over his shoulder. 'We will never find anything like this. Perhaps we should return to the fort?'

Arminius smiled reassuringly at his nervous cousin.

'You are right of course Rolf. We will never find them. I am relying on them finding us....'

Suddenly, there was movement all around them. Like silent phantoms, heavily armed warriors seemed to rise up from the very ground around them. Noiselessly, they appeared from the mist on both sides of the track, their drawn bows pointing at the two riders. Startled, Rolf's hand reached for his sword.

'*No!*' hissed Arminius urgently. 'Keep you blade where it is.'

Arminius raised his hands slowly towards the nearest Ampsivarii.

'I am Herman, son of Segimer, king of the Cherusci. I seek urgent council with your great leader Segestes.'

The warrior's eyes narrowed with suspicion. After a moment of indecision he reluctantly waved most of his ambush party back to their hiding places in the mist. As they lowered their bows and disappeared as quietly as they had arrived he turned his attention back to the two waiting riders.

With the point of his spear he motioned them forward, adding a flick of his head in the direction of the track ahead.

Sullen faced he growled. 'Surrender your weapons to my men Cherusci, then follow me. No tricks...or you die!'

Standing on the raised council platform Segestes glared down in silence at Arminius and Rolf, as the warrior who had been both guard and guide whispered into his ear. Spiked on poles behind him, two heads stared blindly across the wooden platform, their eyes gouged from their heads. The cheeks of one was torn and the other looked badly crushed

The Ampsivarii's leader nodded as he listened to the guide. Beside him an old man dressed in animal skins also listened intently to what the guide was saying. The old man was wizened, his ancient skin looked grey, like stretched parchment. He wore a fur headdress adorned with the white skull of a wolf on his head. On his leather belt hung the small bones of forest animals. Staring balefully at the two Cherusci he hissed something into Segestes' other ear then, with a claw like hand he angrily waved a bone rattle at the two men sitting silently on their horses. The Ampsivarii king laughed and slapped his thigh. He turned to Arminius and Rolf. With a knowing grin he said.

'You wear the swords of the invaders. My soothsayer says you are Roman spies and he wants to spill your blood on our sacred stones.'

Segestes' dark eyes bored into the two men.

'Vorlec is wise to the ways of outsiders and there is more than a ring of truth in his council...So tell me Cherusci spies, why have you travelled so far... and what do you want here?'

Arminius answered quickly.

'Brave and noble Segestes, it is well known among the tribes of your warrior's fierceness in battle. We come here respectfully to ask for your help with a very serious and urgent matter. I wish to discuss a thing of great importance which will enrich both you and your people.'

Arminius bowed his head respectfully. This was a dangerous moment. Appealing to the Ampsivarii leader's vanity would only take him so far. Segestes was well known among the other tribes spread across Germania as a treacherous opportunist. As yet untroubled by Rome, his involvement would not be offered for a high and noble reason like freedom from tyranny; he would be swayed only by the booty of rich pickings, if he did ultimately agree to give his support to the rebellion.

'With your permission we seek an audience with you in private, away from the prying eyes and ears of lesser men....'

Intrigued, Segestes thought for a moment then slyly nodded.

'I will listen to your words Herman, son of Segimer, but I warn you, if Vorlec smells out even a single lie.' With a savage grin he turned and pointed towards the heads behind him. 'Our angry Gods will be appeased with the sacrifice of your miserable lives.'

Surrounded by his bodyguard and closely attended by Vorlec, Segestes sat in the gloomy smoke filled interior of a small council chamber in silence.

'So Herman, son of Segimer, now I sit among trusted friends. Explain to me why you are here, and why I should spare your lives.'

Arminius explained his plan to destroy the Romans. He had quickly decided that truth was his only hope of surviving this meeting. To be caught with a lie or half-truth on his lips would invite the same fate as the Romans who had died at his order. Taking fate in his hands Arminius told Segestes of being taken hostage as a child and explained in detail the cruel oppression of his own people by the

Romans. There was fire in his eyes when he spoke of his own burning hatred of Rome.

When Arminius finally finished speaking Segestes looked towards his soothsayer. Vorlec and the chieftain whispered to each other before Segestes spoke.

'For now, your lives will be spared. I will seek a full council before I decide to join your attack upon the Romans.' He waved his hand towards the council chamber's entrance. 'In the meantime, you will enjoy my hospitality until I have decided.'

The Ampsivarii's leader clapped his hands. A young woman stepped from the shadows and respectfully bowed before him. Tall and slim, she was barefoot, wearing a long threadbare dress of plain brown material. Her long blond hair was woven into pigtails, drawn together into a tight bun. Arminius started momentarily. He thought her quite beautiful. As he stared, he couldn't help but notice the girl's face looked tense and frightened. Her beauty was marred by her bottom lip which was cut and swollen; one side of her face was discoloured by a large purple bruise; there were dark circles under her green eyes.

With a dismissive flick of his hand Segestes waved the two Cherusci from his presence.

'Take our guests away and see to it that they are given food.' He growled. 'And remember your place.'

The girl cringed slightly. She bowed again and silently motioned the two men to follow her.

As they turned away, Segestes looked towards the leader of his bodyguard. He inclined his head towards the disappearing backs of Arminius and Rolf. The bearded warrior nodded his understanding. Accompanied by three of his men the bodyguard leader quickly turned and followed the others as they stepped into the bright sunlight outside.

Followed closely by the guards, under the curious gaze of huddled Ampsivarii women and children, the girl led Arminius and his cousin through a warren of huts to a small wicker lean-to on the edge of the settlement. Throwing back the hanging hide which served as a door she beckoned them inside. She entered behind them and stooping down, picked up two wooden bowls which lay in a dim corner. As the girl wiped out the bowls, Arminius took in his surroundings. It was a far cry from the clean mosaic floors and brightly tiled walls of civilized Roman society. The interior was sparsely furnished with just a wooden cot filled with a thick bed of dry bracken set on a compacted mud floor. A thin blanket lay crumpled at one end of the crude bed. Wiping the bowls again on her dirty apron, she placed them on the ground beside a small cooking fire in the middle of the shabby room. Suspended just above the glowing embers was an iron cauldron half-filled with grey bubbling liquid. She scooped some into each bowl with a wooden ladle and handed one to each man.

Arminius nodded his thanks and lifting the bowl to his lips, sipped at the steaming broth. It tasted of rancid animal fat and little else. He caught a look from his cousin, who appeared to be trying to suppress a shudder of disgust. Arminius lowered the bowl and spoke to the girl.

'What happened to your face, who hit you?'

The girl shook her head rapidly and walked swiftly to the entrance. She stopped suddenly and turned. For the most fleeting of moments she stared at Arminius. It was a strange look, and for an equally fleeting moment it unsettled him. Throwing back the curtain she left the dwelling. Rolf turned and watched her disappear. He shrugged.

'She's pretty but not much of a talker is she?'

Night had fallen hours earlier. Below a star studded sky the two Cherusci remained confined in the hut under close guard. There had been no message of agreement from Segestes and no further sign of the girl since their scant meal earlier in the day.

Arminius looked at his cousin, who was sitting in the shadows. Keeping his voice down to a whisper he said.

'It looks like Segestes is taking his time over his decision. Do you want more broth?'

Rolf grunted. The fire had gone out and he couldn't stomach the thought of swallowing more pieces of fat and the slimy scum the cold cauldron contained.

'No. It was bad enough when it was hot...'

Arminius nodded. Rolf was right.

'It's strange about the girl. She seemed terrified of Segestes but wore no markings of a slave?'

In the darkness Rolf replied in a whisper. 'Perhaps that's how the Ampsivarii treat their women?

'Perhaps you're right?'

Arminius shrugged in the darkness and went back to thinking of the girl.

Suddenly, there were heavy footsteps outside the hut, followed by muffled words exchanged between guards. The leather curtain was thrown back and one of the Ampsivarii warriors thrust his head through the gap in the doorway. He growled at Arminius and Rolf.

'You, come with us.'

Both men were on their feet in a moment. They left the gloom of the hut and followed the guard. He led them back to the council chamber in the middle of the village. The guard turned to the two men and pointed at the doorway.

'Go in.'

The council chamber was illuminated by burning torches and crowded with more than twenty older Ampsivarii men. A fire burned brightly in the middle of the circular chamber. Smoke drifted lazily through a round hole cut high in the thatched roof. The men around Segestes sat murmuring to each other on the floor with their backs to the wall, so all could face their leader and be heard. Most fell silent when Arminius and Rolf entered. Segestes sat opposite on his wooden throne. Seeing the two men enter he clapped his hands for silence. He came straight to the point.

'It has been decided that we will help you against the Romans, but my people will not fight under your command. I will decide where and when we will strike. Any tribe who stand in our way will die. I will not tell you when or where I choose to attack. Whatever we seize from the Romans is ours by right and will not be shared with others. Prisoners will be ransomed only if I decide it so; they will be mine to do with as I please.' Segestes stared intently at the two Cherusci. Scowling he demanded an answer.

'Do you agree to my terms?'

Arminius nodded. Negotiation would be dangerous with this man. Having the wild Ampsivarii attacking supply columns and isolated outposts at random over the next months was exactly what he wanted.

CHAPTER 14

'Yes Segestes, it is agreed. Your terms are fair. Your people should profit from their fight....When will you begin to move on the Romans?'

Segestes stroked his untidy beard for a moment. A cruel smile played across his lips.

'It will be soon Herman, son of Segimer, as soon as we are ready.' The Ampsivarii looked towards one of the guards; their meeting seemed to be at an end.

As Arminius and Rolf turned to leave, Segestes held up his hand and growled.

'Wait!'

Both men stopped and turned back to face him. Segestes stood up.

'It is the custom of my tribe that we make blood sacrifice to our Gods before going to war. I think it only fitting that you join us at the ceremony, to bring their blessings on our new alliance.'

There were nods and murmurs of agreement among the elders who stared up at the two Cherusci. Now was not the time to offend the Ampsivarii leader or his council. Arminius bowed slightly and spoke gravely.

'It will be our honour to be a part of your sacred rite.'

Segestes motioned to his elders, who stood up and began to file out. As the last of them left the guard grunted to the two men to follow him outside.

In the flickering torchlight, from the corner of his eye Arminius saw suspicion drift across his cousin's face, but he ignored Rolf's concern and whispered nothing to reassure him. Beckoning them to follow, the guard led them in the opposite direction, away from the girl's hut towards the outskirts of the Ampsivarii village.

The elders were filing one by one into a large hut which was surrounded by a ring of wolf's skulls mounted on wooden posts. Above each gleaming skull a burning torch flickered in the darkness, throwing shadows and light across each one. From inside the hut the two Cherusci heard a deep and unearthly growl. The guard grinned at them. He said.

'Feel for the wall and stay close to it. Keep silent and wait for the ceremony to begin.'

Both men smelt a rancid and overpowering musk of something inhuman as they entered. It was very dark inside. Arminius sensed rather than saw others close to him. He felt Rolf's hand brush his shoulder as they both stopped abruptly with their backs tight against the wicker wall. There was another echoing growl just below them, louder this time as the unseen beast smelt the men around it. Arminius and Rolf could hear something big and powerful sniffing the air as it paced back and forth, but still the darkness defeated them; they could see nothing.

The hoarse and crackling voice of Vorlec suddenly filled the blackened chamber.

'It is time to make sacred sacrifice to the Gods of war to ensure our victory.'

It was the signal. Two Ampsivarii entered, holding burning torches before them. They stood to one side as light spilled into the chamber. Arminius's eyes were immediately drawn into the depths of the pit before him. Pacing back and forth, a huge bear lumbered, its shaggy head raised high as it sniffed the air. The monster's slavering jaws and teeth dripped in the torchlight. It let out a deafening roar of excitement and reared up on its hind legs. Behind the beast, Arminius saw gnawed bones littering the bottom of the pit. His eyes narrowed with realisation. The bones were human.

Vorlec stood on the edge of the pit and waved his rattle magically over the bear below. He cried up to the heavens and chanted his prayers to the Gods of destruction, as a boy beat a slow rhythm on the tightly stretched skin of a drum.

The elders had arranged themselves shoulder to shoulder in the darkness, with their backs to the round hut's wall. Like Arminius and Rolf they stood several feet back from the edge of the deep pit. There was the gleam of anticipation on their faces as they began to chant their responses to Vorlec's exaltations.

The noise in the chamber grew louder as the drum continued to beat. Vorlec exaltations were drawing him into a growing frenzy. He shivered and shook to the rhythm of the drum; his cries got faster and echoed over the pit and the snarling beast it contained.

Suddenly both he and the drum stopped, filling the chamber with a foreboding silence.

There were muffled curses and the sounds of a scuffle outside the entrance. A struggling figure was half carried and half dragged inside. In the light of the torches Arminius recognised the man's garb instantly; he wore a torn and dirty tunic of the Legion. The wretched legionary was tightly bound hand and foot. The captive saw the beast pacing across the pit and let out a cry of pure terror. Vorlec grinned triumphantly. He laughed and savoured the man's rank fear. As his guards held the soldier in their vice like grip, Vorlec began to mutter incantations as he smeared dark liquid from a clay gourd over the terrified man's face and body. Both

Arminius and Rolf caught the smell of the viscous fluid. Only one thing smelt like that. It was the powerful odour of blood.

When he was satisfied he had covered his victim with sufficient magical swirls and symbols, Vorlec passed his rattle over the cringing legionary for the last time. Despite the chill in the chamber his face and arms were covered with glistening sweat. Vorlec turned and faced his leader. Through half closed eyes he watched Segestes, whose cruel smile betrayed his enjoyment of the prisoner's terror.

Segestes nodded grandly towards Vorlec to show his approval. The surrounding elders began their chanting again. They looked towards the terrified legionary and gestured into the darkness of the pit.

Segestes stood and slowly drew his sword. He raised it towards the roof and the star filled heavens outside. The elders quickly fell silent. The hungry bear paced back and forth growling and snarling with growing excitement and hungry anticipation. It too had smelt the blood. The deathly hush among the gathered elders passed as Segestes lowered his eyes towards the terrified legionary.

'Your sacrifice will bring us great fortune Roman. The Gods will be with us!'

Wild eyed, the prisoner didn't understand what the chieftain was saying, but he understood his fate. A terrified sob escaped from his trembling lips. His fearful face filled with dread as hot urine ran down his legs. It collected in a steaming puddle around his naked feet.

With a bloodthirsty sweep Segestes slashed his sword down towards the waiting bear. The laughing guards understood. With a scream of pure horror the struggling legionary was pitched forward, into the bone littered depths of the waiting pit below...

'Return these men's weapons and horses.' Beneath a sky pinpricked with points of light, outside the sacrificial chamber Segestes turned from his men to Arminius. 'You will leave.' He cast his eyes around his assembled elders. His eyes glittered with feral anticipation. 'Vorlec says our Gods are pleased with our sacrifice. They are with us now, and we have a war to arrange.'

Rolf and Arminius rode carefully through the darkness, the shining moon lighting their way. Their guide had left them, having seen them onto the track which would lead them back to the border fort. Each man was lost in his own thoughts until Rolf broke the silence between them with a whispered question.

'Why do we need the Ampsivarii savages to begin attacking now Herman? Won't that put the Romans on their guard and make things more difficult for us when we launch our own attack?'

Arminius nodded in the darkness.

'Yes indeed, it will alert the Romans Rolf. But that is exactly what I want to happen.'

Confused, Rolf turned his head towards his cousin.

'I don't understand?'

Arminius grinned to himself in the darkness.

'When the time is right and we are ready to launch an all-out attack, I want the strength of the Legions to be drained. Using the Ampsivarii will split them and reduce the number of cohorts we will have to fight when the time comes. When Segestes begins his attacks and Roman losses of men, food and material begin to rise, Varus must move quickly to reinforce all the smaller garrisons defending strategic settlements throughout Germania, in case they are overrun and destroyed by the Ampsivarii rebels. The old General's plan to increase trade will come to nothing if he cannot maintain order in the province. I have no doubt that we can convince the tribes who are already with us to add to the drain on Roman manpower by demanding protection from the wild tribe that is raiding from across the border. That is after all, the other side of the Pax Romana agreement. Rome promises armed protection to those who submit to her dominion.'

Rolf nodded, it was a cunning plan, but he could see a weakness.

'Surely the Romans will withdraw their men as they usually do before winter comes, and then march all of them to safe winter quarters over the Rhine?'

Arminius shook his head.

'No Rolf, I don't think so. Now that trade has started flowing freely in the province, as we have secretly arranged with our allies to permit, Varus cannot leave such a valuable network of trading settlements undefended anymore, even during the snows of winter. He will be obliged to leave sufficient soldiers stationed throughout the province on a permanent basis to keep trade flowing freely.'

Rolf looked at his cousin with admiration. If it worked, it was a simple but brilliant plan, but he still had one more question.

'But what of the soldiers who guard the settlements? I thought we would banish the Romans forever before winter comes?'

Arminius's eyes glittered in the moonlight.

'The garrisons are remote and isolated from each other Rolf. There will be no hope of relief. We will send men to surprise and destroy them one by one, at the same time the Legions are being cut to pieces.'

They rode on in silence but then Arminius added.

'We will need to show our allies the futility of open war. I must arrange a demonstration for them and then show them the path to victory.'

The men continued in silence, picking their way carefully along the track to avoid injuring one of their horses' legs in a concealed pothole or hidden warren. There was still a long way to go. A lame animal would severely delay their return, and Arminius had other things to plan and do.

The journey continued uneventfully. The night remained dark and still, save for the occasional bark of a prowling fox or distant hoot of a hunting owl. Rolf was happily chewing on a hunk of stale bread when Arminius suddenly whispered.

'There's something moving behind us Rolf.'

Rolf stopped chewing, turned in his saddle and stared back into the darkness.

'I see nothing cousin. Are you sure?'

Arminius replied softly. 'Yes, I heard something earlier, just after the guide left us and went back to his village.'

'What did you hear?'

'It was an odd sound... Perhaps it was a stone being dislodged on the track behind us? Then I heard something again, just moments ago.'

Arminius thought for a moment. Whatever was tracking them must be taken as a threat. Slowly he drew his sword. Rolf saw the movement and reached for his own. Arminius held up his blade and whispered softly.

'No Rolf, keep your sword sheathed but be ready. When we reach the next bend in the track, take my bridle and lead my horse while you continue forward. I'll slip down and seek cover in the trees, and wait for whatever is following us.'

Rolf nodded. Minutes later, the track veered sharply to the left. Arminius passed his reins to Rolf. Arminius slipped soundlessly from his saddle and landed lightly on the ground beside his walking horse. Without a word he turned and in a low running crouch disappeared silently into the trees close beside the track.

Arminius didn't have to wait very long. A single shadowy figure stole quietly along the track on foot. A blade glistened in the stalker's hand as he hurried after the horses.

When the hooded figure had passed, Arminius stepped out from behind cover. Matching the fall of his feet with the figure in front he quickly closed the short distance between them. Arminius could have easily killed with a thrust of his sword into the back of the figure, but he wanted answers. Perhaps their true purpose had been discovered by a spy in the pay of Rome? Was it an assassin following them? He had to know why someone was creeping after them in the dead of night, deep as they still were in Ampsivarii territory.

Arminius was close enough to hear the gasping breaths of the stalker now. Taking no chances from the dagger the figure carried, Arminius swung the flat of his blade at the hooded head only a few feet in front of him. It connected with a dull and muffled thump. The figure instantly fell stunned to the ground. Quickly scanning the surrounding darkness for accomplices Arminius thrust the point of his sword towards the figure's neck as he wrenched the hood from the stalker's head.

A terrified shriek pierced the night as the material was ripped away.

'No please, don't kill me!'

Arminius' jaw dropped. The moonlight shone across blond hair and the bruised face beneath it. To his utter amazement, lying frozen with fear beneath his raised sword was the slave girl from the village.

'*You!*'

Still dazed from the blow to her head, the girl burst into tears. Arminius heard Rolf galloping back up the track towards him. Alerted by the girl's piercing shriek, Rolf had drawn his sword and returned, ready for a fight.

Gasping between sobs, the girl remained where she lay. She had lost her dagger when Arminius had struck. She held her empty hand to her head and rubbed it gently.

Rolf climbed down from his horse and walked over to his cousin. Staring down at the prisoner Rolf laughed softly.

'Looks like you have caught yourself a pretty little fish cousin.'

Fighting to recover some dignity the girl struggled to sit up. She glared at Rolf with a withering stare. With a flash of angry defiance she flared at him.

'I am no fish, Cherusci bastard!'

Both men grinned. The girl had spirit.

Still grinning Arminius asked. 'What's your name girl?'

Rubbing her head she replied. 'My name is Thusnelda and how dare you attack me.'

'You are lucky I didn't kill you.' Arminius glanced around him. 'This is no place for you to be creeping around like a thief in the night.' He stared into the girls eyes. 'Now tell us Thusnelda, why were you following us?'

The girl looked sulkily at her captors.

Rolf added. 'Speak truly now girl, before we return you to your village.'

Fear returned to the girl's eyes as the words left Rolf's lips. It was the same fear she'd displayed when she stood trembling before Segestes in the Ampsivarii village.

Thusnelda's hand flew to her mouth. Tears brimmed suddenly into her eyes again. She cringed.

'*No Please!* Don't take me back. He'll kill me for sure if I return now.' Both men heard genuine terror in her faltering voice.

Startled by her frightened reply Arminius held up his hand to reassure her.

'All right, calm yourself. What happens next depends on telling us the truth Thusnelda. Why were you following us, and who will kill you if we take you back?'

Thusnelda wiped the tears from her face. Breathing deeply, she composed herself. When she felt calm enough, she began her story.

'I am promised in marriage to the son of a friend of my father's, but I defied him and refused to marry the man. My father wants me to marry a stupid drunken beast, and I hated him from the first moment I saw his ugly face. I begged him, but my father wouldn't listen to me so I ran away, but they caught me and took me back. My father beat me for shaming him.'

Her hand went involuntarily to her bruised face. 'I am due to be married when the moon wanes but I couldn't face the thought of being joined to such a brute and bearing his children. I'd rather die than suffer his touch.' Thusnelda shuddered with revulsion in the darkness.

Arminius glanced at his cousin, and then quickly looked back at the frightened girl.

'So why did you follow us?'

In the darkness, Thusnelda sighed. Arminius felt her eyes boring into him.

'When I first saw you, I was forbidden to speak to you, but I felt...something. I felt safe when I was close to you. I don't understand it, I don't even know you, but I desperately needed someone to save me. Time is running out and you were my only chance. I came after you to plead for your protection!'

Arminius stared at the girl with unashamed surprise. He felt his heartbeat quicken in his chest. He hadn't admitted it to his cousin, but the girl's face hadn't left him since he'd first seen her. Something had stirred in him too.

This unexpected turn had taken him by surprise. Looking into her lovely face, for once he permitted himself the luxury of his heart ruling his head. Before he agreed, there was a question he must ask, but he feared he already knew the answer.

'Who is your father?'

Thusnelda let out a frightened sob. 'You already know him...my father is Segestes, Lord of the Ampsivarii!'

There was silence from both men. Arminius felt trapped. He had no doubt the girl's fears were right if they returned her to her father. Having seen the twisted pleasure on the Ampsivarii leader's face during the human sacrifice, Arminius harboured no doubt that Segestes was capable of murdering his own daughter over her defiance; if Segestes found out that they had smuggled Thusnelda to safety, there would be trouble but it was too late to change his plans now... It was unthinkable to return her to her father, so Arminius had to think fast.

'Very well Thusnelda. I will give you my protection and see you safely from Ampsivarii territory. We will re-join my escort and take you to my father's village. I know he will give you the sanctuary of my tribe if I ask him. After that...' He shrugged. 'We'll see.'

Arminius stood up and climbed back onto his horse. Staring at the girl he reached down and offered her his hand.

'You'd better ride with me.' Hastily he added. 'We'll make better time that way.' Thusnelda smiled and gratefully grasped his hand. He hauled her up and waited until she was sitting safely behind him. She reached around his body and grasped the front of his cloak. Resting her head gently against his broad back she smelt his musk and felt the warmth of his body.

Gruffly Arminius spoke over his shoulder.

'Pull up your hood and keep your face covered girl. As long as your father doesn't know you've escaped with us, he will search in all the wrong places for you. I will report to my superiors that I have taken you hostage, but until we are far from your father's territory it's vital you are not recognised in our company.'

Arminius turned to his cousin. Clearing his throat he said urgently.

'We must go quickly Rolf.'

Rolf raised an eyebrow. With a knowing grin he whistled softly at his cousin's audacity.

Arminius ignored him. Tapping his horse's flanks he led off into the night. In the darkness, for once, Arminius was smiling too

CHAPTER 15

Light filtered silently through the broad valley; dawn's watery sun cast long shadows across its browning autumn mantle.

Hidden in the dense canopy of trees on the hillside, three men lay concealed, spying in silence on the village below. A narrow silver stream sparkled and splashed through its deserted centre. The men could see smoke rising lazily from holes cut in the apex of a few thatched roofs within the sleeping Tencteri village. Somewhere in the settlement a dog caught their scent and barked a warning, startling a cockerel to lift its head towards the clear sky. It crowed loudly.

'Well at least something's awake down there' whispered one of the soldiers, blowing softly into his cupped hands to ward of the early morning chill. The stiff red plume mounted across his helmet betrayed his station as a Centurion of the 18th Imperial Legion. Close beside him lay Optio Praxus, the veteran Centurion's second in command. A few feet to his right lay Tribune Lucius Flavia Crastus, a young staff officer.

Much to Centurion Rufus' annoyance the young inexperienced Tribune had been temporarily attached to the

2nd Cohort to gain some much needed field experience. To add to Rufus' frustration, on the direct orders from General Varus, he had placed all six of the Legions' young Tribunes in temporary command of the last weeks tax gathering missions across the province, before the three Legions finished their summer duties and returned to the warmth and safety of their winter quarters, built on the west bank of the mighty River Rhine.

True, admitted Rufus silently to himself, these junior Tribunes were of officer rank but usually acted as assistant administrators in charge of pay and the equipment stores within each Legion. They were secretly laughed at; not considered real fighting soldiers by any of the men serving in front line Cohorts. When Rufus and several other Centurions heard the news at officer's call the previous day they had all groaned inwardly. They were equally mystified by the sudden change of policy, but with the usual resignation of experienced soldiers they accepted that orders were orders whether the Legion's Centurions liked them or not, especially when they filtered down from the very top.

It had been a difficult forced march through the night. The track through the forest had been poor by Roman standards and the sickle moon had done little to lift the darkness beneath the thick canopy as the Century marched through the vast tract of forest towards their distant destination. But now, the Century had arrived safely at the very edge of the pacified Germania Magna province, deep within the hunting grounds of the Tencteri tribe, situated on the northern edge of the known world.

Still staring down at the silent village Centurion Rufus sniffed absently and rubbed his chin, deep in thought. Abruptly, his mind made up he looked towards the man on his left.

'Seems a bit quiet down there somehow?' Still rubbing his chin he shrugged to himself. 'Still, there's been no trouble with the Tencteri tribe for years now but it's probably best you take three sections and sweep the tree line beyond the village. When you signal the all clear I'll bring the rest of the lads down from this side of the hill.'

Optio Praxus nodded. Remaining low he slid back to recover his broad oblong shield emblazed with the 17th Legion's emblem of a running boar. Tribune Crastus stood up and coughed.

'I believe I am in command here Centurion... am I not?'

The Optio froze. Rufus stared for a moment in silence at the young Tribune. The chain of command in the Roman Legions was clear cut. Tribunes, even junior ones, outranked

Centurions by a country mile, no matter how young, snot nosed or inexperienced they might be.

Rufus nodded. He suppressed the sigh he felt rising deep in his chest. The twenty two year old Tribune had been with the 17th for only a few months, but already had fallen into the trap of believing himself both master tactician and leader of men. Rufus had seen this happen all too often before to bother getting angry any more. The boy came from a good family, who owned a huge winery on the banks of the River Tiber. Rufus had come across his type more than once before: with plenty of money behind him, suffering from the usual wealthy class maladies of arrogance and overconfidence. Having done a short tour in the army the Tribune would soon be heading back triumphantly to Rome, a hero to his family. While his father still lived, he'd probably spend the next few years slithering his way into some cushy job, probably a secretary in the Forum or an administrator in one of the Ministries at Rome's heart. If he could pick up a decoration or two during his short term with the 17th, well, so much the better for his future prospects in Roman society.

Common sense said to check around the outskirts of the village before committing his main force, but there was no point in arguing. The Centurion held up his hand towards Praxus.

'Hold there.'

He turned his attention back to the impatient Tribune.

'Exactly what *are* your orders...Sir?' he enquired straight faced and just a little too formally for the young Tribune's liking.

Crastus' eyes narrowed, unsure if the veteran Centurion was being insubordinate. He failed to see the silent grin spread across the Optio's face behind him. Rufus' expression remained impassive.

The irritation of the moment was clear in the Tribune's voice.

'I will bring the entire Century forward, and we will approach the village in extended skirmish line. You will both wait here until I return with the men. Understand?'

As the Tribune turned and strode off through the trees towards the legionaries waiting on the other side of the hill, Centurion Rufus stood up and thrusting his outstretched fingers forward, saluted with a straight right arm. 'Yes Sir, perfectly clear Sir.'

As Crastus disappeared quickly into trees up the forested slope, Rufus turned his head towards his Optio. His eyes narrowed to slits as he growled.

'And you can wipe that bloody silly grin off your face my lad... or you'll find yourself in charge of latrine duty when we get back to camp.'

'Steady lads...keep the line straight.'

From his vantage point on the left of the line, Centurion Rufus kept one eye on the heavily armed legionaries marching shoulder to shoulder in extended line down the hill. The early morning sun glinted off their burnished helmets and segmented armour. Each man's leather bound shield that protected his body from shoulder to calf was held close to the left hand side of their bodies and each long pilum throwing spear was held smartly at the regulation angle of 20 degrees all the way along the line. Centurion Rufus kept his other eye fixed on the silent village ahead. If the boy Tribune wanted a parade, he might as well make damn sure his men followed the close order drill they had practiced so many times before. The last thing Rufus wanted was the snot-nosed Tribune to find an excuse to punish him or his men when they returned to the Legion's forward base around sunset.

'Steady lads, you know the drill. Watch your dressing...'

Rufus allowed himself the luxury of a satisfied smile. Since he transferred in from the 3rd Legion and took command of his men ten months earlier, he had sweated them daily and deliberately hammered a new confident snap into their military drills. Many of his battle hardened men boasted more than ten years with the Eagle but even the most experienced among them would shirk repetitive training unless a firm hand was maintained.

Centurion Rufus had almost immediately raised eyebrows among his senior officers and not a little dissatisfaction within his own ranks after carefully reviewing his new command. Unsatisfied with their general appearance and standards he ordered extra sword drills, inspections and personally led daily route marches soon after assuming command. Ignoring their grumbles, endless hours spent on the Legion's practice arena thrusting against a wooden post with the gladius, the army's standard issue stabbing sword, and throwing countless practise pilum javelins had tightened slackening muscles and improved fitness and reflexes throughout his entire 80-man Century. An old soldier like Rufus and his experienced Optio Praxus both knew the truth of it. Their soldiers could make any number of clumsy mistakes in practice and live to tell the tale, but just one error with their shield and swordplay could cost them their lives in the deadly maelstrom of close quarter combat out here in the wilderness of Germania.

Now they had left the trees behind them it would take another minute or two for the Century to cross the broad sloping meadow before reaching the first line of crude daub and wattle huts. Rufus grew more concerned with every step. By now at least one of the locals should have heard or seen them coming and roused his neighbours. That's what usually happened inside a pacified village when an army patrol arrived unannounced. Surrounded by excited and curious children dressed in filthy rags his men would search the settlement for weapons then herd the villagers together and sort them out into family groups. The head of each household would be separated, forced to line up and pay the taxes set by Rome's Treasury, while his soldiers looked on and kept watch for any dissent from their families.

They probably wouldn't pay up in gold and silver Rufus thought absently to himself, judging by the unkempt state of the huts in front of his marching line of men. The locals would probably trade off their debt in livestock or grain; either was perfectly acceptable in the correct quantities. The Tribune would no doubt enjoy sitting behind his tax collectors table, officiously scratching records on a series of clay tablets as individual payments were made. Jupiter help any poor sod the Tribune caught who came up short when their turn came to pay. Overseeing that Rufus though ruefully to himself, was about all the little snot was good for.

Rufus was torn from his thoughts by a loud horn blast from the centre of the marching line. It was the signal to stop. Like his men, the Centurion halted. He stepped back two paces and looked towards the line's centre, to see what the Tribune wanted. At the other end of the line, Optio Praxus did the same. The boy had insisted that he should control the advance, and had taken prime position in the line's centre next to the Century's signum standard bearer and the Conicen, who carried the large circular buccina horn across his shoulder used for conveying orders to men beyond earshot of shouted commands. The Tribune was waving Rufus to him.

Centurion Rufus turned back to the soldier at the end of the line. Gruffly he snapped.

'Legionary Severus, you will take control of the wing. If I'm not back before we advance, make sure you keep the line straight... or you'll answer to me.'

Legionary Severus snapped to attention.

'Yes Sir.'

Rufus had been watching Severus closely recently. He had impressed his Centurion with his military skills on a number of occasions, not least when Severus had saved him from drowning several months earlier. Rufus was considering putting his name forward for promotion to Optio in another century within the Cohort. The final decision could wait for now though, Rufus thought. Satisfied that the veteran understood his duty Rufus hefted the weight of his own shield and gripping his sword's wooden handle tightly in his right hand he doubled swiftly towards the centre of the line.

Within moments he skidded to a halt besides the waiting Tribune, panting slightly after sprinting forty yards under the full weight of his shield and armour.

'Your orders Sir?

The Tribune regarded him coldly.

'Send a section forward and wake the villagers up.'

Shocked, Rufus took an involuntary step backwards.

'But Sir, regulations say to always use at least four sections...'

'Silence! The young officer snarled angrily. 'Don't you dare quote regulations to *me*. You will carry out my instructions or I'll have you in front of the Legion Commander on a charge of disobeying my order.'

Surprised and stung by the rebuke Rufus remained silent for a moment. The book said four sections forward when reconnoitring a small settlement but arguing between officers was bad for the men and the senior officer's side was always taken anyway if a Centurion was brought before the Legate, the Legion's Commander, on a disciple charge.

Rufus snapped to attention.

'Yes Sir!' His eyes flicked to his right. Out of the corner of his mouth he hissed.

'Number one section... double forward into the village... wake 'em up!'

Five minutes later, a runner returned from the edge of the village. He planted himself directly in front of his Centurion and was about to make his report when the Tribune spluttered.

'Damn your impertinence legionary! You will report to the senior officer present.'

Momentarily confused, the legionary stared back at his own officer for guidance. Rufus gave an almost imperceptible nod. The legionary blinked twice, turned and marched several steps towards the Tribune. Banging his heals together in the regulation manner of the parade square when addressing an officer he snapped to attention.

'Sir, the village is empty. There's no-one home, they've gone...all of them!'

'*What?*' The Tribune's surprise was genuine. 'Are you quite sure? It can't be so! Look, there's smoke coming from the huts.'

The legionary remained at attention and nodded. 'There are still some cooking fires smouldering inside 'em Sir.' The soldier shrugged. 'I saw a dog and a couple of stray chickens pecking about but no sign whatsoever of the Tencteri, or any of their livestock for that matter. Even the grain pits are empty. There's nothing...?'

The Tribune ground his teeth in frustration. No Tencteri meant that any chance of collecting taxes was gone. He'd have to return to his Legion's headquarters empty handed and admit his mission was a failure.

The Tribune whirled on Rufus. He had no intention of allowing this stain to tarnish his family name and or his own reputation in the eyes of the Legate.

'This is your fault damn you! When I get back to headquarters I'm going to...'

The rest of the Tribunes truculent rant stopped abruptly. From the other side of the valley the booming blast of a dozen war horns rent the still air. The powerful baritone blasts echoed mournfully across the valley as hundreds of near naked warriors suddenly burst from cover, streaming like a foaming tide from the trees only a hundred yards across the valley floor from where the halted line of legionaries stood. They yelled their war cries and waved axes, spears and swords above their heads, which glinted chillingly in the early morning sun.

Wide eyed, the startled Tribune looked back at the Centurion, a mixture of surprise and fear in his eyes.

'What the...?'

Rufus had had enough of the priggish fool standing uncertainly before him. It was time to snatch back his command. Ignoring the floundering Tribune he bellowed at the Conicen.

'It's a bloody ambush! Blow recall! Get the patrol back from the village.' Stepping forward he shouted above the roaring clammer busting on their ears from the other side of the village. 'Century! Form fighting square...*quickly!*'

Not a man among the battle hardened veterans needed to be told twice. Forming on their century standard, the legionaries sprinted to their rehearsed positions and in a matter of seconds the long line was gone and a solid phalanx was formed. It was second nature; a standard fighting tactic they had practiced so many times recently in training. Behind the solid square of shields the men anxiously watched the patrol running for their lives towards the protection of the Roman fighting square. Already the leading warriors were splashing across the stream in a shower of foaming spray. The last legionary was limping badly. He had taken a well aimed piece of slingshot in the back of his leg. Blood ran hot and burning as he frantically tried to hobble away from the village to safety. The wall of howling warriors was too quick for him. He screamed to his comrades for help as he disappeared beneath a frenzy of swinging blades, as the tribesmen broke over him like a crashing wave.

Chests heaving, the other six legionaries disappeared behind the open shields of the square which quickly slammed shut behind the last of them.

Rufus stood calmly with his shield raised at one corner of the square. Watching the approaching tribesmen he drew a deep breath and bellowed.

'Steady now lads...Second rank. *Ready pilums!*'

The second row of legionaries inside the wall of shields tightened their grip on the long wooden shafts of their throwing javelins. They rocked back, drawing their throwing arms behind them as they readied themselves for the next order.

Satisfied, Rufus quickly bellowed again.

'Front rank, draw swords and brace yourselves.'

Each man forming the outer shield wall snatched out his short stabbing sword and tensing muscles crouched slightly behind his shield. Each braced his right leg behind him. With shields virtually locked together, only the deadly points of the gladius were thrust outside the protective screen decorated with the 18th's emblem of the running boar.

From across the valley, the war horns continued to blow, urging the charging warriors to close and kill. When they were just fifty feet from the tight square Rufus' next order rang out.

'Pilums...*Throw!*'

A shower of sleek javelins hissed over the heads of the front rank and arced towards the onrushing mass of tightly packed tribesmen. Even as they left the legionaries callused hands Rufus roared anew.

'Again men...Ready ...*Throw!*

Another salvo of pilums flew from the square, as the first began to smash into their rushing targets. Warriors screamed and went down everywhere as the heavy javelins crashed into the tightly packed swirl of charging men. With a sudden look of shock and pain one howling chieftain dressed in the skins of a wolf took a javelin full in the chest. A gout of bright blood erupted from his mouth as he toppled forward. Pierced by the heavy iron pilum heads, both the dead and wounded dropped to the ground. Those who still lived screamed with pain as they lay skewered and writhing in agony. Their fallen bodies tripped those who careered headlong behind them. One or two javelins were stopped by shields carried by a few of the near naked tribesmen. The heavy iron heads punched through their wicker skins with ease, pulling their carriers off balance and rendering the shields awkward and utterly useless for further defence.

This was part of Rufus' plan, to break the impetus of the initial charge before it broke on one side of the Century's shield square. There was no time for a third volley of javelins, the frenzied tribesmen who had survived the hail of deadly pilums charged forward and crashed into the line of Roman's shields in a blaze of oaths, hissing blades and snarling fury.

Under their Centurion's orders the legionaries stood ready; silently braced and waiting for the first powerful impact. This would be the moment when months of hard training should pay off; providing the shield wall held the highly trained Roman killing machine could begin its deadly work.

The tidal wave of screaming warriors broke on the shield wall with a mighty crash. The barbarians frantically hacked and slashed at their enemies but their swinging blades bounced off the legionary's leather bound wooden shields.

Their first flailing swings momentarily blunted their ferocious attack as their initial rush failed to penetrate the Roman defence. Forced forward, hard against the Roman shields by the onrushing crush of warriors behind them, unable to pierce the wooden wall of locked shields, the closest warriors were forced to reach up and try to stab over the top of the nearest shield. This was the moment the legionaries had been waiting for. As the screaming barbarians stood tall and tried to thrust at the legionary's heads, in that one wild moment each of them failed to realise that they had completely exposed the right-hand side of their unarmoured bodies to the razor sharp points of the waiting Roman stabbing swords.

Centurion Rufus gave no order when the hand to hand fighting began; each of his men knew his duty and was trained for what they must do if they were going to survive the ambush. As the warrior in front and to his immediate right stretched upwards to attack the man standing beside him, the legionary thrust the tip of his sword between his enemy's ribs. Precision wasn't necessary, just hold onto the shield and stab with a flat horizontal blade anywhere into the adjacent warrior's rib cage, or just below it. Separated only by their shields and at most a few inches, the Centurion's men could smell the stink of their enemy's breath and the rank odour of their unwashed bodies as they stabbed.

Inflicting a minor flesh wound was extremely unlikely. In the tight melee, every legionary knew any solid thrust into enemy flesh would almost certainly inflict a mortal wound. The point of the gladius would slice into a lung, puncture guts or pierce a vital organ.

Stabbed barbarians began to scream and fall all along the shield line. Their groans and anguished cries of pain were drowned by the snarling roars of the warriors behind them who climbed over their fallen brothers to push home their own frenzied attack on the legionaries standing behind the wall.

The legionaries fighting against the unrelenting onslaught were beginning to tire. While they thrust and parried, they were engaged in an exhausting shoving match against the mass of barbarian warriors. To hold their position and maintain the vital protection of the shield wall they had to strain against their shields and hold against the push of their screaming enemies.

Centurion Rufus placed a small red whistle to his lips. He took a deep breath and blew. The whistle's shrill scream pierced the cries of the barbarians. Every man in the phalanx knew its meaning. The front rank disengaged themselves and stepped smartly backwards past the fresh rank of their comrades standing close behind them. With swords drawn and shields in place, a new and rested line of legionaries stepped into the desperate fight, quickly replacing the old wall. The exhausted soldiers who had fought so desperately for minutes which felt like hours fell back to the centre of the phalanx to snatch some much needed rest.

Centurion Rufus decided it was time to wrong foot the wild tribesmen. Nodding to the horn carrying Conicen he shouted.

'Blow... Prepare to advance!'

The Conicen nodded and spat down onto the ground, desperate to find enough spittle to lubricate his dry mouth. He put his lips to the horn's mouthpiece and blew two short baritone blasts. Trained to fight in silence every legionary heard the signal. Grimly, they readied themselves for the next order blown from the horn.

Satisfied, Rufus pointed his sword towards the village and bellowed.

'Century will advance...*Advance!*'

Thrusting their shields forward on the horns new signal, the new front line smashed the conical iron bosses mounted in the centre of their shields into the faces of their enemies, then took their first pace forward. The entire phalanx began to move in unison close behind them. As the front rank moved forward the next rank stabbed down at the throats and chests of the fallen barbarians who lay on the ground beneath their feet. It was a cruel tactic but made good tactical sense. A wounded enemy might feign death then suddenly slash at the back of the legs of one or more of the men fighting on the front line. If a hole suddenly appeared in the wall, it would mean the end of the solid defence the Century currently enjoyed.

Standing next to the Conicen, Tribune Crastus ducked suddenly when a piece of slingshot careened off his helmet. The ricocheted slug hit the legionary behind him full in the face. With an agonised cry, blood streaming from just below his eye, the wounded legionary fell groaning to the ground.

Horrified, Tribune Crastus stared transfixed at the man's bloody face. Surrounded by the moving phalanx and trying to hide the burgeoning panic he felt rising inside him the Tribune shouted at the legionaries surrounding the fallen soldier.

'He's done for...*Leave him!*'

Rufus heard the order. Furiously he shouted to the surrounding legionaries.

'*As you were!* Pick him up and carry him into the centre lads.'

Angrily the veteran Centurion whirled towards the ashen faced Tribune as his men picked up the injured legionary.

'We *never* leave wounded men behind...*Sir!*'

Still furious Rufus turned his attention from the open mouthed Tribune and focused his attention to directing the battle which was still raging around him.

The shield wall was tiring; it was time to change the front rank. Rufus blew his red whistle once again. Relieved to be swopped, his front rank stepped back sharply. Some of his men were bleeding and several injured needed the willing help of their comrades to return to the relative safety of the centre of the phalanx.

Rufus glanced about him. The barbarians charge had spilt around its armoured walls and now all four sides were engaged and fighting hard. Their defence was holding and to his relief, no warrior reinforcements had appeared from the tree line.

Ahead of him two legionaries suddenly went down, leaving a gaping gap in the shield wall. Rufus didn't hesitate. He snapped at the Tribune beside him.

'Follow me!'

Rufus stepped over one of the fallen legionaries and locked his shield with the next man in the line. A second later Tribune Crastus was beside him, shield raised and fighting for his life. A huge warrior rose up in front of him and smashed his wooden club down on the top edge of the Tribune's shield. As the bottom of the shield thumped down onto the ground, another snarling barbarian thrust his spear towards the exposed officer's groin. Crastus desperately parried at the spear with his sword but only managed to partially deflect it. The spearhead's sharpened blade cut through his tunic, a fraction below the armour which protected his waist. Crastus let out an agonised yelp as it sliced across his hip. As he fell, Rufus cursed and hacked down on the spear. He recovered the powerful stoke with a backhand slash at the startled warrior's throat. In a spray of blood the warrior recoiled from the shield wall. Another legionary stepped forward to fill the gap left by the fallen Tribune. Lying bleeding on the ground Crastus wailed.

'Please, don't leave me!'

Ducking an axe that cleaved through the air at his head, Rufus shouted an order over his shoulder to the men behind him. There was unguarded contempt in his voice as he snarled.

'Get the Tribune out of here.'

Suddenly the barbarian horns, which had fallen silent during the desperate fighting, blew another echoing signal across the valley. To Rufus' amazement, the barbarians began to disengage and withdraw; sprinting helter-skelter back through the village towards the cover of the opposite tree line.

Recovering from his surprise, Rufus quickly ordered the Conicen to blow the signal to stop. Chests heaving from their efforts the legionaries gratefully came to a halt. Leaning forward, they rested on the top edge of their shields. Moments later Optio Praxus appeared.

'What happened Sir, why did they suddenly run?'

Rufus shook his head. 'I don't know Praxus. We were holding our own but they had us pretty much trapped.'

Taking off his neck scarf, Rufus wiped it across his sweat stained face. Retying the red cloth firmly he said. 'Go and check on the wounded, then get the Century back up the hill quickly. We don't want to get caught out in the open again if they change their mind and come back.'

Still breathing heavily, Optio Praxus nodded as he removed his helmet and wiped his brow. 'Stay formed up as we are until we hit the tree line Sir?'

Rufus nodded again. 'Yes.' He glanced at the silent village. 'We're done here anyway. We'll get over the hill, reform and head straight back to camp...and I want a report on our casualties.' He stared at the dozens of dead warriors who littered the battlefield. Most had fought naked except for the cloaks they wore. Rufus nodded towards the dead outside the phalanx and said thoughtfully.

'Recognise them? From the way they're dressed I reckon they're renegades from the Usipati tribe, but why are they raiding so far from home?' Rufus sucked his teeth and looked back at the deserted village. 'And where in Hades for that matter have the local Tencteri villagers gone?'

Optio Praxus scratched his head. 'Dunno Sir. Now you mention it, it does all seem a bit odd.'

Rufus gave up looking for answers. He said. 'Get the lads moving Praxus. I must get back and make my report to the chief Centurion...None of this makes any sense to me....Why attack, surround us, and then not finish us off?' As he rubbed the back of his neck Rufus stared hard at his Optio.

'No. Something definitely doesn't feel right here.'

From their vantage point high on the other side of the valley, a group of horsemen dressed in woollen cloaks and warm furs had observed the battle. Concealed in the dense cover of the forest of trees they now watched as the Romans withdrew in good order into the distant tree line. Close to the bearded warriors a dozen other barbarians stood silently watching. Each carried a war horn.

Only one of the watching group knew the outcome in advance. He was dressed differently; he wore the uniform of a Roman cavalry officer.

The attempt to overwhelm the Romans had failed miserably. Two to one, a savage charge and raw courage had not been enough. It was a brutal and graphic lesson to each of them, written in the blood of the fallen warriors on the valley floor below.

Arminius turned his head and spoke to the tribal leaders around him.

'Behold my brothers! Now you see the result of fighting the invaders in pitched battle without sufficient men. If we are not blessed with overwhelming numbers, this is what will happen to us when they have both time and room to manoeuvre.'

Each of the seven barbarian chieftains nodded silently. Their faces were grim; they were not afraid of what the future held but there was unspoken concern among them; each knew that Roman revenge would be terrible if they failed. Torture, death or enslavement awaited them if they were not victorious. The invaders would show no mercy.

Arminius shook his head gravely. 'There is only one way to gain victory. We must engage them as my father did long ago.' Arminius rolled his fingers into a fist.

'We fight them the way we know best; ambush, slash and run. We keep snapping at them like hungry wolves; attacking again and again. We don't allow them the luxury of rest.' Grinding his teeth, he smashed his fist into his open palm and snarled.

'Our warriors keep bleeding them until the Romans stand before us afraid and exhausted. We will cut their columns into smaller and smaller pieces until all are annihilated.'

Arminius' eyes narrowed They burned like coals as he watched the last legionaries across the valley disappear from view. As bitter as bile, a lifetime of hatred welled up from deep inside him. He spat the words from his mouth.

'The Romans will come to know the meaning of real terror when they are trapped.' There was silence for a moment, and then, his voice softer, he said.

'There will come a moment of sweet victory for all the tribes.' He stared into the faces of his allies.

One of the chieftains looked at Arminius and asked.

'When exactly will our people taste this victory Herman?'

A savage grin spread across his face.

'It will come before winter's first snows brother, when we slaughter every last one of them in the Teutoburg forest.'

The chieftain's eyes remained fixed on Arminius.

'But how will we force them to enter the Teutoburg?'

Arminius looked down at the slain warriors below, and then stared back at the chieftain. The fire had died in his eyes, replaced now with animal cunning. Almost in a whisper he said.

'Don't worry brother...Leave that to me!'

Chapter 16

Sitting hunched in his chair, Camp Prefect Macros listened with growing concern to Rufus's report. When the Centurion finished the Prefect pushed himself back from the table and stood up.

'None of this makes any sense to me at all Rufus. We've had no reports from the border of unrest or incursions, and apart from the usual inter-tribal bickering; it's been quiet throughout the province since we arrived back in the spring. Now suddenly, out of the blue your patrol was ambushed by hostiles in force?'

Rufus nodded. 'Yes sir, that's about the size of it. It was clearly a trap. The village had been emptied of people and provisions before we got there, and the barbarians were waiting for us.'

Prefect Macros scratched his head. 'Sounds like you were lucky to escape?'

'Yes sir, that's what I think. The lads did well but we lost two men dead. One was killed from the scouting party which swept the village; another died of his wounds on the journey back here. I've got fifteen of my lads with the medicos now having their wounds treated.' Rufus shrugged.

'Nothing too serious, but I'll have to put most of them on light duties until their wounds have healed properly.'

The Prefect nodded. 'Of course, I'll leave that to your discretion.' Rubbing his chin he added. 'How did young Crastus perform?'

Rufus looked down at the ground and said nothing. The boy had panicked during the action, but he was young and inexperienced and criticizing a senior officer was a dangerous path to tread.

Prefect Macros clicked his tongue with irritation. 'Well?'

Rufus looked up. Reluctantly he said. 'He was in command before the ambush was sprung sir, but took a flesh wound shortly afterwards during the fighting. I led when he went down, so I can't tell you much more.'

The Prefect stared at his Centurion coldly. He was an old soldier and knew perfectly well when he was being lied to.

'All right Rufus, I hear your official version. I'll see to it that's what will be recorded on his record.' He turned and walked back to his table. Sitting on its edge he folded his arms and lowered his voice.

'Listen, I was as surprised as you when the General decided to give our young Tribune's operational command, even inside the pacified territories. You and I have spent too many years learning our craft to be put under a novice.' He shrugged. 'I suppose old General Varus thought it would be a good opportunity for them to gain some field experience without any real danger. They'll go home in a couple of months full of daring tales, leading their men on the wild northern frontier, and their families will be in debt to Varus for giving them such a golden opportunity...'

Rufus winced. It sounded about right. He snorted softly to himself. Keeping his voice low he said. 'I'm glad I'm not a politician. The General has to score points while he thinks of his future. Me, I just wonder what tomorrow will bring, and if I'll live that long.'

The veteran Prefect smiled back at Rufus and said.

'Spoken like a soldier...Now, off the record, what really happened?'

Sitting in the quiet of his tent, Rufus winced as he unlaced his sandal and gratefully rubbed his toes. His back was aching and he felt drained. It had been a tough fight and a gruelling march back to Legion headquarters. He had deliberately forced the pace and had removed his Century in good order from the danger of counterattack quickly. The men had grumbled when he had pushed them on, but now they were back safely and the injured were receiving proper treatment. He'd always thought that live moaning legionaries were better than silent dead ones.

Lying down on his cot, Rufus threaded his fingers together behind his head and tried to relax his aching body. Sleep approached but his mind began to wander. A lifetime of soldiering with the Legions was taking its toll. Although he hid it from his men, recently a new ache or pain seemed to appear every morning somewhere in his battle scarred body when it was time to rise.

He had a year left to serve before he could honourably retire from his military service. What then he wondered? He was entitled to a reasonably generous pension and the gift of land from a grateful Senate. The land wouldn't be even close to Rome of course. That was all privately owned by the richest in Roman society. No, as a retiring veteran Centurion he would be awarded land taken from people somewhere within the Empire. Soldiers stationed locally would be specially sent in and the original owners would be driven off long before he arrived to take possession. It was tough on the locals he thought, but there it was, that's how it worked. He would farm the land and support himself and perhaps, even a wife and family of his own? Except for the most senior officers, it was forbidden to take a wife while serving with a Legion. True, he thought some of his brother Centurions and even a few of the men had a woman who followed them as the Legion travelled. Like the traders, money lenders and brothel keepers, they had set up temporary home in the settlement which sprang up close to the Legion's military stockade.

With his eyes closed, as he lay luxuriating about his future Rufus wondered where he would eventually plant new roots. Southern Gaul was his favourite. The soil was rich and the winters were mild. Perhaps he would take a local girl as a wife? It was an appealing thought to have someone to cook for him and keep him warm in bed at night.

Further dreams of the future were abruptly halted when his Optio's head suddenly appeared through the tent's flap.

'Sorry to disturb you sir, but there's trouble.'

Rufus sat up with a start. Sleepily he growled.

'In Jupiter's name I've only just got to bed. What is it now Praxus?'

The Optio winced. His tone remained apologetic.

'It's Legionary Severus sir. Tribune Crastus has had him arrested and put in chains.'

Rufus rubbed the sleep which had threatened to overwhelm him from his tired eyes.

'Arrested?...What do you mean arrested? On what charge?' He demanded sleepily.

Praxus answered quickly. 'Like I said sir, it's bad. It could mean the death penalty for Severus if he's guilty. The Tribune has just charged him with being an escaped slave....'

Rufus dressed in a hurry. Praxus was right. If young Severus was indeed an escaped slave who had furthered his getaway by joining the Legion there was only one penalty, and that was enshrined in Roman military law. The penalty was death.

Urgently buckling on his breastplate, Rufus picked up his helmet and rushed outside. He followed his Optio through the darkness towards the legion's headquarters. Returning the salute from the sentry he rushed inside and spotted the Prefect's clerk hurrying down the gloomy corridor carrying yet more scrolls towards a storeroom.

'Where is Prefect Macros?' Rufus barked.

The clerk spun round and faced the panting Centurion.

'He's gone over to the Provost's office sir, with Tribune Crastus.'

Rufus sighed heavily. Working under the direct command of the Prefect, the Provost was responsible for the wooden cells built to imprison captives and hostages taken by the Legion, and legionaries under field punishment for disciplinary matters.

Rufus nodded and almost ran from the Headquarters, followed closely by Praxus.

The cells were hard against the inside wall of the stockade, close to the communal latrines of the 10th Cohort. The latrine trench was close to being filled in, another was half dug nearby. Praxus gagged at the overpowering stench which rose from it as they hurried past.

Ahead, silhouetted by flaring torches Rufus saw a small group of officers talking together. He recognised the Prefect first, and hurried over to him. Tribune Crastus was beside him. Saluting, Rufus said.

'I've just been informed that one of my lads, legionary Severus has been placed under arrest. Can you clarify the charge for me sir, he's one of my best?'

'One of your best?' The tribune snapped. There was arrogant contempt in his voice.

Startled by his sudden appearance from the surrounding darkness Prefect Macros stared at his Centurion for a moment as he raised his hand to stifle further comment from the young Tribune. Then, considering his words carefully he replied.

'Ah Rufus, yes. I'm afraid a serious charge has been made against legionary Severus. Tribune Crastus recognised him and ordered his immediate arrest. There is considerable evidence, based on the Tribunes statement that Severus is indeed an escaped slave.'

'What evidence would that be sir?'

'Well, the word of a Tribune of course, but he bears scars on his arm, which could be where his slave brand was removed.'

Rufus spluttered. 'But...but he's a good soldier sir. He saved my life a month ago. Based on his past performance I was even considering putting him forward for Optio soon.'

Marcos shook his head. Spreading his hands he said.

'I'm sorry Centurion; the matter is out of my hands. Based on the charges which have been brought against him, military law dictates that in due course the prisoner must be returned to our winter camp, and put in front of a tribunal of senior officers who will decide his fate.' Marcos shrugged and said matter-of-factly. 'General Varus has granted early leave to the three Legates, so we'll have to wait for them to return before arranging the trial. He'll get a fair hearing of course, but if he can't prove his innocence...' He shrugged as his words hung in the air. 'They'll find him guilty and there is only one sentence which fits this particular crime.... He'll be crucified in front of his Legion.'

Tribune Crastus stepped forward. His face was sly in the flickering light.

'And while the slave is on trial Centurion, I expect the Legates will want to know why you were harbouring him in your Century?'

Rufus spun angrily and looked into the smug expression which had spread across the Tribune's face. In another time and another place, the little snot would have felt Rufus's blade in his throat.

Before he could speak however, Prefect Marcos barked.

'That is quite enough Tribune...You are dismissed.'

Crastus eyes glittered angrily in the torchlight. For just a moment he glared at the Prefect. Reluctantly he saluted, turned and stamped off into the darkness.

The veteran Prefect returned his gaze to Rufus. Stepping forward he whispered quietly.

'We both know that little shit is covering his back after the mess he made during the ambush Rufus. I don't know if the charges against your man are true but whatever happens, watch your step, that boy has rich and powerful friends at home. You should know he wanted me to arrest you as well for complicity, but based on what you had already told me, I refused. He's trying to cast a shadow on your reputation of course, in case you make accusations of dereliction or incompetence against him during the tribunal.'

Rufus spat on the ground beside him. Wiping the back of his hand across his mouth he shook his head sadly and said.

'This bloody army isn't what it used to be, when jumped up little turds like that can cause so much trouble.' With a sigh he added. 'If I have your permission I'll talk to legionary Severus when I get the chance sir. He's one of mine and I can't just abandon him. Truth is, he needs all the help he can get.'

The Prefect nodded. 'Of course you can Centurion. I'd do the same if it were me, but to tell you the truth, in this instance I'm glad it's not.'

Chapter 17

It was hot working under the mid-day sun, even deep in the forest. Far from the safety of their summer camp, stripped to the waist the legionaries from the 2nd Century of the fifth Cohort sweated and grumbled as they laboured. Shields and spears lay on the ground, arranged neatly nearby beside each individual's armour but as always, swords remained sheathed on their hips. The new stretch of road the men were engaged in building was only half complete and it was proving to be particularly awkward. Trees in its path had been felled, and the marching road's broad foundation and drainage ditches dug, but suitable rocks big enough to form the base weren't immediately available. To the growing annoyance of the engineer in charge, they had to be carted in from half a mile away. It was proving a slow process and the engineer's schedule was falling further and further behind.

'This won't do at all Centurion. I need much more rock than this.'

The Century's newly promoted commander removed his helmet and wiped his brow. He stared at the frown on the engineer's face for a moment.

'My men are digging them up as fast as they can. To meet your requirements I can't possibly deliver more without having extra men to quarry the rock.'

The engineer stared at the sweating legionaries who were busy unloading the latest batch to arrive. The rocks were heaved from the two wheeled cart by its driver and another legionary. The lumps of stone thumped onto the ground beside the long scar already dug by their comrades earlier that morning. The work detail picked them up awkwardly. Lifting the heavy burdens into place they carefully interlocked each one tightly to its neighbour to create a solid and lasting foundation. Smaller stones would be added later in layers of decreasing size, as the final stages to producing a firm and levelled marching surface for the Legions.

Casting his eyes away from the toiling men the engineer's gaze fell on the fully armed guards who casually patrolled in pairs through the trees around the worksite.

'What about using some of them?' He enquired. 'They'll do.'

The Centurion shook his head. 'Those men are there for a purpose.' He sighed. 'I know this isn't classed as hostile territory anymore, but regulations still state that half the men labour while the others act as their guards.'

Already annoyed by the series of nagging delays which had confounded his tight construction schedule, tormented under the hot sun the engineer's temper suddenly snapped. Angrily he snarled.

'Damn your bloody regulations Centurion! Our progress is falling behind and you deny me the only possible means to make up precious time. You know very well that this area was pacified long ago. There is absolutely no danger out here and I'm telling you now, if you don't release men to collect more stone right now I'm going to report you personally for causing this delay....' He paused and glared angrily at the young Centurion as he waited for an answer.

Racked with indecision the Centurion looked at his men as they slowly walked the wooded perimeter, shaded by the trees from the hot sunshine. The engineer was right of course, this wasn't an area known for trouble and there hadn't been a single incident since his men had relieved the last century five days earlier. The prospect of being hauled up in front of his Prefect, or worse still the Legate on a dereliction charge appalled him. He'd worked and fought too hard to face demotion now, just when he had realised his life's dream and achieved officer rank. As the youngest Centurion in the Legion, a bright future awaited. His mind made up, he was damned if he was going to see it all ruined by blind adherence to a stupid regulation which, he reasoned no-one else would know he had ignored anyway.

'All right, I understand the problem. I'll give you another twenty men from the guard to help quarry more rock.'

The engineer was delighted. His face beamed. 'Well done Centurion, now that's really using your initiative.'

While the Centurion made arrangements with his Optio to remove every other guard and march them to the quarry site, he was unaware that dark eyes were watching his dwindling command from the depths of the forest...

'Is everything set and ready?'

Lying quietly down beside him, Rolf nodded and whispered.

'Yes Herman, the men are all in position and know what to do when you give the signal.'

Arminius nodded thoughtfully.

'Very well.'

Satisfied that everything was ready, Arminius motioned his cousin back from their concealed vantage point in the trees. They slithered down into dead ground on their bellies. Keeping low, both men jumped up and ran in a half crouch towards their waiting auxiliaries. The cavalrymen were waiting among the trees close to the latest completed section of the road, hidden from the engineer and the sweating legionaries by the brow of a low hill.

Taking his horse's reins from one of the men, Arminius pulled on his plumed officers' helmet. Securing it under his chin he signalled in silence for the cavalry squadron to mount. The grinning Cherusci, dressed in their Roman auxiliary uniforms eagerly hauled themselves into their saddles; despite his churning stomach Arminius's eyes had begun to shine bright with anticipation.

He pinched the material of his Decurion tunic and then released it. His face contorted with a moments contempt and hatred.

'Now is the time we turn these uniforms into weapons against our enemies Rolf.'

Arminius exhaled deeply, betraying the relief which engulfed him. 'Finally we can begin to play our own part.'

He turned his horse in the direction of the unsuspecting Romans. Lifting his arm Arminius waved his squadron forward at the walk. With bridles jingling and their horses snorting to the clatter of iron shod hooves the mounted column began to move. Turning his head back towards Rolf he said over his shoulder with a savage grin.

'It is time to make the Roman swine ahead learn their true mistake of entering our land.'

His untouched breakfast before him, General Varus frowned as he finished reading the latest reports from patrols which had recently returned from their duties in the interior. Two strong patrols had come under attack from the barbarians and taken casualties, and most worryingly of all, contact had been lost with one of his furthest border forts. Three full squadrons of cavalry had been dispatched to ascertain the fort's fate, but had not yet returned.

Varus sighed deeply and dropped the last parchment onto the table before him. This sudden explosion of violence didn't make any sense to him at all. Silently he shook his head. In the last few weeks, the omens had all been good. Ignatius, his haruspex had been blessed one dark night by a highly significant dream. Granted by the Gods, the vision had shown him flying beside a great owl through an obsidian sky pitted with shinning stars. Obviously Ignatius explained, the owl was a creature of great physical power and deep-seated wisdom. Ignatius had assured his master that the creature represented him as military governor, soaring free and using his own insight and sound judgment across the entire Northern Province.

The General's trusted prodigy Arminius had given no hint of trouble either. His latest reports confirmed that the tribes within the province were co-operating peacefully. To back up his confidence in Arminius, the evidence he had seen with his own eyes was solid and overwhelming; trade was flourishing across the Province and Varus's road building program was running smoothly throughout the heavily forested tribal lands. The old general rubbed his hands slowly across the white stubble on his chin. He had not received any intelligence of unrest among the barbarian chieftain's. Tax revenue was being successfully gathered on the whole, and the Province's treasury was growing at an acceptable rate.

Varus shook his head. Had he not also given the highest priority to mediating in the constant inter-tribal disputes? Although to a man they didn't like compromise, under his obligations within the Pax Romana to act as arbitrator he had managed to keep the peace among the simple minded tribal chiefs, having found solutions to their sometimes petty and often ridiculous disputes. Ultimately, his wise judgements had proved acceptable to all parties in every single case laid before him in recent months.

His adjutant, Prefect Dalious suddenly entered his private quarters, saluted and broke the General's train of thought.

'Sorry to interrupt your breakfast General, but a patrol has just returned from the border fort we lost contact with a week ago.'

Varus sighed. 'Surely it can wait Dalious?'

The Prefect's face was grave.

'Err....No Sir. I think you had better hear the commander's report immediately. He's waiting outside.'

There was something hidden in the tone of the Prefect's voice that alerted Varus. It sounded like more trouble and the adjutant's expression concerned him. Reluctantly, with a sigh he nodded.

'Very well then Dalious, you'd better send him in.'

On a signal from Dalious through the open flap the 17th Legion's senior Decurion marched in and saluted. His dusty uniform and the dark circles under his eyes bore the marks of a man who had ridden hard through the night without rest. Concern within Varus's chest increased as he eyed the Roman officer.

'Well?'

The Decurion remained at attention.

'Sir, I have just returned from our fort close to the Alara River on the north-eastern border.... It is my unfortunate duty to inform you that we found the fort had been overrun. The entire garrison has been massacred.'

The General's mouth dropped open with surprise. His tone was incredulous.

'What!...The whole garrison, *all of them?*'

The exhausted Decurion nodded. In a sombre voice he continued his report.

'I'm afraid so Sir. The entire Century was gone; cut to pieces. When we arrived two days ago it was a scene of utter carnage. The fort had been burned to the ground and our men's bodies were scattered everywhere. Their weapons were missing and all had been stripped and horribly mutilated. The heads were gone too, but there was no immediate sign of who had attacked them. My men searched the surrounding area thoroughly. The settlement nearby was burned and looted as well. There were plenty of civilian dead but we found no obvious enemy corpses until a dead Ampsivarii warrior was found under a pile of fallen thatch. I believe there was absolutely no doubt it was them that launched the attack and butchered our men.'

Wiping his hand across his tired face he concluded his report by saying.

'I ordered my men to throw out a mounted screen to guard against further attacks and the rest started rebuilding immediately. My men will hold there until relieved....' As an afterthought he added.

'Before I left I recorded the number of our own men's bodies and on my return this morning I checked with our clerks before I came to headquarters to make my report sir. It seems that only three of the garrison are missing and unaccounted for.'

Varus sat stunned for a moment. His surprise was turning quickly to rage. He barked at his adjutant.

'I want every senior officer here for an emergency staff meeting in thirty minutes Dalious.'

He had faced this same grim prospect before in Syria. Rebellion was in the air, and Varus knew he must act quickly to mercilessly crush it before it flared out of control and spread across the border into the pacified lands under his control. The General stood up and walked across to the beautifully crafted marble bust of the Emperor. Mounted on an ornate wooden plinth, it held pride of place in the tented room. A gift from the Emperor himself, the bust had arrived from Rome in time for his recent birthday. Its cold unblinking stare held Varus for a moment. As if making a solemn pledge to the glistening white image of Augustus, the ageing General suddenly snarled.

'I will discuss this situation with my officers in detail and decide on a suitable response to what is a most serious threat to the stability of the province.'

Anger flared again inside him at a situation which if left unchecked might unravel months of subtle diplomacy and the rewards which had begun to flow. General Varus spun on his heals. Spittle sprayed from his mouth as he roared at his adjutant.

'I will teach these Ampsivarii animals a lesson they will never forget!'

Chapter 18

Both the engineer and the young Centurion looked up with surprise when they heard jingling bridles and horses whinnying. A column of mounted horsemen was slowly approaching through a cloud of dust on the newly constructed road behind them. As the column neared, both men instantly recognised the oval shields and plumed helmets of the auxiliary cavalry and relaxed. To their collective relief, it was nothing more than a friendly mounted patrol approaching. As the horsemen entered the clearing the Centurion stepped forward and raised his hand in welcome. The gesture changed to a smart salute when he saw a senior Decurion was riding at the head of the column.

Arminius nodded his acknowledgement as he walked his horse into the middle of the construction site, towards the waiting Roman officers. He was in no hurry; his men split into two separate files and surrounded the outer boundaries of the site. The Centurion walked forward and smiling said.

'Welcome sir. I was not expecting to see you. I had no idea you were patrolling the area.'

Arminius stared coldly at the young officer for a moment, and then looked around at the sweating legionaries who had taken the squadron's arrival to snatch a momentary break from unloading the last heavy rocks from the cart. Remaining in his saddle Arminius looked down and said.

'You don't seem to have many men here Centurion. Where exactly is the rest of your Century?'

The Centurion blanched. There would be trouble if the Decurion reported him for ignoring regulations and weakening the guard.

'Err...I've sent them to the quarry sir.' He pointed to the heavily rutted track which quickly disappeared off into the dense surrounding forest. Almost apologetically he added. 'Our engineer here requested more rock, so I sent more men to quarry the stones....It's not far.'

Arminius shrugged and wiped his hand over his dry lips. His tone was relaxed and friendly.

'It has been a long ride and a dry thirsty morning Centurion. Do you have any water to hand?'

The Centurion nodded. He relaxed slightly as he turned and picked up a half full water skin; perhaps the Decurion, being a brother officer would overlook such a minor infraction. Passing up the skin the young Centurion said with an ingratiating smile.

'Yes sir, here you are. Please use mine. Take all you want.'

Arminius nodded his gratitude and casually raised the spout to his lips. His thirst slaked, he passed it back. It was an innocent act to the watching Romans but hid a deadly signal to the heavily armed German auxiliaries who watched silently and now surrounded them all.

Arminius's breathing became shallow and the beat of his heart quickened. After so many years of bitter torment, the moment of truth was finally upon him. *Now!*

Arminius's hand moved in a blur towards the handle of his sword. As it hissed from its scabbard the blade flashed momentarily in the bright sunlight. Before he could react, Arminius lent forward and rammed it hard and deep into the unsuspecting Centurion's throat.

'Now men!' He snarled as the Roman fell. *'Kill them all!'*

'But general sir, there simply isn't enough time to launch a full-scale invasion into Ampsivarii territory.'

Varus glared at the 19th Legion's Prefect. This wasn't what he wanted to hear.

Like the other senior officers around him, the veteran Prefect had served on too many fronts, and fought in too many battles to soften what he knew to be true. It was his duty to advise his commander, and he had no intention of shirking his responsibilities. Ignoring the scowl on the General's face he continued his tactical appreciation.

'The logistics alone of taking two full Legions of over nine thousand men into the field, and keeping them supplied in hostile territory is a huge task to arrange sir. If we rush our preparations, we could end up with a disaster on our hands.'

Both the 17th and 18th's Prefects nodded their agreement. One of them added.

'I'm afraid he's right sir. Look what happened to the 5th Alaudae Legion years ago.'

Varus nodded reluctantly. The stain of the 5th's disgrace was still a livid scar in the minds of every military man throughout the Empire. The Alaudae Legion had fought the same Germanic barbarians 25 years earlier in an early and ill-fated campaign, which had ended in a catastrophe for both the legion, and for Rome.

In one battle during months of fierce and bloody fighting, the Legion had suffered the ultimate humiliation. The 5th's Eagle was captured and taken by the savage tribesmen. The circumstances of the loss were irrelevant. There was no greater shame in the eyes of Rome's military machine.

When marched into foreign lands, the Eagle *was* Rome. Its very culture and civilisation were symbolised by the golden Eagle. Losing it to wild and uncivilised barbarians meant defeat for the very essence of everything mighty Rome stood for. The dark stain of dishonour had never left the disgraced Legion, they remained haunted by it. The Alaudae survived as a fighting unit, but losing its Eagle left the 5th's reputation, and that of its commander Marcos Lollius damaged beyond repair.

The ageing General Varus knew the catastrophe of the 5th's disgrace as well as any of his officers; he shuddered inwardly. The damage to his reputation and the subsequent political fallout of losing just one of the precious Eagles under his command was too awful to contemplate. A rash decision now could be his undoing. Closely linked to the Emperor, having such a permanent blemish imprinted on the noble House of Varus was simply unthinkable.

No, Varus decided. His original plan to invade Ampsivarii territory in strength had perhaps been a little hasty. His initial wrath had overwhelmed cold political logic. There must be a better way to act decisively and save face in the eyes of his subordinates, and of course the Emperor himself. Varus pondered as the Prefect continued his appreciation.

'Our campaigning season this year is nearly at an end. As you know sir, the snows will come soon and the winters here bring cold beyond belief. We must march back to winter quarters in just a few weeks or be trapped here until the spring without sufficient supplies.'

Varus nodded. Although he had allowed his three Legion's Legates to go home to Rome early, he was in a way relieved that he had the benefit of these three Camp Prefects to advise him. They were highly experienced veterans and true professional soldiers. Between them, they had no name or family connections to speak of and no future political ambitions that Varus was aware of. He was confident they lacked any hidden agenda to further themselves at his expense if things went wrong.

There was silence in the briefing room. Varus looked up from his contemplation with a start. All three Prefects were staring at him intently, each of them waiting for his final decision. It was time to firmly grasp the nettle of command he thought, and be their General.

'Gentlemen, thank you for your sound advice. Your points concerning supply and closeness of winter are well made. Clearly, now is not the time to invade Ampsivarii territory in force, and punish those responsible for the massacre at the Alara River.' General Varus stood up. Grasping his hands behind his back, he continued.

'A full invasion will take careful planning and preparation, which should be carried out during the coming winter months while we are safely in our permanent quarters west of the Rhine. There is however a case for launching a punitive raid beyond the border now. I want the Ampsivarii to feel our wrath. Settlements which are discovered are to be burned and barbarian foodstuffs confiscated or destroyed. Many Ampsivarii will starve during the coming months; perhaps winter's cold and empty bellies will teach them an early lesson. The Cohorts I send in can also map the territory, in preparation for an early invasion and proper spring campaign against them next year.'

The Prefects nodded their agreement. It was a good compromise and sound plan. One of them raised a finger and asked.

'What of the massacred garrison on the Alara sir? We need to replace them urgently.'

Varus stared at his adjutant for a moment. Pursing his lips he said.

'Good point Dalious. We had better send...half a Cohort as replacements. Three Centuries should be more than enough to hold the new fort when it is completed.

That's triple the men that were there before, but one thing...they will have to remain there throughout the winter.

Each of the Prefects winced. They knew it would not be a popular duty.

'The men won't be too happy staying out there on the rim sir.' One of them said.

Varus replied irritably.

'Of course they won't like it, but we must maintain a strong and permanent presence from now on, or these raids might continue, even in the depths of winter.' He shrugged and stroked his chin. 'As far as I know, there are no units currently under collective field punishment, so to be reasonable to our men; we'll get the Centurions to draw lots.'

The 17th's Prefect pounced. 'From which Legion will we take them sir?'

Varus grinned. Ignoring his adjutant, he stared at the three Legion's Prefects in turn.

'Gentlemen; I think it fair if not just lowly Centurions put their future in the hands of fate.... You can decide which Legion provides our winter guard on the Alara. It is my order that you three Prefects will draw lots first.'

A deathly hush had fallen over the construction site after the screaming had stopped. Most of the Romans died where they stood under the heavy hissing blades of the auxiliaries. The sudden charge had caught the legionaries by complete surprise. Few even had time to understand what was happening, let alone defend themselves. Confusion turned to horror on their sunburnt faces as the legionaries were ridden down and slaughtered by those they considered comrades-in-arms. A few of the outer guard had tried to make a run for it, but Arminius's archers placed silently before the ambush was sprung, found them easy targets.

Arminius swung down from his horse and wiped his sword on the dead Centurion's tunic. The dark wound in his throat still oozed where Arminius's sword had pierced it. The dead officer's armoured chest and the ground around him were covered in a dark stain of blood. Arminius watched the blood drip and puddle as he searched his feelings. He had killed men before in battle. In Pannonia they were his enemies and were trying to kill him; it had never occurred to him to strike down a fellow officer who wore the same uniform.

Arminius suddenly snorted at his weakness. Angrily, he cast aside his stinging conscience. These weren't thoughts worthy of a man sworn to rid his lands of the hated invaders, he angrily told himself. This was the first time he had directly raised his hand against Rome, but he wondered how many more would die under his blade before the fighting was over.

Rolf suddenly appeared beside him. He stared down at the lifeless corpse at his cousin's feet and spat contemptuously at it. His eyes still shining with the light of battle, Rolf's voice was a sneer as he said.

'They squealed like pigs as we killed them Herman.'

Arminius nodded in silence. Clearly, Rolf wasn't troubled by a single shred of guilt or the slightest prick to his conscience. Arminius was relieved. He looked up sharply.

'None escaped then?'

With a wolfish grin and rapid shake of his head Rolf replied.

'Not one got away cousin, all are dead.'

Arminius nodded. 'That is very good Rolf.' As if swabbing away the last vestige of regret, he wiped his hand across his face. It was time to move on to the next stage.

'We must strip the bodies of armour and weapons quickly.' He pointed to the deserted wooden cart. Still in its harness, the mule which had spent the morning patiently hauling stones from the quarry was now resting with its head down, using its powerful yellow teeth to crop a tasty patch of grass between its broad hooves.

'See to it that two of the men gather all the weapons and armour onto that cart. Have them safely deliver it to our own people when we are finished here.' Arminius swept his arm across the silent glade of the dead.

'Take the heads but make sure they are discarded and hidden in the woods.' His face clouding with sudden concern he added. 'Ensure our men take no personal trinkets or booty. Our greatest strength in the next weeks will be surprise. If even the smallest trophy is discovered by the Romans on any of our men we will be undone.' Arminius stared hard at his cousin. 'You understand Rolf, we had the advantage of total surprise on our side today... and we must keep it that way.' He nodded towards the rutted track leading into the trees. 'Tell the men with the cart to follow after they are done here.'

Arminius sheathed his sword and grasped the pommel of his saddle. Before remounting he stared coldly again at his cousin.

'The squadron will ride to the quarry Rolf. I want the rest of them slaughtered before we return to camp.' His dark eyes narrowed. 'You understand don't you? Not a single Roman is to be left alive!'

Chapter 19

In the cramped prison cell, Centurion Rufus's eyes narrowed in the semi-darkness.

'Well Severus. Is what they say true?'

Huddled on the floor at the back of the cell, filled with utter despair the legionary sighed and nodded silently. Stripped of the right to wear his uniform, he now wore just a stained loincloth and tunic, and heavy iron chains manacled around his wrists and ankles.

Rufus stared at Severus for several seconds. The pathetic figure's nod confirmed his guilt. Seeing the gesture Rufus scratched his head.

'Frankly, I don't know what I can do to help you Severus. Under military law you have the right to have an officer speak for you when the time comes at your tribunal.' Rufus shook his head slowly. 'I don't know your story, but I can certainly give you a character reference as your commanding officer if you wish it.'

Severus looked up sharply and nodded eagerly. 'Yes sir, please.'

He sighed deeply. 'I'm sorry to involve you in any of this sir. I don't want to get you into any trouble because of me.'

Rufus snorted. 'Bit late to worry about that now lad. If I'm going to be any use to you at all, you'd better tell me everything from the beginning; from the time when you first ran away from your master's house.'

Severus stared at his Centurion. He chewed on his bottom lip for a moment, and then in a halting voice began to tell his tale.

'I was born into slavery sir. My mother and father were both slaves; the property of the House of Crastus. I grew up on the estate you see. Old man Crastus owns a huge vineyard estate just south of Rome. He also owns over a hundred slaves who mostly work in the fields tending thousands of his bloody vines. As soon as I was old enough, that was my job. Every day, we'd all work from first light until sunset taking care of those damned plants and picking the grapes when they were ready. The estate's overseers were real bastards. They'd use the whip on us for even the slightest thing and they stole the food out of our mouths whenever they got the chance and sold it. Some of the others worked in the winery where they trod grapes and made the wine, and there was a few who work in the family's villa as house slaves.'

Rufus nodded. He supposed that's how it usually worked among the rich. Having spent so many years serving the Eagle in one theatre or another, he'd had very little contact with any slaves or slavery in general for that matter.

'I fell in love with one of the house girls' sir. I...I didn't mean to, it just sort of happened after I was ordered from the fields and given the job labouring on building a new roof on one of the villa's outhouses. The girl, Anna was her name sir, used to sometimes bring us water. We snatched conversation whenever the overseers weren't looking and were...well, just kind to each other.' he shrugged...' and we just fell in love.'

Rufus had been a soldier all his adult life, there had been no time or opportunity for love. To him, this was unknown territory. He simply nodded and said.

'Get on with your story soldier.'

With a heavy heart and eyes downcast, Severus continued.

'My master was a widower. He took his enjoyment as he pleased with the house girls' sir. He kept only the prettiest close to him in the villa. The old bastard had forced himself on Anna plenty of times. It wasn't her fault, she had no choice, she belonged to him. She hated his touch, the beatings he gave her for his own pleasure...and the things he made her do.'

With a pleading look in his eyes he added.

'Trapped like she was sir, Anna told me she was close to ending her torment by taking her own life. I couldn't bear to see her in so much pain so between us, we decided to run. We were going to start a new life together far away, free from slavery.'

Rufus nodded again. 'So what happened?'

Severus sighed. 'I remembered one of the old men who worked with me in the fields had once said he had heard of a man who lived to the north. He reckoned the man was skilled with a blade and could remove our brands. We wouldn't stand a chance if they remained. The runaway catchers would hunt us down and take us back if we still wore the Crastus brand. When I asked him to tell me where this man was and how we could contact him, the old man knew instantly we were planning to run and said he'd only tell us if he and his son could escape with us.'

Rufus said. 'So you took them with you?'

Severus shrugged miserably.

'What else could I do sir? We cut off our collars and broke out one night after Anna had stolen two silver goblets from the villa. They looked pretty valuable and we planned to sell them, or at least trade them for the removal of our brands.' Severus stared down at his scarred forearm. Dark memories rampaged back as he continued. 'We tried to run all night to get as far away as possible, but the old man kept stopping. He was just too old and tired to keep up so we hid all the next day and decided to only travel by night. Trouble was, there were patrols everywhere and the old man slowed us up so much, we didn't get far enough.' Severus sighed at the memory of those terror filled days and nights. 'We were sleeping in a disused farmhouse when the slave catchers came. I think the old man must have fallen asleep on his watch so there was no warning. It was chaos when they burst in... I was dead lucky; I was round the back taking a leak when they came for us. We all got separated in the confusion.' He sighed and shrugged miserably again. 'Somehow I managed to get away.'

A tear rolled down his cheek. 'That was the last I ever saw of Anna and the others. I hid for a while in a culvert and returned to the ruin after dark. I searched and searched all night but there was no sign of any of them.'

Rufus stared at Severus. He had been moved by the man's pitiful story. As a citizen of Rome and a free man, Rufus was only now beginning to understand Severus's story, and the life of misery which he and the others must have endured.

'Right, so you were on your own. How did you end up serving with the 18th?'

Severus wiped his face. His chains clanked together as he moved.

'I still had the goblets, and by then knew how to contact the man who would cut and burn out my brand. I stayed on the run and it took a while, but eventually I did find him. It was bloody painful, but once he'd done his work, I needed somewhere to hide, somewhere far from Rome. I had no money and nothing left to trade so I wandered the countryside for weeks until the pain stopped and the wound healed, stealing food where I could find it. Once it was safe to mix with people again, the town I ended up in looking for work had a recruiting stall in the marketplace. At the time, half starved as I was it seemed a good way of disappearing... so I joined up.' He shrugged desolately. 'And here I am. That's why my old master's son, Tribune Crastus recognised me.'

Rufus felt the legionary's depression. It was his turn to sigh. 'It's just bloody bad luck all round son.'

Severus looked appealingly at his Centurion.

'What will happen to me sir? Do you think there's any chance?'

The Centurion shook his head slowly. This poor little bastard was one of his men, one he owed the debt of his life. Rufus knew he could walk away now and leave Severus to his fate, but within the core of Rufus's own code of honour, loyalty was a door which swung both ways. He expected loyalty from his soldiers, but returned it in equal measure wherever he could. To Centurion Rufus, abandoning Severus in his darkest hour was unthinkable.

'I honestly don't know lad. I've already spoken to the Prefect on your behalf. He's an old soldier and a good man, but he rightly said this has now become an official army matter and things must take their course I'm afraid.'

Severus hung his head again and stared at his chains. Like his Centurion, he knew the only penalty for runaways hiding in a Legion.

'For now I'll have to go away and think about it some more, and talk to some of the older Centurions. Maybe one of them might know something that will help. I'll go and see the Prefect again. If I ask him, he'll advise me on the letter of military law in these circumstances, and then at least I'll know what to expect, and the correct legal procedures when we get back to our winter quarters.'

Severus nodded. These were some words of comfort and hope, but in his heart Rufus knew Severus was doomed.

Before he turned and left the cellblock Rufus stopped in the doorway and called over his shoulder.

'I'll see if I can do something about some better food for you while I'm at it son. The Provost in charge here is an old mate of mine and owes me a favour or two.

Arminius stood before General Varus and finished making his report.

'The tribal leaders are worried and afraid sir. Many have suffered attacks and without sufficient weapons they fear for their people's survival in the coming winter. They have all asked for you to permit them to re-arm themselves against the Ampsivarii.'

Varus frowned. Things were becoming more complicated with every new report he received. The Ampsivarii had crossed the frontier in some strength, and were roaming free across his pacified territory attacking, burning and looting at will. To make matters worse, the barbarians had not limited their attacks solely to the tribes. A road building replacement detail had discovered an entire Century butchered, and a supply column had been raided one night on its way towards his current headquarters.

The punitive raid he had launched into Ampsivarii territory had been unsuccessful. Some tribesmen and their families had been caught and executed, and salt had been ploughed into a few fields to render them useless for growing, but no settlement of any size had been discovered, and the main body of Ampsivarii warriors had not been detected or engaged in battle.

Varus looked at the tall officer standing before him. It was Arminius's turn to frown. A worried look would display his lack of real appreciation of the situation in the General's eyes, and his inability to suggest a solution. The trap was baited, but would the old fool he wondered nervously, fall into it?

Varus rapped his fist on the table before him.

'*No!* Under no circumstances can I permit the tribes to re-arm themselves. It is asking for trouble, you understand? If they don't turn on each other, they might turn on us when we march back in the spring.' Varus rubbed his temples to ease the headache which was building. Exhaling loudly, with a shake of his head he said reluctantly. 'To my mind, there is only one solution to hold the province together during the coming winter.'

'But what can we do Sir?' Arminius' concern sounded grave and genuine.

'It's simple. We will have to establish a new chain of protective forts beside the largest settlements of the interior. We are duty bound to protect those under our dominion, or the Pax Romana will lose all meaning and credibility. We will garrison the forts with our men throughout the winter. Their mission will be to protect the pacified tribes.'

Arminius beamed as if the scales had just fallen from his eyes.

'Of course!' He pounded his fist into his other open hand with feigned excitement. 'Sir, that's a brilliant solution... In a single stroke you demonstrate your concern for the tribes' wellbeing, and keep subtle but total control without giving them as much as a single sword. Your solution will be easy to administer and arrange, and the trading network will be protected and kept safe until next spring, when we return in force. The Pax Romana is fulfilled and the Emperor will be delighted.'

Pleased with his insight and flattered by his prodigy's praise, it was the General's turn to smile.

'Yes, you have it my boy. I will begin issuing orders and making the necessary arrangements today. We must send word to all the chieftains immediately that we will ensure their safety.'

Arminius nodded enthusiastically. 'Perhaps you could even hold a banquet here in their honour Sir, before the Legions march back to the Rhine. It will help cement Rome's friendship with its subjects in Germania, and allay any remaining doubts in their minds.'

Varus thought for a moment as he considered the suggestion. He nodded.

'Yes, that will be the perfect opportunity to display our friendship and generosity, and remind them of the benefits and the reality of being under the protection of Rome.'

Arminius stared at his feet for a moment. Almost embarrassed he said.

'With your permission sir, I would be honoured if I may be allowed to spread word of Rome's new protection and the banquet. May I serve you again as your personal messenger?'

The old general beamed.

'Why of course Arminius. I can think of no man better suited to the task.'

Varus smiled knowingly. He had heard rumours that Arminius had lost his heart to some wild young girl he had rescued from the clutches of her murderous chieftain father in the Ampsivarii homelands. Clearly, Varus thought smugly to himself, the young Decurion nobleman was looking for any excuse to ride out and see her again.

This at least was no lie. Arminius had deliberately lodged Thusnelda far from Roman hands in the safely of his own father's household. It was certainly true that he was keen to see her again, but more importantly Arminius wanted one last council of war with all the allied tribal chiefs, to finalise his plans with them before the Romans broke camp and marched westwards for the winter.

'When shall we hold the banquet Sir?'

Varus pondered for a moment.

'Now let me see...We are due to march for the Rhine in two weeks...Let's make it... Hmm? You will need time to ride out and contact the chieftains.... We'll hold the feast the very night before we leave.'

The audience was over. Varus turned and picked up a scroll. He looked up as he began to unroll it.

'Send in Prefect Dalious on your way out Arminius. I have a meeting to call and detailed arrangements on the new troop movements to make.' Looking down at the scroll again he said. 'Thank you, you are dismissed.'

Arminius saluted. His face betrayed no emotion, but beneath his armoured chest his heart pounded. The feeble minded old fool had fallen for it, hook line and sinker. Soon enough, Arminius thought to himself, Varus would learn he had been duped, but by then he would be surrounded and trapped.

A smile played across Arminius's face as he strode from the Headquarters in search of Rolf. The fate of the three mighty Legions around him had been sealed forever. Soon he thought smugly, they would all die....

Chapter 20

'A banquet you say?'

Arminius's father Segimer looked up from the grinding stone he had been using to sharpen his sword. He ran his thumb along one razor sharp edge. Nodding silently with satisfaction he thought for a moment before he said.

'Why has he invited us? Has Varus discovered the rebellion and plans to take us captive at the feast?'

Arminius grinned slyly and shook his head. 'No father. I don't believe that for a moment. Varus trusts me completely. There has not been a single rumour whispered in his ear about what is about to happen to them all.'

Segimer sniffed. Beneath his mop of long grey hair the Cherusci king licked his lips and smiled. 'We know how to keep our secrets my son.' His face clouded with concern. 'I know the risks you take every day while you remain with the Romans, and so do our people.'

Arminius shrugged. 'What else can I do? If I leave suddenly, the Romans will become suspicious. Trust me father, that is their nature. They live in a world where plots and lies are a part of everyday life. Rome is always awash with rumour and intrigue. The Praetorian Guard who protect Augustus will arrest and imprison a conspirator and his entire family on the slightest suspicion of disloyalty to the Emperor. The Mamertine Prison is full of them.'

Segimer nodded grimly. 'I hope you are right my son and Varus remains unaware.'

Arminius smiled reassuringly. 'We must be bold and accept his invitation Father. I have sent messengers to the other chieftains. They will gather here together in two days time. We will call them to a council and then travel to the feast together.'

Segimer nodded and stood up. He sheathed his sword and walked to the doorway. Casting aside the curtain of leather hide he stared out across the crowded settlement. It was alive with his people. Tents had sprung up everywhere. Smoke from their many cooking fires drifted slowly skywards. Every day more and more arrived from outlying Cherusci settlements. It had started with hundreds but soon they would be counted in thousands.

Arminius's father smiled to himself. His people had been subdued by Rome's iron will since Drusus had inflicted heavy defeat upon them, and a terrible price had been paid by the tribe, but the invaders had never come even close to taming their wild German hearts. For the first time in many years, his men walked with pride and confidence, and carried their weapons openly. Their swagger foretold that the time for vengeance was close and the prospect was clearly relished by all who had answered Segimer's call to arms.

Every trail leading to the Cherusci capital was being watched closely to avoid even the slightest chance of discovery, as the tribe made their final preparations for all-out war. Furnaces glowed cherry red as hastily erected forges rang to the sounds of heavy as new axe and arrowheads were hammered into shape. Old shields were being repaired and sharpened wooden spear points hardened in the fires by those too poor to own iron weapons. Strong young men, sons of his warrior caste elite, who had been just boys when the Romans slew their fathers, came now wearing shirts of chainmail and hefting heavy swords. They too thirsted bitterly for revenge against the men who had come from far away.

As preparations for the rebellion gained momentum, the burning lust for Roman blood filled every warrior high born or low. Poorer men isolated from larger communities had also suffered tragedy at the hands of their oppressors over the years. Many had seen their women raped or their children go hungry when the tax gatherers had finished with them. Too many of them carried the painful scars of much loved little ones who had died of starvation when the previous years' snows had come, as the Romans feasted far away on food stolen from even the lowliest among them.

Arminius joined his father, who had stepped outside. Together, filled with hope, they proudly watched their people in silence for a moment. Segimer was first to noticed Rolf striding towards them through the throng. Beside him, Thusnelda walked quickly. She wore a shy enigmatic smile on her face. The Cherusci king grinned to himself. He remembered the same smile from long ago on his own woman's lips when they had first become one. The girl's radiance was meant for just one man, who stood tall beside him. Segimer wondered quietly to himself if perhaps it had something to do with the knowing whisper he had received from one of his grinning bodyguard, after his son was seen disappearing into Thusnelda's hut the previous night during the darkest hours of the wolf. Segimer acknowledged his nephew and the girl as they approached. As he nodded his welcome to the approaching couple he whispered to his grinning son.

'Well then Herman, tell me, is it true that you have taken the girl as your woman?'

Arminius's eyes danced suddenly with mischief. First staring at Thusnelda, then at his father he stayed smiling, but to his ageing father annoyance remained stubbornly silent.

The feast was going well Varus decided. Beneath an array of flickering oil lamps the chieftains had listened intently as the General had reassured them of his soldiers' protection throughout the rapidly approaching winter months. They had all played their part and growled appreciatively when they had eaten their fill, and he had finished his speech. Now they seemed intent on nothing more than talking loudly in their native tongue and drinking themselves into a profound stupor on his seemingly unending supply of wine. Slaves and servants dashed back and forth, nervously refilling goblets as the wild chieftains drunkenly pounded the table, belched loudly and demanded more. Now discarded by Varus's guests, gnawed hunks of bread, boar and venison bones lay scattered across their table and one man was already asleep, head back and snoring loudly to the great amusement of his drunken companions.

Sitting beside Varus, wearing his dress uniform, his adjutant looked on at their uncivilised behaviour with thinly concealed disgust. Their noise and drunken laughter was growing steadily. Angrily he whispered into his General's ear.

'These are nothing but animals from the forest sir. I've seen better table manners when the servants feed my pigs at home.'

Varus' smile was calm and kindly. Resting his hand gently on the Prefect's forearm he replied quietly.

'Yes, I know what you mean Dalious. We have a long way to go before we can consider any of them remotely civilised, but for now we must be grateful that they sit peacefully at our table without trying to kill each other, and freely accept our wine, and of course our troops' protection.'

Dalious nodded reluctantly. 'I suppose you're right sir, but it sticks in my craw to break bread with any of them. The stink wafting across the room is enough to turn my stomach.'

Varus grinned, but before he could reply there was a loud disturbance at the banqueting tent's entrance. The Centurion guard commander marched in and saluted smartly before his General. Varus inclined his head in acknowledgement, ignoring the growing shouts and raucous laughter which filled the tent. He said.

'Yes Centurion, what is it?'

The guard commander made his report.

'Sir, another chieftain has just arrived and is demanding to enter. He wouldn't give me his name but insists he has the right to attend and asks to be allowed to speak before you.'

Varus looked at his adjutant in surprise.

'I thought you said all the tribal leaders we invited had already been accounted for?'

Prefect Dalious looked confused.

'They have sir... I checked the list personally after Arminius had confirmed their attendance.' He shrugged. 'Perhaps it is some minor chieftain one of their kings has deliberately slighted by not including?'

Varus nodded. 'Yes, knowing how petty they can be that sounds highly likely.' His face darkened. 'But it may cause trouble.' He stared at the drunken row of fierce looking bearded men opposite who showed no interest in the Centurion's arrival. The General turned his gaze back to the waiting Centurion.

'Show him in will you? Make sure he is disarmed and have some of your men provide a close escort to him. Place your entire guard on instant readiness outside in case one of our guests takes exception to his arrival.' As an afterthought he added. 'Bring in one of our interpreters; I want to understand what he says.'

The Centurion nodded, saluted again and strode quickly from the tent.

Varus sighed and shook his head slowly.

'There's always something...'

Moments later, the Centurion returned with the missing chieftain. Like the other guests the man wore his hair long, was heavily bearded and clad in furs. Led before Varus by the Centurion he was flanked by two burley legionaries who stayed close beside him. An auxiliary followed behind them.

Sitting further down Varus's high table beside the 18th's Prefect Arminius stiffened when he saw who it was that had entered. The noise in the room suddenly quelled to hushed murmurs of surprise, as one chieftain after another elbowed the man sitting beside them and focusing with difficulty pointed at the new arrival.

The man planted himself confidently in front of the General. Varus stared at the new arrival. There was something in the man's bearing and a look in his eyes which unsettled the ageing General. Was it madness he saw staring back at him?

With his hands on his hips the man spoke.

'Greetings Roman. I have come far to speak with you... My name is Segestes... I am lord of the Ampsivarii.'

Sudden Anger boiled in Varus's veins. How dare this upstart barbarian stroll so casually into his Headquarters when there was such a heavy price on his head? Despite his age, the General was on his feet in a flash. Throwing his arm forward he snarled at the Centurion.

'Seize him!'

The two guards grabbed Segestes arms and held him tightly. The Centurion drew his sword and held its edge to the Ampsivarii's throat. Segestes didn't struggle. To Varus's surprise his prisoner simply threw back his head and roared with laughter. His barbarian guests, including Arminius's father Segimer were also on their feet, but they were waving their arms, pointing at the rogue Ampsivarii in their midst and shouting to each other excitedly in their guttural tongue.

The General had had enough. He was in command here. He held his hands aloft and roared.

'SILENCE!'

A hush fell, broken only by Segestes's now muted chuckling. As Varus and his senior officers glared at him, the mirth on the man's face changed to the darkest of scowls. Staring intently at Arminius, still with the centurion's blade at his throat he licked his lips. Segestes turned his head slowly towards General Varus and began to speak.

'Without my permission, a band of my young warriors have launched raids into your lands Roman.' He lied. 'I have only just learned of their attacks and wish no quarrel with you. I intend to punish those responsible and have come here freely to speak with you, as I desire only friendship between my tribe and the people of Rome.'

Arminius sat silently, his face impassive, but with each serpentine word uttered by the lying Ampsivarii the knot growing in the pit of his stomach tightened.

Varus stared at Segestes in silence for a moment. Was this man simply mad, or was he telling the truth he wondered? He had certainly placed himself at the General's mercy, apparently in good faith. Curious, Varus decided there could be no harm in hearing him out. With an imperious flick of his hand he snapped an order to the guards.

'Release him!'

Segestes shook his shoulders to shrug off the last touch of the Romans. As the centurion sheathed his sword, the silence in the tented chamber was absolute. The chieftain's heads were clearing quickly; they were on their guard now and sobering fast. The stench of betrayal filled their nostrils; each of them realised the danger which had suddenly enveloped them as conspirators to the rebellion, since the Ampsivarii king had arrived.

Varus was pleased that he had regained control and that his guests had obeyed him so quickly. He mistook their sullen obedience; it was fear which had begun to beat in their hearts. Roman justice was cruel and swift. If their deceit was exposed they would be lucky to survive the night.

Varus looked at the Ampsivarii lord and simply said.

'Pray continue.'

The feral grin returned to Segestes face. If the Roman couldn't, he could smell the fear in the room. His eyes glittered as he gazed at each silent chieftain in turn, then fixed his stare on Arminius. Segestes continued.

'Despite the action of a few young hotheads, my desire is not for war but only peaceful co-existence and trade with you Romans. It has come to my ears that tribes have prospered when they deal with your merchants.'

Varus nodded in silence.

'I wish true friendship, and believe only without secrets between us can we achieve this harmony.' His eyes narrowed and glittered dangerously. 'To cement that future I bring warning of rebellion to you by all the men in here....'

Segestes thrust out his arm and pointed straight at Arminius. He bellowed

'The rebellion will be led by HIM!'

Suddenly, there was uproar in the room. A table crashed to the ground as every guest Varus had invited was back on his feet, red faced and roaring with anger. The Roman officers sitting on either side of their general also leapt to their feet and drew their blades. Prefect Dalious yelled out to the guard commander. Almost instantly, armoured legionaries rushed in with their swords drawn and placed themselves in a tight line between their General's high table and the howling mob of Germans.

Arminius looked on open mouthed. Segestes's betrayal was damning and absolute. He knew he had only one chance of survival...he must deny and refute every single word uttered by the Ampsivarii lord. Around him, with swords still in hand, unsure what to do, the Romans backed away from Arminius, surprise and confusion on their faces. Could this possibly be true? Was Arminius, a citizen and Roman nobleman truly be a viper in their midst? It was impossible...and yet?

On a nod from General Varus, Prefect Dalious hammered the pommel of his sword on the wooden table to regain order in the bedlam and noise which flowed around him.

As his banging continued, the noise began to subside. Varus held out his arms and called for calm. Arminius too was on his feet and took up the call for silence. It was vital he was seen by the Romans to be one of them, trying to quell the tempers which had flared out of control. In his native tongue he called on the chieftains to calm themselves and not be afraid. To Arminius's relief, they heard him and reluctantly obeyed. Still muttering darkly in turn, scowling they fell silent.

Arminius ordered them to sit down and remain quiet. Daring a glance at Varus, Arminius nodded towards him respectfully.

His face still betraying his deep shock, Varus returned the nod. He waited until silence had fully returned. Prefect Dalious lent across to his General and whispered.

'Shall I arrest Arminius sir?'

Ashen faced, Varus shook his head. This was perhaps the most critical moment in his work within the province, perhaps even in his long career. A mistake now would unravel everything. There had been no hint or warning of betrayal in any reading of the runes, and Arminius had proved over and over his loyalty to Rome and to Varus himself. The Cherusci prince was also trusted by the assembled chieftains. If he placed Arminius and the others in chains and put them to the torture to search out the truth behind the Ampsivarii's accusations, all trust and good faith would evaporate immediately between the tribal leaders and Rome, and might well spark a real rebellion.

Varus looked at his Adjutant with tired sad eyes.

'No Dalious, I will not arrest a Roman officer who I trust implicitly, on the word of one renegade who I have no reason to trust at all. There are always rumours of rebellion, but I see no evidence whatsoever to support this man's word, or that of his ridiculous claims.'

He stood up as all heads turned towards him. Varus would find out the real reason behind the wild accusations. He suspected he knew the answer already and relaxed a little; he had spies of his own who sometimes whispered secrets. He stared at Segestes, who remained standing defiantly before him. Varus addressed him.

'Segestes, is it not true that my officer here stole your daughter away from you recently?'

Segestes growled as his eyes blazed with anger at this public shaming before the others. Romans had no honour he thought savagely. As faces startled by the news looked on from the high table, rage boiled from him under the mocking smiles of the others. He snarled his reply.

'*Damn you!* When I discovered she was gone I sent search parties to bring her back. Next morning my men found her knife laying on the same track this man.' He glared at Arminius. 'Had used to leave my land.... It is proof. He is guilty of kidnapping my daughter, and I will kill him for the insult.'

Varus nodded sagely. He turned towards Arminius.

'Well, is this true Decurion? Did you steal this man's daughter?'

Arminius stood tall, hoping his beating heart would not burst from his chest as he locked eyes with the general. Perhaps a mixture of lies and truth would help save him?

'It is true sir; I did help Thusnelda to escape...' Arminius needed to be bold; perhaps there was still a chance to save the rebellion, and all their lives. 'She was under sentence of death by her father's order and under the code of honour I know you live by; I believed it was the right thing to do.' Arminius switched his gaze to Segestes. He could see the flames of madness beginning to burn in the man's eyes. Momentarily, savage memories of the bear pit flashed through the Decurion's mind. All that was needed Arminius thought, was another push, another small twist of the knife.

'Since we left, Thusnelda and I have become very close...So close in fact that a few nights ago sir...I made her my woman.'

It was too much and something snapped. With a feral roar, Segestes launched himself towards Arminius, but the guards beside him were ready. They wrestled him to the ground and then dragged him snarling and spitting back onto his knees. In a flash, the centurion's blade was against his throat again.

Varus signalled to the centurion to remove the wild-eyed Segestes from his presence. Swearing and shouting in his native tongue, the Ampsivarii leader was unceremoniously dragged away.

In the sudden peace that followed within the tented banqueting room Varus lent on the table and smiled smugly towards the Roman officers standing tensely to his left and right.

'There gentlemen; there is the real truth behind the slanderous accusations you have heard tonight.' He shook his head. 'There *is* no rebellion. As military Governor, having judged so many tribal disputes over the last months I have come to know and understand how these barbarians think.' He looked towards Arminius with a knowing and reassuring smile.

'This was not about rebellion gentlemen; it is absolutely clear to me that the Ampsivarii wanted nothing more than cold blooded revenge...'

Chapter 21

Part Three

As first light came slowly to the distant horizon, everywhere within the huge stockade of the 18th's summer encampment, centurions and optios barked out new orders to their men. As burning torches were snuffed out, sections of legionaries were already in their third hour of work, doubling to new tasks or busy packing away equipment and collapsing the tents, which had given them welcome shelter during the dark nights of the past six months. Others who had earned the wrath of their officer over some minor infraction were busy filling in stinking latrine trenches, while outside the stockades high walls, sections of legionaries walked the perimeter in line, gathering up the sharpened stakes and scattered caltrops which would soon be used again to protect the Legion in its' temporary marching camps, during the two weeks it would take them to reach the Rhine.

'Get that buckle tightened properly. Come on you idle pair, you're the last two to finish.'

Centurion Rufus glared at the two legionaries who were trying to secure fat wicker panniers on either side of a loudly braying mule. One of the men was hopping in a circle, energetically rubbing his shin.

'Sorry sir. The bloody thing just kicked me.'

Rufus scowled. Pointing his vine cane at the injured legionary he snapped angrily.

'Stop making excuses laddie, or I'll get you a swift transfer to one of the cohorts guarding the new forts this winter.'

The legionnaire palled. He'd been as pleased as the rest of the lads when he heard the news that his centurion hadn't drawn a black token from their Prefects bag, when it came time to choose who was going to remain behind. It was pay parade in an hour, and the last thing he wanted was to stay out in this dangerous wilderness on guard duty for the next long and very cold six months. There was wine, baths and clean women aplenty in the brothels at their winter quarters over the Rhine, and he had no intention of missing the pleasures offered by any of them. Ignoring the pain in his leg, with a muttered curse he quickly snatched at the dangling buckle and threaded the leather securing strop into it. With the aid of his comrade, the injured legionary pulled the retaining strap tight under the animal's belly. Securing the buckle he said.

'There we are sir, all done.'

Tight lipped and still scowling Rufus looked over the mule and its panniers. Each of his eight-man sections had their own load carrying mule, and after pay parade they would begin filling the wicker containers with their sections heavier gear and tentage before forming up and beginning the long march home.

Rufus swept his cane towards their century's tented lines when he was satisfied that the panniers were properly secured.

'Right then.... Both of you get away and report to Optio Praxus. I'm sure he'll want to use you in helping the others taking down the tents.'

The legionaries saluted and doubled away before their officer found a worse job for them, like sorting out the century's overflowing latrines.

Rufus grinned to himself as he watched the two men running towards their lines. One was limping, but they were both making an effort. How could anyone not adore this life he wondered? Good food and pay, plenty of fresh air and the common bond of family and comradeship which every member of the 18th shared.

Leaving the line of tethered mules with a contented spring in his step he turned and began to walk through the back of the 1st cohort's empty lines, towards his own.

The 1st cohort had begun their preparations the previous day. Now, they were formed up for a final spit and polish inspection by the First Spear centurion before mounting the pay parade's guard of honour. Held rigidly by the standard bearer, the 18th's Eagle would be proudly displayed behind the pay tables. Each member of the Legion was required to salute both the paying officer and their Eagle before returning to the ranks.

Rufus had nearly reached his men when a voice called out behind him.

'Centurion Rufus!'

Rufus stopped in midstride and turned. To his dismay, it was Tribune Crastus who had called his name. Rufus saluted and said.

'Sir?'

Crastus walked up to the centurion and lazily returned the salute.

Rufus silently ground his teeth. The boy couldn't even salute properly.

'Ah Rufus, good, I wanted to see you before the Legion marches.'

Eyeing him suspiciously, Rufus remained at attention and replied.

'Yes sir?'

Crastus smiled. Rufus felt no warmth in it, but the little bastard looked triumphant.

'I have just come from the Camp Prefect. I have formally requested that you take full responsibility for the return of my father's slave known as Severus to winter quarters. Under the circumstances, I thought it only fitting that you should hear it from me. I've arranged for you to personally see the slave arrive safely back at our winter quarters.'

Rufus stared coldly as the smile faded on the young Tribune's face. Bad enough the poor lad should be dragged back in chains and disgrace, but to make his own commander act as jailor? It was petty spite, nothing else. A muscle twitched dangerously in the corner of Rufus's eye as he fought to hold his temper. The little bastard was intent on rubbing salt into the wound, and was clearly enjoying every passing moment of it. As he couldn't have Rufus arrested for complicity, Crastus had made sure the centurion would take personal responsibility for seeing Severus back to await his inevitable public execution.

The smug and triumphal smile returned to the Tribune's face as he added.

'Of course Centurion, if the slave escapes, I'll personally see to it that you take his place.'

With that, the meeting was over. Rufus remained still and stared in silence at Crastus until the Tribune's grin faded. Crastus said with growing irritation in his voice.

'I believe it is customary to salute a superior officer Centurion?'

The twitch returned. Rufus thrust his right arm forward with fingers extended but keeping his jaws clamped firmly shut, he said nothing.

With a disdainful and patronizing nod, Crastus turned and headed back towards what little remained of the 18th's tented Headquarters.

His cheerful start to the day ruined, fighting an almost overwhelming desire to gut the little maggot, through clenched teeth Rufus hissed at the rapidly disappearing Tribune's back.

'You snide little bastard!'

Like the infantry cohorts, that Legion's artillery was busy packing up for the long march too. The throwing arms of the great wooden ballista catapults had been firmly secured by the legionaries who served them, and the heavy contraptions' wheels had been liberally greased, ready for the many miles they would have to trundle on their way to the distant Rhine. Teams of oxen were being brought into position to haul the artillery pieces at the head of the long baggage train which would follow the marching legions. Smaller dart throwing pieces were also being loaded by grunting sweating artillerymen onto their own transit carts in preparation for when it finally came for the signal to move out.

In the cavalry compound all was ready. They would provide both a forward and rear-guard to the massive convoy, and a screen to protect the long vulnerable flanks of the column which would stretch for many miles, and take hours to pass a single point along the route.

In one corner of their mounted compound, Arminius and Rolf stood making final adjustments to their horses tack. His mouth dry, Rolf listened wide-eyed as Arminius finished recounting the events of the feast to his cousin.

Rolf's face darkened.

'Are you sure he truly believes you still loyal and faithful Herman?'

Patting his horse's neck Arminius smiled.

'I'm absolutely convinced of it Rolf. Believe me, after what happened last night I'd already be dead, or be in chains facing the torturer's hot irons if the old fool didn't have complete faith in me.' He shrugged. With a half smile he added. 'And still considers me almost a bastard son.'

Rolf raised an eyebrow and grinned back.

'Who plans to take his father's head...Hmm. Some son, eh cousin?'

Secure in the knowledge that their secret remained safe and the deadly trap was set and ready, both men laughed as they climbed into their waiting saddles.

Even marching six abreast, it would take the entire 17th Legion more than an hour to cross the start line and begin their long march towards winter quarters. The 18th would follow immediately afterwards, with the baggage train close behind. At the head of each Legion, their Eagle was carried before them by the Aquilifer, resplendent in his flowing lion's mane headdress. Only the bravest and most dedicated legionaries ever held the respected and much revered rank of Aquilifer. He was the Legion's standard bearer who had made the most solemn blood vow to protect his precious burden, and gladly sacrifice his own life if necessary, to defend it.

The 19th Legion would be the main marching rear-guard, followed closely by a ragtag stream of several thousand civilians, merchants, illegal but quietly ignored families, prostitutes and slaves, who were the last part of the long column, which when fully extended and moving would stretch from start to finish for well over ten miles.

It was usual practice during transit to send detachments of engineers several miles ahead, in advance of the first legion to quickly chop up and clear any obstacles like fallen trees along the route or make hasty repair to pre-built bridges along the established supply route, should they require maintenance. The engineer's key role was to keep the long winding column moving.

General Varus and his staff officers rode at the head of the great procession. Where they led, the slow moving column would follow.

Varus's freshly plumed helmet shone in the bright morning sunlight. He was riding a magnificent Arabian stallion; a prized gift from King Herod's eventual successor when Varus had been provincial Governor of Syria. As both Governor and Roman General he considered it important to look resplendent in front of the men on such an important campaign occasion. He rode adorned in his full dress uniform, wearing a white purple edged cloak and his armour's detail picked out in glittering gold. He was their General; he had led his three proud Legions into the wild heart of Germania months before, and now, satisfied that all was well in his province, he was finishing the mission by personally leading them safely home for a well-earned rest.

With years of campaigning experience behind him, General Varus knew the long journey back would be tough on his men. They would be travelling through safe and long since pacified areas, so he had decided the previous day that his legionaries, much to their collective relief should move in relatively casual marching order, rather than be at constant high alert dressed in full fighting kit. Even with the aid of the section mule, each man was carrying in excess of sixty pounds of his own body armour and weapons. Personal equipment was bundled and carried securely tied to a wooden yoke pole slung across one shoulder. Even the men's' two throwing javelins were fastened onto the yoke, as they wouldn't be needed during the long march to the Rhine. Armour was worn, but buckles were loose. With shields strapped to their backs, to aid balance under their heavy load, helmets hung around the legionaries' necks and rested comfortably and easily against their chests.

As the last of the 17th's marched across the start line, the 18th Legion prepared to move. With an order barked by its first centurion, the 1st cohort protecting the Eagle came to attention with a thunderous crash of hundreds of hobnailed sandals, on the iron hard parade ground beneath their feet.

Rufus was watching closely. Taking his cue from the leading cohort, he turned to face his men. He roared.

'CENTURY...SHUN!'

As they stood rigidly to attention before him, Rufus eyed them with his usual scowl, waiting for even one of them to make the fatal mistake of moving before he bellowed their next order. Not one of them did except disgraced legionary Severus who shuffled uncomfortably behind them. He was tied behind the only mule with a long rope tether bound tightly around his wrists. The mule, led by one of Rufus's men was carrying marching rations and would accompany the century. The other section mules were mixed in somewhere amongst the huge baggage train that would follow the 18th in the procession of the column.

'Century will move to the right and form 6 man marching file....RIGHT...TURN!'

In one smooth practiced drill movement, despite being hampered by their heavy load, the eighty men quickly slid into a six abreast marching column.

Rufus waited patiently until the last of the 1st cohort marched passed him. With a snapped order his men followed in step with their comrades, out of what was left of the Legion's dismantled summer camp, and began the long march home.

Chapter 22

Riding behind their General at the head of the column, two Prefects were engaged in a heated conversation concerning the events from the night before.

'But what if Arminius is a traitor?' asked one.

The other rubbed his chin. Staring absently at the long straight road ahead he replied.

'Doesn't matter what we think does it? The General has made up his mind, and that's all that counts.'

The first Prefect shrugged.

'I suppose you're right. There's not much one man can do anyway, against twenty thousand soldiers.'

Unconvinced, his companion nodded anyway. He had sat close to Varus at the feast the night before and remained troubled by Segestes' ominous warning.

'Don't forget we've lost the best part of half a Legion guarding those new damned forts in the interior.'

With a grin, the other replied dismissively.

'Yes, but even so?'

Their conversation was interrupted by the pounding of horses' hooves behind them. Arminius and a full squadron of mounted auxiliaries thundered past, making their way towards General Varus and his attending staff officers.

As he came close to the General, Arminius eased the pressure on his reins until he was beside the old man dressed in his finery.

With a smart salute, Arminius said.

'Sir, I have ordered a mobile screen of cavalry to protect the column's flanks, but after last night, I want to make absolutely sure that there are no nasty surprises in front of us. With your permission I will take my squadron and scout ahead.'

Varus nodded. 'Yes, that's an excellent idea Arminius.'

With a curt nod, Arminius spurred his horse forward, followed in file and a cloud of dust by his entire squadron. He had business elsewhere, and needed an excuse not to be tied to the slow moving column as it ground onwards. It would make slow progress as it circumnavigated the great forests towards the first waypoint a week's march away at the bridge of boats at Casta Vetera, which spanned the wide River Wasser. From there, the column's planned route would take it on towards the next distant checkpoint on the River Lippe.

High above, clouds from the east drifted lazily across the blue sky. The weather remained fine, but the most experienced legionaries debated as they marched, on what might happen over the next few days.

'You're wrong you know. Doesn't look like rain to me.'

One of the 18th Legion's veterans, marching beside the other men of his infantry section muttered something unintelligible. His friend tramping beside him looked up and sniffed the air knowingly.

'Five sesterces say I'm right mate. I reckon with luck we won't see rain for at least another week.'

Shifting the weight of his equipment into a more comfortable position across his back the other legionary looked up into the sky, then replied.

'All right, you're on. I reckon it's going to piss down!'

They marched on in silence for a while before one picked up the conversation again and asked.

'Reckon we'll get a break soon?'

His companion shook his head. With a grunt he said.

'No chance mate. You know the score Lesterous. We march a standard sixteen miles until mid-afternoon then stop and build the marching camp for the night. The old General wants to sleep safe in his tent and as usual has got it all worked out with his officers who's going to do the hard work. Let's face it; they don't have much else to do.'

His mate grinned as he absently felt for the entrenching tool strapped behind him on his wooden yoke.

'Yeah, I know what you mean. Bet we don't see any of them digging the bloody ditch around camp when we stop later on.'

His mate sniffed. 'I'm not putting any money down on that.' With a sigh he whispered from the corner of his mouth. 'That's one wager you'd definitely win old son.'

Somewhere ahead in the first cohort a deep baritone voice began to sing a favourite marching song. Morale was high and the men of the second cohort quickly joined in singing the familiar words.

'We are the men of the eighteenth legion
Be off with you, get out of our way
When the orders come and the infantry advance
Only victory ends our day

Our javelins fly at the enemies of Rome
Our pride is in the legion
The Emperor commands and we will die
In every blood-soaked shit filled region

We follow the standards, and heed the trumpet's call
From the barbaric forests of Germany, to the distant shores of Gaul
Across the deserts of Judea, we'll fight them big and small
*We are the fighting infantry....*THE EIGHTEENTH CONQUERS ALL !

As the Legion sang, concealed deep in the forests ahead, hunting trails and ancient pathways were filled with bands of barbarian warriors making their way towards the rendezvous Arminius had set them. Most were little more than savages; uneducated and unwashed wild men of the forest, hardened by years of battling the elements and their unforgiving surroundings. They were tempered by the harsh life the forest forced them to lead. All carried what sharp weapons they had. Everywhere, freshly ground edges glinted on axes, knives and recently sharpened spear heads.

Among them several groups were dressed in the chainmail and helmets of German auxiliary light infantry, who until the previous day had served in the Legion's ranks as mercenaries. Paid off and not required during the coming winter months, the Romans had discharged them until the following spring. Usually, the men of the auxiliary would re-join their families and live out the harsh winter months in their own native settlements, but not this time. Now things were different.

In the utmost secrecy, Arminius had spoken passionately to the men of the native auxiliary cohorts. With his brave words of victory and freedom, he had won them over to the rebellion. Now when the signal came, their swords and spears would be willingly used against their former Roman paymasters.

Shortly before the sun dipped on the grey horizon, the great marching camp was finished. Vertical walls of felled trees surrounded it, and outside the constructed defences a deep ditch protected by sharpened stakes became the tired legionary's home for the rapidly approaching night. Work details allocated by their centurions' had returned from gathering firewood and fresh water. As the men pitched their tents safely inside the palisade and began cooking their evening meal, sentries patrolled on the elevated platform of the newly built walls, sharp eyed and ready to raise the alarm if attack came.

Within the Eighteenth Legion's lines, the men of the second cohort were making the most of their opportunity to relax. Hungry after the day's long march and the labours that always followed, they attacked the day's soup and bread ration enthusiastically, as they sat in small groups around smoking cooking fires chatting to each other. One of the legionaries had removed a sandal and by the light of the fire was picking at a corn which had been giving him trouble during the day's march. Wincing at the pain in his inflamed toe, absently he said to his mate beside him.

'It's a shame about Sextus getting caught like that. I've known him for years and he's always struck me as being a good soldier.'

His mate spat into the fire. The gobbet hissed in the embers.

'Yeah, I know.' He thought for a moment. 'Look, he might be a good bloke, but he's still a bloody slave. I didn't sign up to soldier with the likes of him. You know the rules.... I reckon he's for the chop; they've got him bang to rights.'

Still working studiously on his corn, the other legionary sniffed.

'You're right I suppose. I'm guessing they'll give him short shrift when we get back...Still think it's a rotten shame though, all the same.'

High on a nearby hill, hidden by the darkness under the dark canopy of the forest Arminius and Rolf lay watching the vast spread of twinkling camp fires below.

'There are so many Herman.' Rolf whispered softly in awe. 'Can we really defeat that many?'

Arminius's stare narrowed. His eyes stayed focused on the great sprawl of the three Legion's temporary camp.

'Yes Rolf, I'm sure we can.'

His confidence was tempered with concern however. Turning his head towards his cousin he enquired.

'Which tribes have arrived at the rendezvous so far?'

Rolf stiffened. He had spent the afternoon waiting at the arranged glade deep in the forest beside the confluence of two woodland streams, welcoming and counting the tribesmen as they arrived.

'Our own people were first to come. I think we have about eight thousand Cherusci in total. There are about the same number of Bructeri and perhaps five thousand Angrivarrii.'

In the darkness, Rolf couldn't see the concern that clouded Arminius's face.

'What of the other tribes Rolf. Have none of them come?'

Rolf shook his head. 'No cousin, I saw no others. So far, just three tribes have risen and answered your call.'

Arminius sighed. He had expected the others to hesitate in openly rebelling against the Romans. They had all heard the stories told at clan gatherings of the Roman's past cruelty to those who had opposed them. All the tribes had promised support, but even so...

'Will they come to our aid cousin?'

Arminius pondered the question for a moment before replying.

'Yes, I believe they will, but they are waiting to see how tomorrow goes. We have at best twenty one thousand warriors in the field against about the same number of Romans, but we will have one great advantage.'

Rolf turned his head and stared inquisitively at his cousin.

'How so Herman, if the numbers are so dangerously close?'

'It's simple really Rolf. I can best explain by asking you a question. What happens when you hit a log with a hammer?'

Confused Rolf replied.

'Err...It bounces off?'

Arminius smiled. 'Exactly, it bounces off. But what happens if you hit the same log just as hard with a sharp axe?'

Still unsure, Rolf answered hesitatingly.

'Why, the axe will split the log.'

'Yes precisely, that's exactly what happens. Now Rolf, imagine the Roman column is a long narrow winding worm. What happens if you hit it with the same axe again and again?'

There was more than a hint of excitement in Rolf's hushed voice as realisation dawned.

'Why, you chop it into smaller and smaller pieces!'

There was silence for a moment between the two men before worried, Rolf voiced a new concern.

'But how do we attack the Romans before they close ranks and get into their battle formations. You said long ago we cannot defeat them in formal pitched battle.'

Arminius smiled again. It was time to explain the coming day in detail to his cousin.

'I will shortly move out to the clan rendezvous Rolf. Moves are being made throughout the province tonight to attack the Romans who have stayed behind. Tonight, they will all die. At daybreak tomorrow I will explain my plan to our kin and allies then lead the tribes to their ambush positions. If they follow my orders we are assured of victory. But before I leave this place you should know that you have a vital part to play in the coming battle and our ultimate victory...Now listen very carefully cousin, this is what I want you to do at dawn tomorrow...'

Hours later in the darkest part of the night, one of the new fortresses nestled silently beside a sleeping barbarian settlement deep in the Germanic interior. It was freshly built and many days march from the safely encamped and resting legions.

A young Roman sentry stamped his feet to ward off the numbing cold within the fort. To his earlier dismay, he had pulled the midnight guard duty and now, despite his thick woollen cloak he shivered in the chill night air as he hefted his javelin and patrolled one lonely corner of the newly constructed fort. Three hours, he thought. Three more miserable hours, patrolling up and down in a pacified area where every man and his dog were wrapped up warm and fast asleep. It seemed to be such a waste of time, but when he had asked his Optio what was the point, he had received nothing more than a casual shrug in reply.

The pungent smell of fresh cut pine assailed his nostrils. The tree trunks chopped down from the surrounding forest only days earlier were still green and heavy with rich amber sap which oozed from each of the trunks sharpened ends. In a neat vertical wall they disappeared into the darkness before him pointing silently at the blackened sky. He reached out and touched the sticky ooze of the nearest one. Its tacky residue clung to his fingertips as he withdrew his hand. He smiled. The smell reminded him of being a boy at home; the forested valley far to the south of Rome where his father had been a freeman woodcutter. He idly remembered the valley where he had played so happily among the shadows and fallen leaves with his band of friends as a small child.

A muffled noise abruptly disturbed his reverie from long past memories; it was not a usual sound of the night which he had heard so many times before on countless guard duties around the Empire, more like a small pebble bouncing off the platform close behind him. Curious rather than alarmed he wandered further from the comforting light of the burning torches, seeking the source of the disturbance. He stared into the gloom but failed to find what had caused the odd sound; he also missed the two wraithlike figures that rose silently from the darkness behind him. One broad hand closed over his mouth as the legionnaire's helmet was savagely wrenched backwards with the other. A pitted iron blade flashed in the starlight.

With a look of shock and horror on his ashen face the sentry gurgled and struggled under the assassin's vicelike grip as blood pumped in powerful rhythmic spurts from the gaping wound in his neck. In moments his struggles became weaker until with a final jerk and gargled sigh his eyes closed as the blackness around him became absolute. Powerful arms lowered his body quietly onto the platform.

One of the bare-chested killers lent over the palisade. His long hair fell over his heavily tattooed face as he motioned to his companions, waving them forward out of the darkness. They carried roughly honed ladders. The waiting warriors negotiated the deserted spike filled ditch as they quietly drew swords and began to climb into the darkness above. In just moments, they were assembling in numbers on the ground inside the darkened fort. A savage grin and nod from their leader sent them scurrying silently towards neat rows of tents filled with peacefully sleeping legionaries whose centurion, just weeks earlier had been unlucky enough to draw a black token from his Prefect's brimming bag.

Chapter 23

As dawn broke, light and activity grew within the Roman's marching camp. Centurions rushed about their lines banging on the side of tents and shouting for their men to get up quickly.

Centurion Rufus had roused his century early and was barking orders at his men to begin dismantling their tents and get them stowed away on the waiting mules.

Before he had roused the first man however, Rufus had checked on Severus. Army regulations dictated that when on the march his prisoner should spend the night tied to one of the century's wagons. He had found the ex-slave stiff and cramped, lying uncomfortably on the damp ground behind the century's tents. Staring down at Severus in the half light Rufus sniffed and said quietly.

'I'm probably breaking Jupiter knows how many regulations just being here, but this might make you feel a bit better.'

Making sure he wasn't being overlooked, Rufus slipped his prisoner a large chunk of bread he had acquired during the previous evening. As Severus bit hungrily into his breakfast Rufus added.

'We'll be moving out in an hour or two and something in your belly should make you feel a bit better.'

Still chewing Severus looked gratefully at the bread and said.

'Thank you sir. I really appreciate this.'

Before Rufus could reply, a booming blast came from the guard horn on the main gate.

Startled by the sudden echoing note Severus asked.

'Trouble sir?'

Rufus shrugged. 'I don't know lad, but that was an alert. Get that bread down you quick before anyone sees you eating it.' The centurion rubbed the stubble on his chin thoughtfully. 'I'd better go and see what's up.'

As Rufus turned to walk away, one of the auxiliary cavalry detachments thundered inside the palisade at a full gallop just after the camp's main gate had swung fully open.

As most of the horsemen slowed their snorting mounts, their officer and two riders continued to gallop across the vast encampment, until they reached General Varus's headquarters area. Reining in hard and almost sliding to a halt the riders dismounted and rushed inside.

Rufus looked darkly back at Severus.

'I don't like the look of this...Something's definitely up...I think I'd better go and wake the lads up, smartish.'

The tension in the room was tangible as General Varus addressed his hastily convened staff officers briefing.

'Gentlemen. The recent rumours of uprising among some of the tribes have been confirmed.'

Shock and surprise registered on the senior officers' faces. Surely not now, when the season's campaigning was at an end?

Deeply concerned at such unexpected news they began to murmur together but Varus held up his hand to quell them.

'A patrol came in this morning and reported they have discovered a large concentration of Ampsivarii warriors camped deep inside the forest....Here, let me show you.'

Varus turned and uncovered a stretched animal hide which hung on one tented wall. It was a map showing their route through Germania as far as the floating bridge across the distant River Wasser. Their marching path over the next ten days was marked clearly. Heavily inked in, it showed the Legion's planned direction followed the main supply route the quartermasters had been using for resupply during the summer campaigning season. The supply route was shaped like a huge horseshoe, circumnavigating a heavily wooded region shown in the map's centre. Varus thumped his fist into the middle of the hide.

'The enemy are concentrated in here Gentlemen. I suspect their advance guard has been using this region as a base to launch their recent hit and run attacks; that's why we have failed to find them. Clearly, they have been moving at night and as a result we have been searching in entirely the wrong areas for them.'

Heads nodded before him. The unexpected news explained a great deal. The Ampsivarii had been far too adept at avoiding the numerous foot and mounted patrols which had searched unsuccessfully for them since the raiding had begun.

The General continued his appreciation.

'The report I received stated that as of yesterday they appear to have built up their forces in secret and can now be counted to approximately five thousand.' The General's face was grave. 'We still of course outnumber them heavily but if we are to take them by surprise we must move decisively gentlemen; if we act promptly, we can nip this rebellion in the bud, and as a bonus save perhaps a full week of marching.'

Concerned, one of the Prefects asked.

'Sir, how can we find them in that tangle of forest? It's difficult terrain as I remember.'

Hiding his annoyance at having to state the blindingly obvious Varus smiled.

'That's quite simple really. The scouts will lead us in. Their commander reports they have found an excellent route which should suit our needs with very little work by our engineers.'

Varus turned from the map and resting his fists on the table before him, he stared at the assembled officers.

This was the perfect opportunity to retire on a triumphant note. After two years bringing peace and consolidation to his province, Varus had received a message among dispatches from Rome the previous month under the Emperor's own private seal. It granted him permission to finally retire at the end of this campaign season. Bone tired after so many decades of service, he read the dispatch in private with mixed feelings. Even to mark his retirement from public duties, Varus doubted Augustus would grant him the honour of a full Triumph, with the opportunity to parade himself and his victorious legions through the streets of Rome. Even so, his social standing as a victorious Roman General would be greatly enhanced, and his reputation in the eyes of the Emperor and members of the Senate immeasurably consolidated. Haunted by his experiences in Syria and the political fallout that followed, nobody would dare to plot against him again.

'My plan is, if I may say so quite simple in its execution. We march to the enemy encampment and immediately launch a sudden and devastating assault in overwhelming numbers. The Ampsivarii won't know what hit them when they feel the combined power of three concentrated Legions attacking them.'

Another Prefect stared at the General in uncomfortable surprise and some confusion.

'But General Sir. Who will guard the baggage train and civilians while we destroy the enemy?'

Varus returned the stare, but at best it was patronising. How could a mere Prefect possibly understand the grander stratagems and tactics of one of the most admired living Patricians and Generals of Rome, he wondered. Struggling to hide his growing anger at such obvious military ineptitude, he momentarily wished his Legates were with him instead of just their lowly subordinates. The Legates he was convinced would certainly have seen the audacious brilliance of his masterly and decisive plan.

'The baggage train will follow us of course.' He shrugged at the minor distraction. 'We can leave a small infantry detachment to protect it.' The reassuring smile returned. 'They will be in no danger of course with the added advantage of the cavalry screen.' Varus pushed himself off the table.

'When the operation is over we mop up then simply continue straight on to the other side of the forest, pick up the supply route on the far side and march on until we reach the Wasser. We can afford to rest for a few days then, before pushing on for the Rhine....' Varus held his reassuring smile.

'There is one other important point which you should know gentlemen. I have sent orders via our scouts for Arminius to raise his tribe and come to our support. There is no love lost between the two tribes and we can expect between five and seven thousand Cherusci warriors to assist us. We may well not need them, but they will make a valuable reserve if we do.'

The briefing was at an end. Summing up, General Varus added.

'Now gentlemen, you have your orders. The 17th will lead, followed by the 18th and 19th. See to it that your centurions are fully briefed on the change of plan; I want to begin the march in one hour, and hit them at first light tomorrow.... Thank you gentlemen, you are dismissed.'

As the Prefects and staff officers saluted and filed from the command tent, Varus called to his adjutant.

'Send in the Decurion who brought me the report will you Dalious?'

Minutes later the junior Decurion arrived. Having been announced, he marched in smartly and saluted.

'You sent for me sir?'

Still considering the implications of his future in Rome, Varus looked up.

'Ah yes, indeed I did.'

He walked over to the stretched hide which hung on the wall. He pointed to the map.

'Show me exactly where this track you have discovered cuts into the forest.'

The Decurion smiled as he stepped forward to stand close to the General

'Of course sir, it is easily found.'

As the general turned to inspect the map, he failed to notice a fleeting flash of pure malevolence on the scout's face. It registered only for a split second and then was gone as quickly as it had appeared.

The auxiliary officer pointed to a spot a little further along the supply route from where they were currently camped. He tapped his finger beside the supply route's heavily inked track.

'Just here sir. It's only about six miles ahead. This is where we can enter the Teutoburg forest.'

Rolf's eyes narrowed imperceptibly.

'And surprise our enemies.'

Chapter 24

The skies began to darken as the head of the great marching column turned away from the main supply route and entered the edge of the vast Teutoburg forest.

General Varus had forbidden the Conicens from using their circular horns to pass signals. Surprise he reasoned was the key to success, and announcing their arrival would lose a critical advantage. Instead, he ordered that only mounted horsemen should pass his messages and orders down the long line of marching men.

As the leading 1st cohort of the 17th legion left the open plain and marched their Eagle into the forest, they were immediately cocooned on both sides by dense stands of birch, spruce and ancient gnarled oaks, which seemed to twist and climb almost to the grey skies above. The path was firm but surrounding visibility was badly restricted by tall tree trunks and a dense layer of vegetation as tall as a man which carpeted the surrounding forest floor.

From the dark clouds overhead a light drizzle began to fall onto the Romans as they marched deeper into the eerily silent forest in tight column. It felt cool and refreshing to the marching men of the column. Autumn was upon them and only gentle hiss of the drizzle and the soft rustle of the slowly changing green and russet canopy above overcame the deathly hush which filled the immense and primordial Teutoburg.

Riding just ahead of the Romans as scouts, sitting firmly in his saddle Rolf walked his horse forward in company with one of his most trusted auxiliary kinsmen. Their winding route ahead was clear and easy to follow.

Rolf's companion looked over his shoulder at the Romans behind him, then back at his commander. He whispered softly in his native tongue.

'When will Herman spring the trap Rolf?'

Rolf looked around before replying equally slyly.

'Not yet. We are ordered to draw the entire column deep into the forest so none may escape. Herman has placed strong forces here and there all along the trail ahead, but none may attack until the Romans are fully committed, and all have entered.'

His companion smiled as he touched the hilt of his long cavalry sword, which hung sheathed on his hip.

'Then we kill them?'

Rolf turned and stared into the eager glittering eyes of his second cousin.

'Yes Helmut. Then... we kill them!'

Guided ever deeper by two of Rolf's best men, and little more than a mile ahead a mixed party of the 17th and 18th's engineers were busy clearing the path of obstacles for the approaching column. It was proving to be surprisingly light work. The engineers and their labouring legionaries were making good progress. Despite the close proximity of the surrounding vegetation, the ground beneath their feet was acceptably dry and flat.

During their progress into the forest, the work party had passed several wide pools of standing water which echoed to the croak of frogs and were alive with the buzzing of insects. The track wound around them and the engineer in charge, with time always against him urged his men to ignore the dark ponds and press on regardless.

The drizzle which had fallen for the last hour became steadily heavier. Like the men in the marching column, the engineering party's clothing was quickly becoming soaked by the penetrating dampness. Within minutes, heavy drops of rain replaced the steady drizzle. To the dismay of the men marching in column, rain quickly began falling in great sheets from an angry and rapidly darkening sky. Deep rolling thunder rumbled somewhere far in the distance.

To the chief engineer's consternation, wide puddles were beginning to form in the deluge all along the track, both in front and behind his men. The thick layer of soft humus which carpeted the forest floor was soaking rapidly with the pouring rain and was in danger he realised, of turning to mud.

The path ahead for the engineering party was still quite passable, but only the worst could be assumed when more than fifteen thousand pairs of hobnailed sandals were marching across it. Sharp noises above his party made the engineering centurion glance upwards. His apprehension grew as the wind began to make the canopy sway and creak overhead. Every passing moment saw the weather getting worse.

After three hours of heavy and unceasing rain, the engineer's worries had become fully justified. Heavily laden under individual burdens of 60lbs of equipment, the men in the winding 12 mile marching column had quickly becoming exhausted under their heavy loads. Vital energy reserves were being sapped with the extra effort of maintaining their precarious balance on a track which was rapidly dissolving into a river of thick and clinging mud.

As their centurions barked to keep up, more and more men of the 17th's second cohort were slowly dropping back. It wasn't laziness, simply the difficulty of maintaining the pace set by their comrades in the first cohort, most of who were marching comfortably on the virgin surface of the saturated but still spongy forest floor.

Despite the centurion's best efforts, a gap was beginning to appear between the two cohorts, and the same situation was mirrored all along the column as conditions continued to deteriorate.

Concealed along the edges of the path, bands of barbarian warriors huddled under coarse woollen cloaks, finding shelter from the rain where they could. Arminius had issued strict orders that they were to remain concealed until he gave the signal to begin the first attacks. Hardened by their life in the forests, the men sat quietly and remained hidden. The weather was little more than an irritation to them. This was after all, their home.

Like every man in the column, Centurion Rufus was unaware that every sliding step made by his men was being watched. He yelled at one of his men who had stopped suddenly in the rain.

'Come on man, get a grip. You must keep up.'

Already exhausted after just three hours of marching, the legionary pulled at his leg as he glared back through the torrent of rain towards his scowling officer.

'Sorry sir, but I'm stuck. My foot just sank into a bloody hole.'

The weight of the pole across his shoulder was bending him forward onto the leg which remained firmly wedged in the rabbit hole. Furious with the weather, the army and in particular the filthy stinking mud, the legionary snapped. He flung his heavy yoke aside and dropped his sopping shield into the sludge with a string of sulphurous curses. The men struggling past laughed weakly at his temper and distress. Still cursing, the legionary threw himself backwards. With a gurgling plop the mud released him from its glutinous grip and he fell backwards with a sudden and surprised cry.

Rufus had reached the man and tried not to join in the laughter. He wasn't blind; he knew his men needed rest, but the orders were to keep going. Still scowling he roared.

'Laying down for a sleep are you?'

There were sniggers all around them.

'Get up you lazy sod before I stop seeing the funny side of this!'

Red faced, the legionary's back was plastered from head to toe in clinging mud. With great difficulty he picked himself up. Wearily wiping his hands on his soaking tunic he picked up his shield and hefted the yoke back across his shoulder.

'That's better laddie.' Snapped Rufus eyeing him coldly. 'Now get back into line with your mates, and stop dicking around playing in the mud, or you'll be on a charge!'

It was a similar story all along the column. Units were becoming mixed up despite gallopers who occasionally brought orders for individual units to catch up. Several centuries at the back of the 19th Legion had even been overtaken by the lighter elements of the baggage train.

Now ahead by several miles, ranging far in front of the disorganised column the engineering unit had come to a full stop. The track which had started so wide and promising had gradually narrowed. Now it was squeezed between sopping craggy outcrops of rock rising thirty feet above them on one side, and dense and seemingly impenetrable forest on the other. The scouts had urged the engineering centurion on, reassuring and promising him that this was just one bad area and the track cleared again just a short distance ahead.

The weary centurion removed the dripping helmet from his head and wiped the rain from his face. He had been forced to call a halt before a tangled lattice of moss covered fallen trees; their decaying trunks wedged together between outcrops of rock, which without back-breaking work would permanently block any chance of further progress. Exasperated he called to the men behind him.

'Right lads. Bring up axes and crowbars. I want this obstruction cleared as quickly as possible.'

His men stumbled forward. To their dismay, the obstruction was interlaced with a confused jumble of vicious thorn covered vines.

As his men's axes began thudding into the sopping trunks the engineer sighed to himself. He'd been in plenty of difficult terrain during his long career, but despite his best efforts he couldn't remember anything quite as bad as this.

The legionaries grunted with effort as they swung their heavy axes down into the logs. Woodchips flew everywhere as sweat mixed with rain trickled into their eyes and down their faces. When rewarded with a final snap, other legionaries stepped forward and levering them free, dragged each heavy log aside before rolling it well clear of the path. The task proved to be exhausting and time-consuming labour, but on the constricted path it was the only possible way to keep moving forward.

With growing irritation at the slow progress their officer watched as the last trunk was rolled free. Satisfied that the path was now clear he signalled his men forward. Absently wondering what lay ahead, he cast about looking for the two guides who had failed to warn him of this latest and unexpected obstacle. Through the continuing deluge and thunder which rumbled and echoed across the heavens, he looked everywhere but couldn't see either of them. Angrily he snapped.

'Has anyone seen those bloody auxiliaries?'

His men paused for a moment. Heads turned then shook. Engrossed in clearing the path, not one of the sweating men had noticed the pair slipping silently into the depths of the surrounding forest only minutes earlier...

Arminius smiled with grim satisfaction from his hidden vantage point, as he watched the struggling efforts of the tail of the rapidly disintegrating column. He had already counted the passing of all three Eagles, and the men who were doing their best to follow them. Their ranks look ragged. The usually smart close marching centuries and cohorts were clearly in trouble. Instead of being closed up and one long regulation line of six men abreast, Varus's army was breaking into groups of tired and dejected looking men. Sometimes, there were several minutes of silence below on the carpet of mud before the next dishevelled unit passed by.

The end of the baggage train was close to him now.

Whips cracked and drovers shouted, urging on their struggling beasts. The wagon wheels bit deeply into the churned mud, disturbing buried roots and adding to the drovers' problems of trying to catch up with the Legions. There were soldiers among them, but many looked tired and vacant. Some were limping as they struggled on through the clinging mud. The confused mix of different shield emblems suggested they were simply stragglers from different Legions; injured men that were unable to keep up, who had slowly dropped further and further back from their own tired units, which grimly struggling on somewhere ahead.

Arminius had chosen his vantage point with great care. He was two miles inside the forest. Now that the last of the slow moving baggage train was passing by, only the civilians who had worked at the Legions' summer camp were still to come. They held no interest for him. Lost and afraid, they could easily be rounded up when the fighting was over and added to the tribesmen's haul of booty. Their fate was sealed, some would be taken as slaves, others ransomed for gold.

He stared up for a moment at the dark skies. Sudden lightning flashed across it. The foul weather was totally unexpected, but he silently welcomed the God's bonus of such generous bounty. Arminius turned and walked silently between the densely packed trees to the other side of the hill.

Untying his horse, Arminius climbed into the saddle. He ordered a messenger to run back along an old hidden hunters' path which ran almost parallel to the Roman's route. The messenger was to signal the hidden men guarding the end of the track where the Romans had entered the Teutoburg to seal it off, then advance and begin harrying the tail, creating fear and forcing it ever deeper into the forest. Arminius wanted no survivors escaping back along the way they had come.

Carrying his wooden spear parallel with the ground, the messenger eagerly loped off to pass the order as Arminius turned his horse and kicked its flanks. The Romans had blundered deep inside the trap, and now he thought as he galloped along the track, it was time to spring it.

Chapter 25

Having ridden less than a mile, Arminius reached the first group of waiting tribesmen. Surrounded by a huddle of his men their leader stood up. Shaking drops of the rain from his cloak, he walked forward as Arminius rode into their midst.

'It is time.' Arminius called gravely. The Bructeri leader nodded and turned. Drawing his sword in silence he motioned to his warriors to follow him. Breaking into a run they headed off into the trees towards the unsuspecting column.

'Come on, keep moving you lazy bastards!'

The centurion commanding one of the 19th's centuries was worried. He hadn't seen sight or sound of the units in front or behind him for nearly an hour. Despite shouting himself horse bellowing threats and even using blows from his vine cane, his men were flagging badly. Even so the centurion knew his duty. Despite the constant rain and sucking mud he had to keep them moving until they reached their rest at the day's marching camp. Somewhere far ahead, he judged the front of the column would be close to stopping now. It was comforting to know that they would follow standard procedure and begin laying out the Legion's overnight base. As more and more centuries and cohorts reached the day's stop point, they would slip off their packs and begin building the defensive stockade, while others dug the surrounding ditch which would keep them all protected for the night to come.

Although there was still difficult marching ahead, his men would need every minute of sleep they could get tonight, after marching for hours in such awful conditions. What a difference it had been when they marched off that morning he thought. His men's spirits had soared. There had been plenty of smiles and even occasional laughter in the ranks, but not now, not anymore. His entire century looked exhausted. All around him, his men dragged themselves on through the mud like part of a defeated and retreating army. What else could he do he wondered, that he hadn't tried already to lift their morale and keep them going? He wiped the rain from his face and looked up at the dark sky. If only, he thought angrily, the damned weather would ease up for a while.

As his men trudged on in silence, one of them suddenly looked up. Blessed with exceptionally sharp hearing, he had picked up a strange sound which didn't belong. It was odd, like a muffled rumble. Not like the thunder overhead, more like the continuous rumble of hundreds of distant cartwheels rolling down a hill. Stranger still, it wasn't coming from above, but from higher up the slope on one side of the dripping forest.

The legionary looked up and said to the man closest to him.

'Do you hear that?'

His companion growled. Head down, he was too tired for stupid conversation.

'What?'

'That noise...listen.'

With a loud tut, the second legionary raised his head.

'What noise...I can't hear anything....'

That was the moment the first barbarians burst from the covering trees. It wasn't thunder the legionary had heard, but the drumming of hundreds of feet running down the forest slope beside them.

Eyes wide with surprise and horror, the sharp eared legionary bellowed a frantic warning.

'Attack...We're under attack!'

But it was too late. Sprinting through the trees the first warriors crashed into the thin line of struggling legionaries. Hacking and slashing at them, the Bructeri allowed no time for the century to deploy, or even defend themselves against their speed and sudden ferocity.

The track was immediately filled with blood and the screams of dying men. A few of the legionaries managed to draw their swords and fend off the rain of blows from the nearest tribesmen, but there were just too many flashing blades around them. As one frightened legionary fought desperately with sword and shield, he was stabbed in the back with a Bructeri spear. With a grunt the man pitched forward, face down in the sucking mud.

Further up the track, the centurion frantically bellowed for his remaining men still on their feet to rally to the century's standard, which had been thrust behind him into the mud. He tried to defend it but was quickly overwhelmed and brutally slain by a dozen wild-eyed warriors who stabbed him repeatedly with their fire hardened spears. Seeing their officer fall, the last remnants of the century despairingly tried to run for it, but even without their packs they were still weighed down with sopping armour which wasn't designed for sprinting. The fleetest of them only managed to make a few yards beyond the edge of the track before the surviving legionaries were surrounded by howling warriors and brutally slaughtered to a man.

In the sudden silence that followed, chest heaving with his violent exertions the Bructeri's leader snatched at the abandoned standard. Lifting it high into the air with one hand, he raised his blood-stained sword in the other and let out a deafening cry of victory, which was echoed by the roaring warriors around him.

Beyond sight and sound of the century's slaughter, further along the line, other centuries and cohorts came under different attacks. Stones and lead slingshot peppered ragged ranks and clanged off shields and armour as the legionaries desperately tried to defend themselves from the deadly missiles. Totally unexpected, the first volley had taken many in one century of the 19th. The barbarian's whirring slings were usually used for hunting. In skilled hands most tribesmen could hit a roosting bird or small deer at fifty paces. Slow moving men were bigger targets, and much easier to hit.

Their centurion had been the first to die with a stone between his eyes. His Optio saw him suddenly judder and fall. The young Optio frantically tried to reorganise his men. To his horror he quickly realised the slingers were firing from both sides of the track.

'Pair up lads and watch each other's flanks.'

The men had stalled. He had to get them away from the killing ground where they were trapped, but there was a problem...

'The wounded! Protect the wounded, we can't leave them behind.'

There were men lying half submerged in the mud, a hotchpotch of bodies scattered all around him. Many were dead but some of them were howling with pain. They clutched at bleeding wounds where the solid shot had broken a bone or penetrated unprotected flesh after it had hissed invisible and deadly from the trees.

'Come on boys. Pair up and grab a wounded man!'

Beginning to recover from their shock, his men responded. It was a drill they had practised many times, but for most, this was the first time they had done it under real enemy fire.

One switched his shield to the other arm and crouching down to make themselves the smallest possible target, keeping close together they sheltered behind their wooden shields and sloshed through the mud to the nearest wounded man. Planting their shields either side of him, they used their free arms to drag him to his feet. Tightening their grip on the lifesaving shields they pulled their howling comrade further up the track, and hopefully out of the line of fire.

There were too many slingers scattered among the trees still launching their deadly projectiles to mount a counterattack, so the Optio roared out an order he hoped would save them all.

'Century will withdraw...Come on boys! Follow me up the track... at the double!'

All along the straggling line attacks were being made on isolated Roman units. Those annihilated were silent. Those still under attack couldn't pass warnings forward or back. Noise of individual battles was deadened by the distances opened up between separated units, the storm overhead and the trees which surrounded them. Many, like Rufus's century just trudged on; totally unaware they were marching into the middle of a war.

For once, Rufus had thrown regulation to the wind. Normally, he followed the book to the letter but the horrendous conditions meant casting it aside temporarily and instead, thinking for himself. He had decided to ignore regulations and ordered frequent short stops to allow stragglers to catch up. He had lost contact hours earlier with the rest of the cohort and decided that his priority was now to keep his men together. At peace or not, his was a fighting unit, and it couldn't and wouldn't function strung out and exhausted. The lack of contact in both directions, and the dreadful state of the track made him suspicious that the rest of the Legion was faring little better than his own men; they must, he reasoned be just as hampered by the storm.

The centurion's emergency briefing that morning had said the plan was to get to the marching camp where the Legions would rest before launching an all-out assault on the rebels at dawn next morning. Rufus's priority was to be on the start line when the attack went in, and if he was late getting to the marching camp that evening, well he thought with a shrug, so be it.

Leading from the front with rain dripping from his helmet Rufus turned and walked backwards. He glanced into the faces of the men nearest him. They looked dog-tired to a man, but thanks to his relaxation of the regulation that ordered stragglers be abandoned, the formation remained together and tight. He looked towards the back of the marching century. The mule in the middle of the small column suddenly brayed loudly. Severus remained tightly bound by his tether behind it. The prisoner looked even more miserable than the others as he slithered along thought Rufus. Seeing the movement from the head of the column his Optio waved from the rear rank. It was the signal that all was well. Satisfied, the veteran centurion turned back and with a resigned sniff, marched on.

Shortly afterwards Rufus was daydreaming. His future beckoned and his thoughts were filled with the little farm in Gaul he would have one day. Suddenly his dreams were torn from him by a bloodcurdling cry from the surrounding forest. It quickly became a deafening guttural roar from both sides of the track. In an instant Rufus knew it wasn't an animal sound; it could only have come from many hundreds of human throats. At the same moment there was a whistling hiss and sudden hard thump against his shield. Rufus ducked without thinking. A dark shower of arrows hissed from the tree line. Honed by years of combat Rufus reacted instantly.

'Form tortoise!'

The tortoise was essentially a defensive formation by which the middle ranks of legionaries would hold their shields overhead, except for the front and back rows, thereby creating a kind of shell-like armour, shielding and encompassing them against missiles from all sides and above.

The last shields clanged into place a split second before the arrows hit. Inside the tortoise it sounded like an even heavier shower of rain peppering them. His shield held before him, Rufus peered through the slit above it. There was movement in the trees. A dark sea of barbarians was rushing towards his defensive box from the forest.

With their javelins still tied to their yokes there was only one thing for it. He yelled at the top of his lungs...

'Draw swords!

It was mid-afternoon. The head of the column was untouched by the carnage; completely unaware of the fierce linear attacks going on behind them in the depths of the forest. Like the staff officers around him, General Varus was cold and soaked to the skin. Stretching tired muscles, he lent forward in his saddle. Looked back he called out to his adjutant.

'We should be getting close now and this looks as good a place as any for the marching camp Dalious. We'll halt here and make camp.'

From his own horse, Prefect Dalious saluted. His General was right. The area ahead was the clearest stretch of land they had come across during what he had to admit to himself had been one of the most miserable day's marches he could remember. It would be tight, but he was sure there was sufficient space to fit in all three legions.

'Yes Sir. I'll see to it right away.'

With a nod of acknowledgement, Varus gave a slight tug on his horse's reins. The stallion obediently stopped with a snort and shake of its wet head. Varus waited until one of his orderlies placed the dismounting step beside his animal. Gratefully, he climbed down and once safely on the ground stretched again and yawned. It had been a long and difficult day and he was looking forward to dry clothes and something hot to eat.

He glanced at one of his attendant staff officers and said.

'Go and find those auxiliary scouts for me will you? I haven't seen them for a while. I expect they've probably gone on ahead to reconnoitre. Send a galloper if you must and get them back quickly. I must learn the enemy's dispositions.'

Prefect Dalious returned from issuing his orders to begin building the night's camp. General Varus turned and addressed him once again.

'When my tent is up I can get out of this wet uniform. Call a staff officer's meeting in one hour. I want to start planning the details of tomorrow's attack.'

Chapter 26

As forward elements of the 17th Legion began to build their marching camp some miles ahead, vicious hit and run attacks continued along the entire length of the column as it snaked its way slowly through the dense forest of the Teutoburg.

By the late afternoon Arminius had re-joined his own auxiliary cavalry. He was engrossed in planning an ambush against one of the largest Roman units who, according to a messenger, still marched along the forest path and would arrive soon. So far, reports brought to him by other messengers suggested the day had gone well; his wild army had inflicted heavy casualties on an increasingly desperate enemy. Now he needed something special. He had decided something spectacular was needed to persuade the other watching tribes that the seemingly invincible Romans could be beaten. Many tribal leaders still required a tangible sign of victory to finally convince them to throw in their hand and join his rebellion in their thousands.

Among the trees in the small wooded valley, on the far side of the mud soaked track Arminius had carefully hidden almost two thousand of his best Cherusci warriors. Heavily armed, they were led by noble members of the Cherusci's warrior caste; his fiercest and very best fighters. His men were impatient for battle but they waited under strict orders to stay hidden, remain silent and wait for the signal before launching their attack.

Alerted by the blood-soaked and mutilated bodies of their comrades which they had counted in their thousands, the 1st cohort of the 19th Legion was closed up, fully prepared and ready to fight. In their midst, the precious Eagle was borne by the Legion's standard bearer, a grizzled veteran who had fought and protected it on many distant battlefields during his long years of service. Although his lion's mane headdress was soaked like the rest of his uniform and armour, he carried the Eagle's staff proudly. The Eagle was part of him; in fact it was a very important part, more precious to him than his own heart or the blood which it pumped through his veins.

The skies remained grey and overcast but the rain had begun to ease a little. A short distance up the track Arminius finished explaining his plan to the Cherusci chieftain who would soon lead the charge down the hill from the other side of the narrow wooded valley.

'So you understand Karl? When the signal comes, your attack must be fast and savage. I want you to strike them like a lightning bolt thrown by the Gods. You must hammer them; don't stop or show mercy, and hold their complete attention. Is that clear?'

Nodding his shaggy grey head the old warrior grinned eagerly. He growled.

'Yes Herman. Our men are ready and know what you expect of them. We will attack like demons and cut them down like corn falling before the scythe.'

Arminius placed his hand on Karl's shoulder. His cold stare was deep and intense.

'Today, ultimate victory may well rest on us and the noble members of the Cherusci warrior caste.' Arminius's face was grave. 'For years to come, the battle we will soon fight will bring honour to our people, and heap shame onto the heads of our enemies.'

The tension in his face eased a little as a grin of anticipation began to spread across it.

'The message we send to them will echo forever through the great halls of Rome.'

Arminius dropped his hand.

'Now go back to your men Karl...watch the track, and await my signal.'

Lucius Plinius was confident. As highly decorated and much respected first centurion of the 19th Legion, he knew the calibre of the men who served in his cohort. Not a man among them boasted less than ten years' service with the Eagle. They were battle hardened veterans and the array of bravery decorations they proudly wore proved their courage beyond a shadow of doubt to any who might make the grievous mistake of questioning it.

As he marched at the head of the reinforced cohort beside the standard bearer carrying the 19th's precious Eagle, Lucius Plinius's confidence was tempered with growing concern at the number of dead they had passed from the 17th and 18th Legions. The carnage was clearly the result of a large scale barbarian rebellion. It was clear to Plinius that the tribes must have been hitting the extended column hard all day.

So far, with his double sized cohort of nine hundred men, despite the condition of the track, the enemy had made no serious attacks on his own unit; resorting simply to occasional sniping by slingers and archers hidden in the dense tree line close by.

The ground began to rise gently as the 1st cohort entered the heavily wooded valley. It was a perfect place for an ambush Plinius thought, but what alternative did he have but to lead his men straight through it? Marching off the track and around the valley was unthinkable. The trees were so tightly packed on either side of the rapidly narrowing path; they would soon be reduced to marching in single file if he tried to take his men around. He had no choice but to keep his troops together, stay in tight formation and press on. Plinius hoped that the enemy had missed the opportunity of using what he considered an excellent ambush point.

Arminius watched the Eagle as it was carried slowly past him by the standard bearer on the muddy track below. He cast his eyes beyond the track, and could see no one hiding among the trees. He nodded to himself with satisfaction; it remained unnaturally quiet in the valley; it was almost time to begin the attack.

A little way ahead, the Cherusci holding axes tensed. The huge oak tree they had worked on all morning still stood tall, but was only held from falling by a network of taught ropes above. The trunk was almost severed; white chips carpeted the ground around its broad base.

The noble commanding them slowly stood up. Concealed by the massive tree trunk he was watching for the head of the column to reach a white rock placed on the side of the track. As the Romans approached the marker he turned and whispered to his men hoarsely.

'Ready yourselves...'

His men knew what to do. Grinning broadly, several spat into their hands and picked up their heavy felling axes. As the noble Cherusci watched, he lifted his arm. The others were ready. Suddenly, his hand chopped down through the air.

'NOW!'

His men swung their axes with all their strength and sliced through the straining ropes. For a second nothing happened, then with an ear splitting crack the last sinews of the trunk shattered and slowly at first the massive tree began to topple towards the marching Romans.

The men in the cohort's advanced guard heard the cracking noise first. They looked nervously about them as they tried to define its source. Suddenly to their right, in a shower of falling leaves the canopy began to shake and swirl as the ancient oak crashed through it towards them. Most of the advance guard had no chance to react before the huge tree fell on them.

As the trunk crashed to the ground there was a mighty roar from the startled column's left. Screaming their guttural battle cries, brandishing swords and axes, a moving carpet of warriors suddenly burst from cover and charged straight at the surviving Romans.

Lucius Plinius screamed at his men to deploy into double line formation. As the front rank's shields clanged together, the second line hurled their javelins at the sea of charging warriors. Despite the shower of deadly missiles, huge numbers of howling warriors remained unscathed and crashed into the line where they began hacking and slashing in a frenzied attempt to get at their hated enemies.

The men who formed the escort to the Eagle, with swords drawn had instantly surrounded it, forming a solid phalanx circling their precious charge and the lion's mane of its standard bearer.

Plinius frantically called for the rear centuries to close up. The extended line would only hold for a few seconds more under the ferocity of the murderous onslaught. With another ear splintering crash, a second tree fell across the far end of the column, crushing many and isolating the last fifty men who were quickly surrounded and hacked to pieces beneath a rain of swinging blades and axes.

The first centurion was shouting himself hoarse, trying to issue orders above the din ranging all around him. His men were falling all along the line but so he noticed with grim satisfaction, were many of the barbarians.

Some of his men scrambled back into the phalanx when they heard the order to withdraw, but almost half still battled furiously with their screaming enemies, unaware that the desperate order to rally had been issued.

Plinius knew his cohort was in danger of being overwhelmed unless he could get his men's attention and pull them back around the Eagle. He snarled at his Conicen, who carried the large circular buccina horn across his shoulder.

'To hell with orders. Blow rally *NOW!*'

The horn trumpeted out a series of short notes. The men fighting desperately in the line heard and understood the signal. As they tried to disengage and rally to the Eagle, many were cut down as they made a run for it. They didn't know they weren't the only ones waiting for the buccina's signal.

On the other side of the valley, Arminius drew his sword and yelled to his two cavalry squadrons formed into a long line on either side of him.

'CHARGE!'

The mounted auxiliaries surged forward down the hill, swerving their snorting mounts between the trees and urging them towards the furiously fighting men, and the intense din of battle.

1st centurion Lucius Plinius noticed the movement and realised to his overwhelming relief that reinforcements had arrived in the nick of time and would save them all. It was a standard tactic. Any second, the line of thundering cavalry would swerve left and right and attack the barbarians on both flanks and more importantly, from the rear. In the ensuing chaos, that would be his moment to launch a counter attack, order his men forward and crush the now surrounded enemy. Turning to the men around him he bellowed.

'Take heart lads. Our cavalry have arrived! Fight hard and prepare to advance!'

A cheer rose from the phalanx as relief surged through every one of them.

Plinius waited for the cavalry to begin enveloping the barbarians, but was suddenly alerted by the screams of his men behind him. He turned. To his horror, the cavalry detachment hadn't ridden out to the flanks, but instead were urging their mounts forward and hacking down left and right with their long swords into his own men. Lost for a moment in utter confusion, Plinius realised too late that the auxiliaries had switched sides and were cutting his men down and driving towards the phalanx's centre. His stomach turned to ice when the truth dawned on him. Panic rising in his voice he shouted.

'The Eagle! The bastards are after our Eagle!'

His warning came too late. As the barbarians continued to fight and savage what was left of the forward fighting line, the heavy horses behind them were forcing a widening wedge into the rear of the defensive phalanx. More warriors on foot were streaming down the same narrow paths used by the horsemen moments earlier. Romans screamed and fell in a spray of blood beneath the flailing cavalry blades, as more and more roaring tribesmen surged forward from all directions and joined the desperate carnage and slaughter amidst the mud on the track.

Caught like a nut between two hammers, the last legionaries fell onto ground which was soaked and running with their comrade's blood.

The outcome was inevitable. Only a few Romans stood huddled around the eagle now, surrounded by a pile of their dead comrades bodies, and the closing ranks of their fur clad enemies. Lucius Plinius stood back to back with the standard bearer. Both men were badly wounded. Blood flowed freely from deep slashes in the 1st centurion's arm, and the standard bearer fought on bravely with an arrow embedded deep in his thigh....

His sword still gripped tightly in his blood-splattered hand, Arminius rode slowly across the track in the deathly hush which had fallen across the battlefield. The 19th's golden Eagle lay across the 1st centurion's body, still gasped in the hand of the dead standard bearer, who fulfilling his sacred oath had been the last Roman to fall. He had fought desperately to protect it until a spear pierced his heart. Around them, the forest floor and track was carpeted with the bodies of the cohort. Warriors ranged among them, callously laughing as they dispatched any wounded legionary they found feigning death; eagerly helping themselves to whatever booty and weapons they could discover among the bodies of the bounteous dead.

Arminius climbed down from his horse and walked into the middle of the silent ring of Roman corpses. With the smell of fresh blood filling his nostrils he bent down slowly and savouring the moment, grasped the Eagle's staff. He pulled but even in death the standard bearer's hand still held it in a vicelike grip. With a frown Arminius swung his sword and lopped off the Roman's clenched hand. It fell to the ground with a soft thud as Arminius straightened, wiped the blood from his blade and recovered his prize.

Elation surged through every fibre of his body. His plan had worked. His men had done the impossible. They had captured that most revered symbol of Rome and all it stood for...They had taken a Roman army Eagle.

More powerful emotions of relief and exaltation surged through him as he hefted the staff and raised the Eagle high above his head. It was a symbol he would parade before the doubting tribal leaders later. But now he decided was not the time.

Arching his back he breathed in deeply and bellowed a single triumphant cry which filled the quiet valley and reverberated across the silent battlefield...

'REVENGE....!'

Chapter 27

The day had turned to dusk. It was almost dark when Rufus and what was left of his century first saw the beacon of torches glittering around the Legion's marching camp. Many of his men who could still walk were helping the limping and sorely wounded. Some had hurriedly bound their injuries with torn strips of cloth to stem the blood which stained their ragged clothes. The carrying yokes were gone, dropped hours ago far behind them and abandoned deep in the forest. The men were utterly exhausted.

Rufus had led them from the ambush after a desperate fight to save their skins. The barbarians had made a mistake as they first charged down the slope from the trees. Eager for their share of booty, the small group of warriors blocking the century's advance had joined the fight too early. Rufus saw the gap open. It was his one opportunity to save his command and he took it instantly. He formed his men into a fighting wedge and smashed his way out of the trap. There had been a running battle afterwards where many of his men had been picked off one by one by their pursuers. It was only in the last hour that there had been any relief for Rufus and his men, when the warriors had finally given up after losing interest in chasing them any further.

The century's mule had taken an arrow in the shoulder and fallen. Trapped by his bonds, Severus had screamed for help. One of his friends who remained loyal had slashed the tether as he ran past. Heart pounding, Severus had managed to remove the loosened rope from his wrists and snatch up the sword of a fallen legionnaire, as he ran for his life with the rest of them.

Bone weary, Centurion Rufus led his men through the heavily guarded gate and entered the marching camp. Wounded men lay groaning on the cold damp ground as far as he could see in the gloom and the nearest torch's limited spill of light. His mind almost numb with exhaustion Rufus turned to call out an order to his Optio, but remembered sadly that Praxus was dead, killed by a barbarian arrow through his eye. There was no time to mourn the loss now, that would come later if he survived the night, Rufus thought ruefully. He turned to the struggling line of exhausted legionaries behind him.

'Help the wounded to the Medicus lads. Keep your eyes open when you go to our lines and see if you can find some food. Get your weapons clean and sleep as soon as you possibly can. I'll join you when I've made my report.'

Not one of his men had the energy to reply. With a nod from a few almost asleep on their feet they disappeared wearily into the darkness.

Severus was the only man to remain in the shadows. He was as drained and exhausted as the others. Unsure what to do next, he mumbled.

'Err, what about me sir? Where shall I go?'

Rufus shrugged. Severus was still under open arrest but what to do with him given the day's events? One thing was for certain Rufus thought; eyeing the inky darkness around the stockade's wall and the savage horrors which lurked beyond it, he was certain Severus wouldn't try to escape. After a moment he replied wearily.

'Buggered if I know son. It's probably best to go and join the rest of the lads for now, while I go and find out what's been going on today.'

As Severus turned to go, Rufus said with one tired eyebrow raised.

'As you are still a prisoner, I think you'd better lose the sword, don't you?'

The mood was sombre at the senior officer's staff meeting. Reports had been collected and causalities counted. The news was not good.

'Eight cohorts gone?' General Varus's voice was incredulous.

His adjutant nodded.

'I'm afraid so General. All three Legions have sustained heavy attacks all day. I have had reports that the enemy were assembled in huge numbers. The cohorts that survived have been dismembered and in some cases lost over half their men; others were completely wiped out... or are still missing.'

Prefect Dalious fell silent. He looked down at his feet and shuffled uncomfortably.

The assembled officers stared at Dalious until General Varus enquired.

'Is there something else on your mind Dalious?'

The Prefect looked up. Licking dry lips, reluctantly he said.

'I'm afraid so Sir. Lucius Plinius and the first cohort of the 19th are among the missing.'

The General's eyes widened with shock and anguish.

'The Eagle?'

With a deep sigh Dalious shook his head.

'We've no idea where it is Sir. The last men in before dark reported seeing a heavy concentration of our dead a few miles back, but the bodies had been stripped and we've no way of knowing if it was the 19th's 1st cohort...but I believe it might well have been.'

Varus swallowed. If an Eagle had been lost the shame could ruin him politically in Rome. His face remained impassive but his mind was suddenly thrown into turmoil. Defensibly, he replied

'Or on the other hand it might not have been... Lucius Plinius is a resourceful officer and may well have found somewhere safe to ride out the night.'

The disgrace of losing an Eagle under his command would tarnish the General's good name forever. Even his close family ties with the Emperor wouldn't save him from falling from Imperial grace, if he didn't quickly find a way to lift the curse. There was confidence in his voice, although inside he didn't feel it. Hopefully Varus continued.

'He could turn up at anytime without warning. There are still units arriving are there not?'

Dalious nodded silently. He hoped his General was right about the fate of the 19th's Eagle, but his old soldier instincts filled him with the gravest doubt.

Varus had made his decision. It would buy him time as he searched for a way to save his honour. His eyes narrowed as he stared into the faces of the surrounding officers

'No... We mustn't damage the men's morale. I want them simply posted as missing for now...Is that clear?'

The officers nodded. Like Dalious, they silently harboured doubts on the Eagle's fate, but the men's morale was vitally important and there was no need to do it harm with supposition or by dealing on unconfirmed rumour. Varus said.

'Take heart gentlemen. Remember that although we have lost men today, Arminius will arrive soon with thousands of loyal Cherusci to help us.'

General Varus swept several half full cups from the table beside him and unrolled the same hide map he had used to brief his officers before they left the summer camp.

Resting both hands on the map, Varus looked up.

'Now gentlemen, I have some hard decisions to make. My appreciation of the situation so far is that the rebels have got wind of our plan and launched spoiling attacks against us with the view of delaying us bringing them to battle.'

One of the senior centurions looked up from the map and enquired.

'To what end sir? Why should they do that?'

Varus smiled.

'I came across the same tactic in Syria. The rebels there tried to delay my Legions to cover their own withdrawal, but

I fought through their ambushes, caught up with their main army and annihilated it when I took Jerusalem.'

The 1st centurion and staff offices around him nodded. The general's victories in Palestine when he governed there were legend. Varus stared into their drawn faces in silence. He needed another victory quickly. He was sure it would be enough to overcome the shame of the 19th's loss of their Eagle. Perhaps, it might show Rome what a truly tough fight it had been and conceivably even reinforce his own military genius to those who counted in Rome. Varus continued.

'As I see it, we are faced with three choices gentlemen. Our first choice is to stay where we are, reinforce our defences and send for reinforcements. I am discounting that option. If we stay here, by the time our messengers return with men from the two Legions stationed at the Rhine forts, winter will be upon us, we will have run out of food and the enemy will have melted away.'

One of the Prefects interrupted.

'But sir, we have so many wounded...Surely we must stay here and wait.'

Varus held up his hand.

'Yes, thank you Aquilinius, I have read the casualty reports. I will come to the issue of the wounded shortly.'

Clearing his throat, Varus continued.

'Our second option is to try and outflank the barbarians. I have discounted this plan as well. We are unaware of the enemy's' dispositions, and the local terrain will not lend itself to a set piece battle. We simply couldn't blunder about and try to hunt them all down in this close country, and then put them to the sword.'

Varus tapped the outstretched map with his hand.

'We must use the terrain to our advantage gentlemen. Speed is the key here. It is my intention to leave this camp with the Legions before daybreak tomorrow in total silence, to avoid alerting the enemy and push on to the other side of the forest. As you are aware, the ground is flat and open on the other side. We will draw the barbarians out of the forest... and then we will crush them.'

Prefect Aquilinius nodded like the others. It seemed a good plan but how could they maintain the necessary speed to accomplish Varus' strategy? He caught the General's eye.

'But how can we move quickly enough, and at the same time keep the baggage train and all the wounded protected sir?'

Varus looked down at the map for a moment, and then his head suddenly snapped up.

'Being a General is a heavy burden sometimes Prefect Aquilinius. I carry the responsibility of representing the

Emperor, my Legions and all of Rome for that matter, while out here on campaign. My ultimate duty is to give victories, whatever the cost.'

The Prefect shook his head.

'I'm sorry sir; I don't think I fully understand your point.'

Varus sighed. This was the only way to save his honour and family name. He must cast aside all other considerations; he must fight the coming battle and win. Feigning a heavy heart he said softly.

'To accomplish success and strike quickly I have been forced to make the hard decisions I mentioned earlier...Therefore I have decided we must burn the baggage train, and I'm afraid there is no other choice...we must abandon our wounded.'

There were sharp intakes of breath and muttering all around him. Looks of disbelief surrounded Varus. Like the other officers assembled around their General, Aquilinius was aghast. The General's order was breaking a fundamental principle which within the fighting Legions, was cast in stone. The wounded were never left behind.

Ashen faced, his voice incredulous, Aquilinius stammered.

'But...but this is simply unthinkable sir. The barbarians will show them no mercy. Our wounded will be slaughtered...And what of the civilians who follow us. There are hundreds of women and children among them. Are they to be abandoned as well?'

To extricate himself from potential disaster, Varus needed time to manoeuvre. He was confident that the barbarians would waste valuable hours raping the civilian women and pillaging the remains of the supply carts. He also expected to gain even more precious time while the barbarians engaged themselves in torturing and slowly killing his wounded.

Their eyes betrayed them. There was suddenly a palpable feeling of mutiny in the air among the senior officers standing before him; the General could almost taste it. He knew he must act quickly to crush the growing dissent. Suddenly Varus hammered his fist onto the table. The room hushed instantly after the ringing blow. The anger in the General's voice betrayed his seething fury at having his future threatened and his decisions questioned by a mere Legion Prefect. Varus snarled.

'*I am in command here!* Your duty is to obey my orders without question. If you cannot, I will find someone else who will!'

Glaring, Varus searched the faces of each of his officers as the blunt threat hung in the air. Through gritted teeth he hissed at them.

'Do I make myself perfectly clear...gentlemen?'

Chapter 28

Although the mood was strained and sombre in the Roman headquarters, several miles away it was verging on the riotous in the Rebel's hidden encampment.

Tribesmen swaggered about by the light of roaring fires, proudly displaying their newly captured swords and javelins. Men laughed and spoke in loud voices of their fighting abilities and the prowess they had shown when killing the enemy. Many staggering unsteadily between the blazing fires; drunk on wine looted from an abandoned Roman wagon. Some swung heavy blades and axes through the empty air, re-enacting fights to the death they had become embroiled in during moments of the fiercest fighting of the day. There were auxiliaries mixed into the throng who loudly joined in the celebrations with their brothers.

Nearby was one of the many sacred groves which peppered the forest. Inside, within rings of consecrated stones the priestesses spoke to the Gods, and made offerings of blood to the spirits of the dark forest. The high priestess had demanded sacrifice to appease the angry Spirits. Soon, she was promised, prisoners would be brought; they would have their fill.

Still wearing his uniform and armour Arminius warmed himself against the chill night air, sitting beside a fire at the edge of the encampment. He bit into a charred hunk of venison one of his men had passed him. Beside him, Rolf sat inspecting a minor gash on his forearm, taken from a Roman gladius during their fierce attack on the Eagle. Rolf wasn't annoyed by the wound and wore it proudly; he had killed the legionnaire who had given it to him, and afterwards sought out his body and taken his head.

Behind the two men, with dried blood staining its staff, stood the Eagle. The base of the staff had been rammed into the damp earth and at the other end the Eagle glittered brightly, reflecting the light thrown out by the numerous fires of the victorious tribesmen. Arminius had sent word that he had taken it to all who still doubted the rebellion. He challenged each of them to view it, if they had the courage. He was sure that would bring them all to see his treasured prize.

Rolf bound a cloth around his arm. He looked up at the laughing cavorting throng of men before him.

'The men are drunk Herman. Will we try and put an end to it?'

Arminius chewed on a piece of gristle, and then spat it into the fire. As it began to smoke and sizzle in the glowing embers he looked at his cousin. With a smile he said.

'No Rolf, let them have their fun. It is our way after battle to celebrate victory and the wine they fill their bellies with is captured booty.... Have you ever tried to snatch a bone from a hungry dog?'

Rolf continued to stare at the celebrations as he nodded with a grin. With a shrug he yawned and lay down in front of the fire, pulling his heavy cavalry blanket over him.

Before he closed his eyes in search of sleep, yawning again he asked.

'We fight again tomorrow cousin?'

Arminius nodded, staring intently into the flickering fire. The answer was in the flames.

'Yes Rolf, we will kill many more once the sun has risen.'

Arminius was soundly asleep when he was roughly shaken from his slumbers by one of his own auxiliaries. Dawn's first glow was lighting the horizon. The auxiliary crouched down beside him. There was alarm in the man's voice

'Herman, wake up. There is much smoke coming from the Roman's camp. They are burning their wagons.'

Still confused by sleep, Arminius opened his eyes. He sat up as Rolf began to stir on the other side of the smoking embers of their fire.

Rubbing his eyes Arminius asked.

'What do you mean...what smoke?'

'The men you ordered to watch the Roman camp have come back and roused everyone. The Romans slipped away in the night and their supply wagons are left behind and burning. Our men want to go to the camp and take what they can...'

The grave news fully woke Arminius with a start. He jumped to his feet. Angrily he said to the auxiliary.

'No! We must not waste time looting, that must wait.'

Rolf was also awake now, disturbed by the hurried conversation beside him. Sleepily he said.

'What is it cousin, what's happening?'

Arminius looked down at him and said.

'The Romans try to flee Rolf. I should have seen this coming...We must go after them quickly before they find their way out of the trap.'

Rolf threw his damp blanket aside and stood up as Arminius continued.

'I must stop our men or the rebellion is in danger. Quickly now, gather our nobles and bring them here to me.'

At the hastily called council, tempers were frayed among the crowd of incensed and hung-over Cherusci nobles. News that they were to be denied valuable booty had soured the previous evening's elation.

'But Herman, it is our right to take what we win in battle.'

Another growled angrily.

'Aye, Ulrich's right. How else are we to enrich ourselves?'

Someone at the back called out.

'If we don't take our spoils now, the other tribes will take them.'

There was a general growl of agreement from the Cherusci chieftains.

Arminius held up both hands in supplication.

'No, you must listen to me. This is exactly want the Romans want. By leaving their scraps behind they want us to squabble like dogs over their leavings. While we plunder their supplies...they will use the time to escape.'

Sour faces around him told Arminius the nobles disagreed.

One of the oldest nobles, a close friend of Arminius's father stepped forward and spoke.

'Then let us leave men to put out the fires and guard our spoils Herman.' He turned to the others. Sternly he addressed them. 'If we are to rid our lands of the Romans, we still have much fighting and killing to do. Like you all, I know my men will fight harder if they are assured of getting a fair share of the spoils when the fighting is done.'

There was silence for a moment while the other nobles considered the compromise. War brought valuable booty which could be traded for other things, but he was right. If they didn't slaughter *all* the Romans, they would be back in the spring and take a terrible revenge. Grudgingly, heads began to nod; despite their sore heads, the nobles could see the wisdom of it.

Arminius breathed a silent sigh of relief. Grasping the hand of the elder he said.

'Thank you Adalbert, as always you bring your sage council to our tribe when it is needed most.'

The crisis passed, Arminius addressed the assembly.

'It is agreed then. We will detach two hundred men to guard the booty while the rest of us pursue the Romans. If they find any Romans still there,' he shrugged 'they can amuse themselves by killing any prisoners while they guard our treasure. The Romans believe they have tricked us by leaving before dawn but don't let it concern you, they haven't. We already know their only route, and I have positioned our Angrivarrii brothers along the difficult path that they must tread. The ground in front of the Romans is low lying and filled with swamps. The Angrivarrii are fewer in number than us, or the Bructeri, but they have been following my orders and using the last two days wisely,' he grinned. 'They have been preparing some surprises for the Romans which will slow them down until we can get ahead of the column.'

In the belief that leaving camp two hours before dawn would give them the chance they needed to escape, the survivors of the three Legions marched on as light began to brighten the eastern horizon. Although sleep had eluded most, at least they had had the chance to rest their exhausted bodies.

The night had been filled with ugly and tragic scenes before the survivors had slipped quietly from the marching camp.

The wounded were attended to. Those with superficial injuries had their injuries stitched, sealed with hot irons or tightly bound. Those too grievously wounded, who could no longer walk were given a stark choice. The stricken men were offered a swift death at the hands of the Medicus, or the forbidding alternative, to take their chances of mercy from the barbarians when they arrived in the morning. Fearing hours or even days of terrible torture, most realised their situation was hopeless and chose to take a swift death and die by Roman hand. The Medicus placed an iron chisel against the nape of the wounded man's neck. The brutal impact from a hammer on the butt end of the chisel severed the spinal column just below the skull, delivering instant and painless death.

Before the Medicus arrived, old comrades bid gravely wounded friends' farewell, knowing the fate which awaited them. Tears of sorrow were shed by hard men tempered in the crucible of battle. They had shared their lives together; they had fought and bled beside these good friends, who now lay in pain and devoid of hope; these were friends they must gently say goodbye to for the very last time.

There had been much wailing among the civilians when they heard that they were to be abandoned. Those women who had men serving in the Legions' ranks pleaded for the sake of their children to be spared the fate which all knew awaited them, but to no avail. Stern faced centurions ensured that the general's orders were obeyed to the letter;

civilians were herded from the camp in the middle of the night at the point of grim faced legionaries' swords.

The artillery was burnt and the wagons were set on fire after they had been thoroughly searched for spare javelins. They were removed and issued to a waiting line of tired legionaries. Even the arrow like artillery bolts were removed just before the ammunition wagons went up in flames. The barbed iron darts were lashed to long poles and quickly issued. Every javelin would be needed when the next day dawned.

Although it had stopped raining during the night, the clouds remained hanging dismally in the dark skies above. They shielded the forest floor from moonlight; a welcome addition to the enveloping darkness as the Romans stole silently from the camp. Those sections which still had their pack mules stuffed leaves and grass into the bronze bells which hung around the animal's necks, to deaden the sound normally used to find the beast if it strayed. Stumbling and cursing, the men marched through the inky darkness and tried their best to stay close to the man in front.

When the path through the forest became light enough to see, it began to rain again. At first, the marching men barely noticed. There was a new energy in them, galvanized not only by their dread of the forest, but also by a new emotion which few had really felt before during years of military service.

It was gnawing fear in the pit of their bellies which drove them on and fuelled tried muscles.

The rain increased with flashes of forked lightning and the rumble of distant thunder. The rain lashed down in ferocious torrents on the snaking column. The wind had picked up until it gusted ferociously. The trees around the column were whipped by it; they swayed, creaked and groaned all around the marching Legions. In the slippery mud it became difficult to stay upright as the marching men struggled against the wind's awesome and unrelenting power.

Leading the column, General Varus had dispatched his engineers once again to reconnoitre their way ahead and clear obstacles which might delay their flight westwards.

Chapter 29

Despite the foul weather, the column made reasonable progress in the first hours after dawn, but once again the track deteriorated into a trail of slime and mud. Gallopers urged the units to stay closed up but inevitably gaps between units began to appear and widen, once again.

To replace the fallen from the previous day, Rufus and the forty men he still commanded had been attached to the 18th's 1st Cohort. The General had given the highest priority to protecting the remaining Eagles.

The 18th's first centurion Marius had been gravely wounded, but as a senior officer he had been granted dispensation and a place crammed uncomfortably onto one of the few carts the column had taken with them.

Severus marched silently among the century's survivors. With Rufus' permission, he had donned the armour and helmet of a legionnaire who had died of his wounds during the night. Rufus reasoned that under the circumstances, what with the drovers and civilian men being issued weapons and invited to join the column, the general staff up ahead needed every sword available, and he wasn't prepared to waste the services of a fully trained and experienced man by retying his bonds.

The Romans sent ahead by Varus to reconnoitre approached the silent swamp with caution. Their auxiliary scouts had vanished the day before; now they were on their own.

There was clearly a path of sorts running into the marshlands, but it looked narrow and treacherous. The tall trees in front of the engineering party began to thin in number, making the constant half-light brighter and visibility just a touch easier. The gnarled trees scattered in the vast swamp were surrounded and partly submerged by deep pools of dark stagnant water swollen to higher levels by the recent rains. They went on as far as anyone in the detachment could see. A bird screeched unseen from somewhere deep inside the swamp's fetid interior; a piercing shriek picked up by other waterfowl startled by something unseen and lurking in its forbidding depths. The pungent smell of rotting vegetation wafted towards them though the heavy rain-filled atmosphere; the air was filled with the putrid stench of stomach-heaving marsh gas.

The engineering centurion's Optio stared at the sombre wetlands with dismay. Beneath his rusting armour he turned to his commander. After the tumult of the previous day there was more than a hint of apprehension and despite his best efforts to hide it, even a trace of fear in his voice.

'Surely there's time to find a way around sir? The journey so far has been bloody awful, but this looks...much worse.'

The centurion shook his head. His face was grave and resigned to what must be.

'No. Our orders are clear. We are to find a way straight through this cursed forest.' He cast a quick glance over his shoulder and then turned back to his Optio. 'The barbarians are hunting us. They're sure to come back and attack again at any moment. Without cavalry support we've simply no time to scout out an alternative route and go around whatever lies ahead.'

With silent foreboding he stared at the point where the track disappeared into the ancient primordial swamp. Trying to suppress a shudder, he shook his head and muttered reluctantly.

'There's no choice I'm afraid, our duty is clear. We have to go in.' Grim faced he added. 'Order the detachment forward, will you?'

Like a ravenous spider concealed in the centre of a vast fetid web, the Angrivarrii watched and waited for the unsuspecting Romans to enter their dank and menacing trap.

As the vanguard of the 18th Legion's 1st cohort, Rufus and his legionaries trudged wearily on.

Among his men, personal loads were much lighter now. Their equipment was long gone and few carried shields. Most had discarded them as they ran for their lives after the previous day's attack. Rufus was concerned about the loss, but there was nothing he could do about it. His men were trained to fight with sword and shield but now they would have to make the best of it. He had thought about charges, but decided against it because slowed by the extra weight of rain sodden shields he doubted he would have had more than a handful of men to command, given that the fleet footed barbarians pursued them carrying little more than a sword or spear. To stand and fight would have been suicide, even with a shield.

Suddenly, gallopers approached. There were four of them. With dismay, Rufus instantly recognised the man who led them.

Tribune Crastus raised one arm to signal a halt to his bodyguard. Then, like the other mounted legionaries he hauled hard on his reins. The horses slithered to a stop in a spray of mud, liberally splattering Rufus and the front of the vanguard with fat gobbets of slime.

Eyeing him coldly, Crastus watched as Rufus saluted. Lazily returning the salute the young Tribune said self-importantly.

'Ah yes, Rufus. 1st centurion Marius died of his wounds less than an hour ago and I have been ordered by Prefect Marcos to take command of the 1st Cohort, until we reach the other side of the forest.'

Rufus watched as the Tribune and his men rode further back along the column towards the standard bearer and his party. His darkest suspicions were confirmed. Things were obviously more desperate than the senior officers were letting on. To put a raw inexperienced Tribune, who was considered by the 18th's tough centurions as little more than a spoilt and spiteful boy in charge of protecting their precious Eagle sent a cold shiver down Rufus' spine. He shrugged to himself. The chain of command didn't always work he thought morosely, as he set his jaw and trudged wearily on.

Having sorted out their differences over booty, Arminius and his men were making good time. They used hidden tracks running through the deepest forest to bypass the Romans. Moving silently, the lightly equipped Cherusci and Bructeri horde passed by unobserved, beyond sight of the slow moving Roman column as it approached the swamp. Using men who had spent their lives hunting the marshlands as guides, the barbarian army quickly outflanked the Romans. Their guides led them on through the depths of the gloomy swamp, using ancient pontiff longii; wooden bridleways laid on the fetid surface. The network had been built by local tribesmen over centuries. Using stout timbers secured with thick rope, the floating walkways provided a hidden highway for the rebels to cross deep bogs and seemingly impassable marshland with ease. In places they had to be cautious however; sliding from the sopping timbers into the marsh could only mean quickly disappearing beneath the dark surface of the surrounding waters and without rescue, drowning quickly in the sucking ooze of the deep mud just below the water's surface.

The attacks the previous day had been piece-meal. Today however, on the other side of the swamp Arminius planned to launch all-out attacks in huge and overwhelming numbers. Even weakened as Varus' army was, it remained potent. Arminius harboured serious doubts that he could inflict a total rout on the Romans before nightfall. He was certain however his men would inflict critically heavy casualties on the fleeing column.

Arminius would need the following day to finish the Romans but if he was right, the disintegrating army of General Varus would have its back broken in the hours of daylight which remained, before darkness once again shrouded the vast depths of the great Teutoburg forest.

Although fewer in numbers the Angrivarrii positioned inside the swamp had a part to play in Arminius' strategy. They would buy him time to get his main force into place and add to the growing Roman casualties, and the exhaustion and growing fear he knew must by now be gripping theirs guts like an iron fist.

The forward engineering party pushed on through the swamp. Only the sound of the swirling water at their knees, or the cry of a distant bird broke the heavy silence which surrounded them. The track in places had disappeared completely after several days of torrential rain. The centurion and his men had sometimes been forced to wade up to their waists through miles of black foul smelling water, before eventually finding the first patch of higher ground where the going would at last become easier.

Free at last of the fetid water, the centurion gratefully called a halt to his fatigued party.

'Looks like we're close to getting out of this filthy swamp lads. We'll rest here for ten minutes, and then push on and find our way out.'

His men were all lying exhausted on the ground when the first arrow struck the ground at the centurion's feet. From a nearby stand of trees, a small group of Angrivarrii boys fired a ragged volley of arrows and stones at the resting Romans. Laughing loudly, they followed the volley with loud cat-calls and rude insulting gestures, pulling up their cloaks and displaying their naked genitals and backsides at the Romans.

After the past days of unrelenting pressure and uncertainty the centurion's frayed nerves suddenly snapped. How dare these barbarian brats attack their rightful masters? Frustrated rage boiled over the Roman as he lost all sense of reason. They would pay for their insults. His eyes blazing with fury he turned and roared.

'By the Gods! I've had enough of this. On your feet men and follow me!'

Snatching out his sword, the centurion ran the short distance across the open ground towards the laughing gesturing boys. His men were close behind. Flecks of spittle sprayed from his lips as he snarled over his shoulder.

'Fan out! I want every one of these little bastards' heads.'

Blinded by his rage, he and his men failed to notice that the boys didn't attempt to run but instead stopped laughing and uncertainly stood their ground. The small Roman party didn't notice as they charged forward, the ground just in front of them had been recently disturbed.

Only a dozen paces from the nearest boy, the centurion unexpectedly pitched forward with a cry of alarm. He disappeared through the thin lattice of sticks and leaves concealing the dark pit below. Suddenly gone from view, his startled cry was abruptly choked off.

Unable to check their forward momentum three more legionnaires fell forward into other concealed pits. Their screams of terror stopped as suddenly as they plunged forward; impaled a heartbeat later on beds of needle sharp stakes the Angrivarrii had fashioned the previous day.

Shocked and leaderless the remaining legionaries looked at each other in momentary confusion, then in stark horror at the screaming band of Angrivarrii warriors who broke cover and charged from the stand of trees in front of them. Uncertain what to do the Romans turned in blind panic from the sword wielding barbarians who outnumbered them by at least twenty to one.

The engineering party suddenly disintegrated into a starburst of fleeing men running in blind terror for their lives. The firm ground around them was blocked by howling warriors and deadly pits. The only chance they had was to flee back into the swamp. As the first Romans launched themselves with a loud splash into the black fetid water, the slowest were caught by the Angrivarrii and savagely hacked and cut down.

The screams behind them added urgency to the terrified men who had already reached the water. None dared look back. Hampered by their heavy armour and the clinging effects of the water, without the slightest regard to where they were going they frantically waded deeper and deeper into the swamp. Bubbles of stinking marsh gas foamed around them as they plunged on through tangles of rotting vegetation and submerged roots.

Half the small party lay dead behind him as the Angrivarrii's leader roared for his howling men to stop at the water's edge. Breathing heavily, he turned and waved the young boys to his side. He gestured towards the struggling Romans, several of whom had already disappeared up to their shoulders in the clinging ooze.

The Angrivarrii chieftain felt cheated. Since the rebellion began, these were the first Romans he had seen but they were so few in number. Disappointed, he wondered angrily where the honour and glory was in killing cowards who wouldn't stand their ground and fight like men.

In the cold water, a fleeing Roman lurched forward as one of his sandaled feet became trapped in a hidden knot of tangled roots. His ankle broken, with an agonised cry the legionary's head plunged beneath the dark surface. Seconds later he re-emerged coughing and whimpering in pain and abject terror. The Angrivarrii chieftain's heart was cold towards his enemy's suffering. Where was their all conquering arrogance now, he wondered? His face filled with hatred and contempt the Angrivarrii stabbed his sword towards the wildly splashing figure who was now trying desperately to stay above the surface. The Angrivarrii eyes narrowed as he hawked and spat towards the helpless fugitive. Looking down at the expectant faces of the boys around him, with a savage grin he swept his hand towards the fleeing Romans struggling in the water. With the nodding approval of his men he snarled.

'Use your bows and slings young warriors... *Leave none alive...Kill them all!'*

Chapter 30

The rain stopped in the early afternoon and the skies began to brighten.

The last of the 19th Legion dragged their exhausted bodies from the clinging horrors of the vast swamp. Some wept openly with relief that their ordeal was over. Others counted themselves lucky but were confused as to why the Gods had chosen to spare them. The harrowing hours spent avoiding stake filled pits, and fighting their way through the stinking marchland had seen too many comrades fall to repeated barbarian ambush. Some of their oldest friends had gone missing; they had become separated and hopelessly lost during the ordeal. Panic stricken; men whose nerves were stretched beyond all reason had leapt from the path into the marsh, trying desperately to get away; seeking any kind of shelter or simply succumbing to the blind desire to get out of range of the deadly and unremitting hail of enemy arrows and slingshot.

When groups of stragglers reached the occasional relief of higher ground they had been attacked again and again with furious hit and run assaults which left the Legion's already stretched ranks dangerously thinned. The murky waters throughout the swamp were littered with floating and half submerged corpses, surrounded by the spreading stain of Roman blood.

Several miles ahead of the 19th's recovering survivors, Rufus and his men trudged wearily westwards. Like many others who still survived after their perilous journey through the swamp, Rufus's century was down to less than twenty men. Half their number lay face down and silent in the vast swamp behind them. They had no shields and no defence against the Angrivarrii arrows; it was down to little more than luck that any now preceded their Eagle and trod the path away from the slaughter in the marshes.

The route ahead had been clearly defined by the 17th's marching feet, who had passed over the same ground only a short time before. In the heart of the Teutoburg, visibility beyond the track remained extremely limited. The forest's uneven floor was covered with a thick mat of green vegetation and only yards from the marching men the gloomy forest closed in, wrapped in a confused crisscross of dark shadows. To the frightened men of the 18th Legion, it gave off an aura of soul sapping despair.

Severus was marching beside his centurion in silence. His eyes were constantly moving. They flicked nervously to both sides of the surrounding forest, probing every tree and bush, watching for the slightest tell-tale sign of enemy movement. His bread bag long empty, Severus's stomach growled with hunger.

Licking his dry lips, he asked.

'Do you think there'll be any food up ahead when we stop Sir?'

Rufus considered the question for a moment.

'There might be something left son,' he smiled wryly 'but I wouldn't get your hopes up.'

Suddenly, birds roosting in the canopy above screeched in alarm as a ripping snapping roar erupted close by in the forest. A huge ancient oak tore through the green wall of the surrounding trees and fell with a deafening crash across the track just twenty paces behind them. The ground shook with the thunderous impact as the gnarled trunk smashed to the ground in a shower of broken branches and browning leaves. There was the sound of more crashing trees behind them along the track, but they were hidden from Rufus and his men by the massive girth of the first tree to fall.

A deep baritone blast of a war horn filled the forest; its sombre note chilled the advance guards' blood. It was followed by blasts from other more distant horns. Rufus and his men suddenly heard a mighty roar behind them, from the throats of a vast host of Germanic warriors.

Followed by Severus, Rufus ran back down the churned track to the fallen tree. There was an arm sticking out beneath it in a spreading pool of blood, but no sign of the rest of the body to which it belonged. One of his survivors stood beside it ashen faced and frozen. Shocked out of his daze by his centurion's sudden arrival the legionary looked up into Rufus' face. He was white and shaking.

'I...I was talking to Paulo just seconds ago sir. He...he was there one minute then... then he was just gone!'

Rufus grabbed the man by the shoulder and shook him. There was no time for finesse.

'Snap out of it lad. Now draw your bloody sword and wake up!' A little more reassuringly he added quickly. 'We need you!'

Beyond the massive trunk there was the growing din of battle joined. The ringing sound of steel on steel and the piercing cry of agonised screams rent the air. On the other side of the trunk his comrades shouted desperate orders and warnings which Rufus understood, but the guttural cries and oaths in the barbaric tribesmen's tongue meant nothing.

The fallen trunk was thicker than the height of two tall men. There was no way over it. Cursing silently in his frustration Rufus looked left and right. The fallen tree's surviving foliage locked a thick tangled mess of snapped branches into the surrounding undergrowth. At its other end a confused web of roots did the same. Angrily he snarled to the frightened men surrounding him.

'This is bloody hopeless, we're cut off!'

Making up his mind on what must be done, renewed energy flowed through tired muscles as he snapped.

'We've got to rally to the eagle men...Follow me!'

Arminius watched the unfolding battle from a nearby ridge. Around him, his cavalry squadrons were eager for battle, but Arminius had forbidden them from moving. His allies, the Bructeri had fought well the previous day. Their nobles and men had died bravely in the numerous battles along the line and he knew it was only right for them to receive a suitable reward. When he had planned the day's attacks, he made sure it would be the Bructeri who would launch an assault on the second Eagle.

When Arminius was victorious, he knew he would need allies bound to him in an uncertain future. The new alliance he had spent months forging between the tribes was fragile. After the Romans were defeated and gone from their lands, he needed the common bonds of spilt blood and glory between them to bind both the Bructeri and the Angrivarrii to his future plans for Germania.

Beside him, Rolf was also watching the developing battle. He could see the swirling groups fighting below. The Romans had neither the time nor opportunity to join together. The fallen trees had done their work. Isolated pockets of men hacked and slashed at each other as far as he could see with no quarter asked or given. As the Bructeri fell before the stabbing Roman swords they were immediately replaced by new warriors lost to the pain of minor wounds by their mind numbing and ferocious battle madness, and an unquenchable thirst for enemy blood.

'The Bructeri fight well Herman.'

Arminius nodded.

'Yes Rolf they have no choice.'

Rolf's face betrayed his lack of understanding. Arminius smiled knowingly and replied.

'They must fight well today Rolf, their tribe's honour is at stake. If they fail to take the 18th's Eagle their shame will spread throughout our lands. Men will spit on the name Bructeri.'

Rolf's face filled with admiration for his leader.

'The Bructeri king will use any number of his men to avoid that, won't he?'

Still watching the ferocious fighting below, Arminius nodded. There was coldness in the smile which played across his lips. The Romans had taught him the meaning of ruthlessness.

'Yes Rolf. We still need the other tribes to rally to us before this is over, but our cause will gain another Eagle today. It will encourage them without shedding a single drop of our own Cherusci blood.'

Below, things were going badly for the 18th Legion. Dwindling pockets of desperately fighting legionaries had scattered and were being cut down in vicious hand to hand combat as wave after wave of screaming warriors appeared from the surrounding forest and swept down to join in on the murderous attacks. The barbarian's tactics were simple and clear. They surrounded each group of desperately fighting Romans, enveloping them by sheer weight of numbers. Heavy axes crashed into those legionaries who still held shields. Arrows hissed across the chaotic battlefield and slammed into the tightly packed throngs of Romans who, as their comrades fell, were quickly reduced to fighting back to back in a vain attempt to save themselves. Their bloody end was certain...there were just too many Bructeri blades hacking into them.

Beyond the fallen tree, the ground had suddenly fallen away forcing Rufus to lead his men on a wide detour to get them to the defence of their Eagle. Suddenly he saw a group of young barbarian warriors racing towards the sounds of battle. So intent were they on joining the fight they failed to notice the band of Romans who suddenly appeared from the undergrowth close on their right. In that critical moment; Rufus had only one possible course of action while he had surprise on his side. He roared to his men.

'Charge!'

Within seconds both bands were locked in fierce combat. Adrenaline surged through the tired legionaries. They were desperate, isolated and alone, fighting for their very survival. Surprised by the sudden attack, the Bructeri troop was caught off guard. Rufus stabbed the nearest warrior in the throat. With a gurgled gasp of pain and surprise the young warrior fell to the ground. Rufus recovered his balance and slashed another. Running forward he attacked his next opponent. He was an older man armed with a vicious looking axe. Swinging it above his head he rushed at Rufus growling like a maddened bear. Rufus ducked as the blade hissed past his head. Now too close to use his sword, Rufus drew back and slammed the rim of his armoured forehead into the growling warriors face. Blood erupted from the rebel's nose and lips as the stunned Bructeri fell backwards. With all his strength Rufus leapt forward and stabbed the warrior in the centre of his unprotected chest. The warrior shuddered and lay still. This was like the fighting Rufus had witnessed as a boy, between rival gangs in the backstreets of Rome. Savage and cruel it was simply kill or be killed; in the charnel house of the blood-stained battlefield nothing else mattered.

Severus was on the ground in trouble. A muscular Bructeri had his hands around the legionnaire's throat. Moments before, the man had lunged at him with a spear. Severus had sidestepped the thrust and the iron tipped head missed his shoulder by inches. With the added reach of the man's spear, Severus's training took over. Instinctively, he knew he had to get in close before he was skewered by the next thrust. The Bructeri realised what the Roman was trying to do and dropped the spear. Growling like a beast he lurched forward and reached for his enemy's throat. His brutal impact knocked both men to the ground and Severus's sword flew from his hand. Sensing victory the snarling Bructeri increased the pressure to the struggling Roman's throat. The Bructeri's strength was immense.

Severus tried but couldn't break his iron grip. As blood roared in his ears he remembered. Releasing one hand from his enemy's fingers he felt down to his left hip. Relief surged as his fingers closed around the handle of his pugio, the sidearm dagger carried by all Roman soldiers. As the world around him began to blur and blacken, Severus pulled the pugio from its sheath. His life-force ebbing quickly he desperately stabbed upwards under the snarling warrior's chin. The blade pierced the warrior's soft pallet and slammed into his brain, killing him instantly.

Severus lay with the warrior's dead weight on him for several moments as he gratefully gasped air into his burning lungs.

Chapter 31

Torn and bloodied bodies lay heaped around Tribune Crastus, the standard bearer and 18th's precious Eagle. What was left of the 1st cohort had been trapped and cut to pieces defending it. They had willingly sacrificed their lives to protect their Eagle and now lay scattered silently on the ground before it. As men fought and died, Crastus stood terrified beside the blood splattered standard bearer. At that moment he cared nothing for the honour of the 18th and wished with all his heart that he could be anywhere rather than facing a horde of uncivilized barbarians who were intent on killing him. As blades rang and flashed around him, he looked desperately for a way to escape. Suddenly he saw it. The remnants of the standard party had been forced back by the sheer weight and ferocity of the Bructeri attack. Just a few paces behind them now, the empty forest beckoned silent and welcoming. The few remaining survivors of the first cohort had forced a narrow channel on both sides behind him which was free of the enemy.

Crastus turned and ran.

Seeing his commander making a break for it, the standard bearer mistook his motives and followed his lead. With only a handful of men left he knew their position was hopeless. He was out of options and now his duty was to save his precious charge by any means possible.

'With you sir!'

Crastus cursed. He heard the shout but didn't stop. He blundered blindly into the cover of the forest, intent only on getting as far away from the hideous slaughter as possible. One of the last men of the 1st cohort closed the gap and bravely fought on to their dying breath.

Still gripping the Eagle, the standard bearer followed his Tribune through the tightly packed trees. Just ahead he could see him sword in hand checking the way forward. Perhaps there was a chance he thought. Perhaps there would be a miracle in this stinking forest after all?

Winded, Tribune Crastus weighed his options as he continued his flight deeper into the forest. The sound of battle was faint now but he could hear the stupid standard bearer pounding along close behind him. If he saved the Eagle he would be a fated hero of Rome, but he knew his chances were nil of escaping under the noses of his enemy. The filthy barbarians were intent on capturing it; it was clearly what they were after. They would hunt the two of them down like dogs until they found them and took it anyway. Crastus shuddered at the thought of being taken alive by the savages who would begin the hunt at any time.

The fools still fighting to the death behind them wouldn't last much longer, he thought nervously. If he was going to save his own life, he must act quickly.

Panting, he stopped and lent against a tree. A moment later, his chest heaving with effort, still carrying his precious burden the red-faced veteran arrived beside him.

Between gasps he said with surging relief.

'You did it sir, you got the Eagle away.'

Still breathing heavily Castus smiled and nodded. Suddenly with explosive force he rammed his sword into the Aquilifer's unprotected throat. The man's eyes bulged and his face contorted to a look of shock and confusion as the blade was wrenched away as he fell to his knees. Crastus drew the edge of his blade across the standard bearer's throat, and with a sneer of contempt, pushed the dying man's body forward onto the forest floor.

The Tribune picked up the staff of the eagle and rammed it into the earth beside the still twitching body. The eagle was in plain sight for all to see. Even the half-witted savages would easily discover it now, he thought smugly.

As he turned and ran further into the concealing depths of the forest, it occurred to Tribune Crastus that with any luck, the barbarians would not even realise that it had been *two* men who had escaped the battlefield with the Eagle.

They would see the corpse wrapped in the Lion's mane headdress and simply assume the standard bearer had bled to death alone on the forest floor.

Five miles ahead, still surrounded on both sides by dense forest, General Varus ordered the column to halt. It was time to build the coming night's marching camp.

Varus needed to carefully consider his options, and discuss them with his staff. Hampered by lack of intelligence from his missing scouts he had been leading his men blindly westwards with no idea of alternative routes, enemy dispositions or how far they had left to travel before they marched into open ground and salvation.

There were unanswered questions which disturbed Varus. Who exactly was leading the revolt? Whoever it was had so far outmanoeuvred him at every turn. He was facing a rebel leader who had marshalled his forces and used the terrain like an experienced General, but there was no one he knew among the barbarian chieftains who even remotely had such abilities?

His spirits failing, he ordered assembly of his senior officers for an emergency staff meeting at dusk. The ageing General was deeply disturbed by the lack of contact with Arminius. Where was the damned man and his supporting cavalry he wondered? Might he be dead or captured, or perhaps Varus thought darkly was there a more sinister explanation to his disappearance? In the back of his tired mind, Segestes's warning at the feast was beginning to haunt him.

It was becoming critical now that Arminius brought the Cherusci horde to his ragged army's aid. Although so far there had been no reports concerning his whereabouts, Varus still had some cavalry remaining under his command. A full squadron of auxiliaries originally recruited as mercenaries from Gaul, led by Roman Decurion Numonias Vala were close by and available. He snapped an order to an aide to find Numonias, and bring him to the General's command tent immediately.

As more groups of stragglers and survivors limped slowly into the half built marching camp Decurion Numonias Vala presented himself before his General. Varus had his head down. He was intently studying a campaign map. Muttering to himself, he ignored the Decurion and still staring at the map slowly shook his head.

Suddenly looking up, through eyes bloodshot with fatigue Varus regarded the Roman before him. There was a moment's uncomfortable silence before the General acknowledged the Decurion.

'Ah yes, Vala. I have two very important missions for you and your men.'

Numonias stiffened. 'At your service sir, but my men are very tired. They haven't been out of their saddles for two whole days and two nights.'

Varus nodded.

'No doubt Decurion, but nevertheless I need you to send a patrol back along our route to find Arminius. He and his tribe of loyal Cherusci are out there somewhere and must be brought to our aid quickly. Do you understand, with all dispatch?'

Numonias nodded. Fighting his own exhaustion, with a resigned sigh he replied.

'Yes Sir.'

Varus nodded.

'Good. Send your best man to command the patrol. I cannot overemphasise the importance of him finding the Cherusci and the rest of our auxiliary cavalry. We need them, you understand, we need them desperately?'

Numonias nodded and said.

'You mentioned two missions sir?'

The General nodded.

'Yes Vala I did....I want you to ride for the Rhine tonight and bring reinforcements.'

Beside the campaign map lay a sealed scroll. Varus picked it up and handed it to the Decurion.

'See to it personally that you hand this message to Nonius Asprenas. He has two reserve Legions who can come to our assistance....Our situation is becoming worse by the day Vala...I plan to fight our way out of this cursed forest but we cannot last forever... Take the freshest horses you can find. Do you fully understand how vitally important it is that you get through to the Rhine?'

Decurion Numonias Vala understood perfectly. Although he hadn't said so, the inference was that without help, the general's army was finished. Lifting his head and looking above his General Numonias said.

'I won't let you down sir; I'll get through to the Rhine somehow.'

It was Varus's turn to suppress a sigh. Beckoning Numonias forward Varus pointed to the map.

'Good. Then let us now consider your best route out of the forest Decurion...'

Rufus and his men trudged wearily on through the forest looking for a suitable hiding place. They were fully alert, tensed and watching cautiously for rebel patrols. There were only six left; the fight with the Bructeri had been both brutal and deadly, but had probably saved the survivors' lives. Their armour and helmets discarded, the fugitives still carried their weapons but uniforms were hidden as they were dressed in looted furs taken from the men they had recently killed. Rufus reasoned that their disguise wouldn't stand up to close inspection, but from a distance it might give them a fighting chance.

When Rufus had run the last rebel through he had initially ordered his survivors back into the forest while he crept forward to divine the fate of the 18th. It had been ominously quiet and that boded badly to the experienced centurion's instincts. Removing his helmet he smeared mud on his face and slithered through the undergrowth on his belly until his breasted a low rise. Gently pulling a low branch aside Rufus had felt his gorge rise as he silently surveyed the ghastly scene before him. His comrades bloodied bodies lay everywhere. The forest floor as far as he could see was carpeted with them.

There were barbarian rebels walking casually among the corpses, stooping to pick up weapons and helping themselves to trophies as they spied them. One of the rebels was crouched nearby with his back to Rufus, engrossed in cutting off the finger of a dead legionary to release a thin gold ring he had spotted during his search of the dead.

Rufus scanned for his Eagle, but he could see no sign of it anywhere. He imagined the barbarians

would be displaying it proudly if they had taken it. Perhaps somehow it had been spirited away under their noses?

His heart heavy, Rufus had seen enough. His duty now was to the few men who had survived their deadly skirmish with the isolated band of rebels. He carefully replaced the branch and began to slither backwards. A branch cracked and abruptly Rufus froze. Not more than fifty paces from where he laid a small band of rebels suddenly burst from the forest. Yelling excitedly to the great multitude engaged in looting they triumphantly thrust the 18th's glittering Eagle high in the air for all to see.

With a growing roar of excitement the warriors began to gather around the trophy, whooping and howling in their savage elation.

As the last of the Bructeri party emerged from the dense tree line, Rufus saw something which made his heart sink lower and his stomach churn even more.

His hands tied behind his back and a noose around his neck Tribune Crastus was led from the forest by a grinning Bructeri who yelled his delight at having a captive. The Tribune's face was streaked with dirt and a trickle of blood, but beneath the grime he looked white with terror. Crastus cowered and whimpered as one of the surrounding Bructeri cuffed him hard on the side of his head. The surrounding warriors laughed as he staggered backwards.

Rufus's eyes narrowed and his jaw tightened. Crastus was a little shit but there was absolutely nothing Rufus could do against so many to save him. It was plain to see that the Eagle and the tribune were both lost, with no possible chance of rescue.

Standing hands on hips before Crastus, in his native tongue one of the older Bructeri growled.

'How did you catch this little rabbit?'

The rebel holding the tether grinned.

'I caught him hiding by a stream close by. There was blood on his sword but he didn't put up much of a fight.' Looking contemptuously at the prisoner he half drew his sword and said. 'What shall I do with him, kill him?'

Eyes wide with terror, a single sob escaped from Crastus.

The older Bructeri shook his shaggy head as he stared at the shivering Tribune. He grabbed the young warrior's forearm.

'*No!* You must take him to the sacred grove of the Ravens.... Our High Priestess has decreed that all captured Roman officers' lives are to be dedicated to the Gods.' With a jerk of his thumb towards the prisoner, knowingly he added. 'His death will bring us great favour with them, and honour the spirits of our ancestors.'

He sneered at the terrified Tribune as his eyes glittered with cruel anticipation. The old warrior knew what was going to happen to the prisoner, he had seen it done before.

'Do not feel cheated Kurt, you have done well. The Roman's death will be neither quick nor easy. He will die slowly locked in a wicker cage, as the priestesses roast him alive over a sacrificial fire.'

The disappointment evaporated from the younger warriors face. Satisfied both with the respect he had earned, and his prisoner's ultimate fate a savage grin spread over the young Bructeri's face. With a respectful nod to the elder he tugged hard on the tether and dragged Crastus away to meet his fate at the sacred Place of the Ravens.

Knowing it was hopeless, Rufus crept silently back to what little was left of his command.

He found them where he had left them, huddled together hiding in a thicket. He could see the fear in their eyes. They too had listened to the ominous silence coming from the ambush site since their centurion had left them, and the sudden unexplained roar of celebration. Expecting the worst, Severus looked up at his commander and whispered hopefully.

'Did we beat off the attack sir?'

Stone faced, Rufus shook his head.

'No lad, none of the first cohort survived. I don't know how many more were lost along the line but there are droves of rebels everywhere....' Almost ashamed, he added sadly.

'And they have our Eagle.'

All five men drew breath sharply at the impossible news. Rufus held up his hand to calm them. Keeping his voice firm but to a minimum he said quietly.

'There's nothing we can do about it. There are thousands of barbarians just a little way over there.'

Rufus nodded in the direction of the ambush site, but decided against mentioning Crastus. His men were frightened enough. If they were going to survive the hours to come, he needed them sharp, not paralyzed with fear at the horrors which might befall them.

'We can achieve nothing by staying here lads. We must move away from the track into deeper cover and hide until nightfall. Once it's fully dark we'll try and slip through the enemy patrols and re-join whatever's left of the column at tonight's marching camp.'

His men's grim frightened faces brightened a fraction at the chance of re-joining their comrades. As their heads began to nod with new purpose Rufus glanced about the silent forest and then added softly.

'That's if we can find it?'

Chapter 32

The small patrol sent by Varus discovered Arminius just a few miles away an hour before the sun began to set. They had no reason to suspect anything was amiss. They rode into the auxiliary cavalry's encampment with a sense of profound and overwhelming relief. Their comrades lay chatting around camp fires, eating and laughing together. A few stood up as the Roman officer and his five-man Gaul escort arrived in their midst, but nothing was out of place or raised any alarm in the minds of the new arrivals.

Bringing his horse to a halt, the junior Decurion stared down at a group of Arminius' men who were closest to him.

'You there! Where is your Decurion?'

Grinning, the auxiliary pointed to the other side of the camp.

'He's over there....*Sir.*'

Irritated by the lack of respect in the tone of the man's voice, but too tired to remonstrate with him the junior Decurion turned his horse and walked it over to where Arminius stood watching him.

The Roman saluted. Still in his saddle he said.

'Thank the Gods I've found you. I bear desperate news sir.'

Arminius eyed him coldly. His entire squadron was on its feet now. They watched in silence, but edged closer.

'Well Decurion, make your report.'

Clearing his throat, the Roman said.

'I am commanded to tell you that General Varus orders you to bring your cavalry and the entire Cherusci to the urgent assistance of the Legions sir.'

As one officer to another, almost in confidence he added.

'We have sustained repeated attacks over the last two days and taken very heavy casualties.'

Arminius nodded in silence. He turned to his men who had now begun to gather in growing numbers around the patrol. Raising his arms above him Arminius roared to them.

'Did you hear that men? General Varus has been attacked and requests our assistance!'

There were roars of laughter and scattered cheers from the auxiliaries who now crowded closely around the mounted patrol. Bewildered by the look of triumph on their grinning faces and the odd reaction to his dire news, the Decurion turned back and stared at Arminius. Confused, he said.

'I don't understand Sir. You must come immediately; we are in a most serious situation.'

Arminius nodded.

'Yes it is a very serious situation, but you will understand very shortly my friend....*Seize them!*'

His men had been waiting. Like coiled springs they leapt at the surprised Decurion, dragging him and his escort from their horses. Disarmed and roughly thrown to the ground, the Roman's expression changed abruptly from confusion to one of shock and sudden fear.

Arminius turned to his cousin who stood beside him. The look on his face was merciless. With a voice as cold as ice Arminius hissed.

'I need information on the state of Varus and what's left of his army. Put this fool to the torture...I want everything he knows...'

Every man has his breaking point. Helplessly tied to a tree the Roman tried bravely to resist the questioning and terrible pain they inflicted on him before he broke. Bleeding and delirious with pain, when his eye was gouged out with the point of a dagger the end came and he could resist no more.

Before Rolf slit the Roman's throat, Arminius had everything. He knew exactly what was happening inside the Roman encampment, but more importantly Rolf and his ruthless torturers had discovered Varus's desperate plan to send his remaining cavalry on a frantic dash for the Rhine.

Time was short; to thwart any chance of the last ditch rescue attempt succeeding Arminius must act quickly. Issuing a flurry of orders, he commanded his cavalry's camp broken, and his men into their saddles.

Only when it was fully dark did Rufus order his men to their feet. The dense canopy and the dark cloud filled sky blocked any starlight from filtering down through the trees from the heavens above. The forest floor was pitch black and deathly silent. Rufus had tried, but when he extended his arm moments earlier he was disappointed that he couldn't see his hand at the other end of it. The canopy rustled above and an owl hooted forlornly in the distance as Rufus gathered his men close around him and whispered.

'Right lads, I know its bloody dark in here but we're going to try to make our way westwards. We can't go anyway near the track because the rebels will be all over it so we must get further away.' He stared into the inky darkness which surrounded them. 'I don't think we'll get far without torches so let's take our time and put some distance between us and the track before we light them and turn west.' Rufus paused for a moment before continuing grimly. 'We're only going to get one chance at this so keep your eyes and ears open... and for Jupiter's sake, stay close together and don't under any circumstances get separated. Because there's no light, rest your hand on the shoulder of the man in front of you to stay in touch. When we move out in a minute we must move quietly and slowly like shadows from the afterlife...We've no idea if there are rebels close by so keep it quiet...any questions?'

Taking their silence as confirmation of their understanding Rufus added one last comment.

'If we get hit...it's every man for himself. Don't stop for anything, just try and get away.'

The party set off in silence heading north. Almost immediately Rufus knew it was going to be more difficult than he had at first hoped when his shin collided with a fallen log in the darkness. Stifling an oath he felt his way over the obstacle as far as he could reach then carefully eased his leg over it. Gingerly applying his full weight to his front leg, Rufus lent forward and carefully lifted his back leg over it as well. He turned and helped Severus as he began to clamber over the fallen log. It took several minutes for all of them to cross and get clear. Rufus didn't rush his men, they were still too close to the track to risk discovery by making any unusual or unnatural noises. Rufus and his men were playing a deadly game of cat and mouse with the unsuspecting rebels; to stand any chance of surviving the night, he couldn't afford to give the slightest hint of their presence to the enemy.

As they made slow progress forward, magnified by the stillness of the surrounding forest, an unseen twig occasionally snapped beneath one of the men's feet; the sound boomed like the crack of a whip and startled, it made them all drop into a crouch and listen intently for any sign of discovery.

Arms outstretched Rufus felt his way slowly forward, stopping and dealing with obstacles as he discovered or blundered into them. It proved to be exhausting work as his senses strained with every pace the men took forward. Night marches were always challenging, and knowing how difficult it was to judge distances travelled without reference points in the darkness, Rufus was carefully counting every step.

Progress was painfully slow. After an hour of cautiously fighting their way through a tangled mass of undergrowth, branches which threatened to stab into unprotected eyes and climbing over fallen rotting tree trunks, Rufus had counted only seven hundred paces through the dank, dripping forest. He whispered a halt so his men could snatch a short rest.

At this rate Rufus knew the men behind the walls of the marching camp would be long gone before he could lead his small party to safety. There were plenty of hours of darkness left, but each one was critical if they were to successfully meet up with the Legions and make their escape. Rufus turned to the shape nearest to him and whispered.

'Severus?'

Out of the darkness the whispered response came instantly.

'Sir?'

'Listen, we can't spend all night moving like this, it's taking far too long. We must be at least a thousand paces from the track by now. We've seen no sign of the enemy, but the problem is that tonight's marching camp might be miles away so we'll have to risk moving with light from some torches.'

Severus nodded in the darkness. He knew the risks, but they were worth taking.

'Yes sir.' He replied quietly, gently rubbing a recently bruised knee.

Rufus said quietly.

'As soon as we get the torches going, we'll turn and start heading west.'

Darkness had fallen when General Varus closed the staff meeting. His heart ached with resignation and sorrow. There had been nothing but bad news. His adjutant had begun the meeting with the latest casualty figures. He estimated there were less than five thousand men left alive under his general's command, and many of them were wounded. The others were missing and must be presumed dead or worse still, captured and in the hands of the barbarians.

There had been a heated discussion as to the merits of pushing on or staying behind the palisade walls and waiting for reinforcement from the reserve Legions on the other side of the Rhine. Varus had angrily dismissed such defeatist talk; he still had a chance to salvage something from this debacle and maintained they could still win a resounding victory before the reserves arrived with the help of the Cherusci.

Varus had sent out small scouting parties on foot. One had returned and reported that they had climbed the highest hill and could see beyond the canopy of trees that the other side of the treacherous forest was close now; it was no more than five miles away.

It was of deep concern to all that since they had left hours earlier there had been no sign of the mounted patrol sent out to find Arminius. The General had committed the last of his cavalry and couldn't now rely on them providing any screening whatsoever to the remaining column. To compound a terrible day, not one but two Eagles were now unaccounted for. The 18th Legion, apart from a few survivors, appeared to have been completely wiped out. The handful who managed to make the marching camp reported that the enemy's tactics had changed. They had attacked in huge numbers. Instead of hit and run, the 18th had been assaulted by wave after wave of rebels until they were simply overwhelmed and slaughtered. Their supply of javelins exhausted, the hungry exhausted men who formed the backbone of the marching columns' centre hadn't stood a chance against the unrelenting attack by so many fresh and ferocious enemies.

General Varus issued his orders for the following day. The three Legion's survivors would leave the safety of the marching camp once again in total silence two hours before daybreak. The seriously wounded were to be left behind. There was every possibility that the entire column would reach open ground beyond the forest as dawn broke. If Arminius arrived with the Cherusci in time, there was every chance that a glorious victory could still be snatched from the jaws of ignominious defeat before the sun set on the following day.

After the staff officers left the command tent and went off about their duties General Varus sat alone in his tent. Tomorrow he thought would be the day when he might salvage the name of Varus. When the omens had been so good, how had so many reversals come about he wondered morosely? Based on past experience, he had done everything right. He was suddenly shaken from his reflections when Dalious re-entered the tent and interrupted his train of thought. Without ceremony his adjutant announced.

'Decurion Vala and his men are formed up by the west gate and ready to leave General. They await your order.'

Varus remained seated. Head in hands and too tired to move, softly he said.

'Thank you Dalious. The order is given.' He lifted his head wearily and looked up. With a slight wave of his hand he said.

'Send them on their way, will you?'

Dalious saluted, turned and strode from the command tent. When he reached the west gate he signalled to Vala.

'You are ordered to proceed immediately with your mission Decurion. May the Gods bring you good fortune.'

Decurion Vala nodded. Grim faced he signalled his twenty men to follow in file and tapping his heels on his horse's flanks trotted through the open gate into the darkness which lay beyond.

Chapter 33

Rufus and his men had been walking all night. Still deep in the primordial forest, they had seen neither hide nor hair of the enemy. There had been one moment of pure terror when they had disturbed a colony of sleeping rooks. The roosting birds had risen in alarm into the dark sky above crowing loudly to each other. Under Rufus' whispered order, with hearts pounding his men had found the strength to pick up the pace and get clear of the disturbed area as quickly as possible before the sound of the birds brought discovery.

In the spill of the light from their burning torches, they slithered, climbed, tripped and cursed throughout the dark hours during their unrelenting flight through the forest. Without food or sleep and utterly exhausted they walked on holding aloft their spluttering torches as if they were living through some terrifying nightmare from which they could not wake.

Rufus had abandoned his initial plan to re-join the column during the night. To even try to find it in the obsidian darkness could only bring them to disaster. Even with their barbarian clothing they would stand no chance if they blundered into the enemy massing somewhere ahead for a dawn attack. He had managed to get his men this far without discovery so he ignored his original plan and kept pushing his men west. Sooner or later they must find their way to the end of the forest. If they found high ground he reasoned, they should be able to see the column somewhere ahead.

During the dark hours long after midnight the air had warmed slightly, well before the first rays of dawn's light showed through the trees on the eastern horizon. Behind them mist had begun to form in the low ground and hollows. It quickly became thicker, floating through the sleeping forest, sending swirling tendrils of white silently between the tall trees. It surrounded and enveloped Rufus and his men as the first light of dawn began to lighten their surroundings. Calling a short break, Rufus turned to Severus.

'This fog will help us. It should offer good cover until we reach the end of the forest.'

Severus nodded. Their luck had held so far, but would it last?

As planned, General Varus, accompanied by his staff officers led the survivors from the marching camp before dawn. To raise morale, he had ensured that the word was passed down the line that the end was now firmly in sight. His spirits had lightened. Vala's cavalry should be well on their way by now, and relief should be with them in just a few days. There was still no sign of the patrol looking for Arminius, but Varus still convinced himself that he would arrive soon.

The vanguard of the column was formed from the 17th Legion. A half century was marching just two hundred paces in front of Varus and his officers. Using torches, they led the way through the thinning forest. After well over an hour of good progress without incident, they suddenly halted. Varus noticed the block of light ahead had stopped moving. Hearing no sound of battle he called a halt and sent a galloper forward to investigate.

The mounted aide returned quickly.

'Sir...it's the cavalry...'

Varus didn't wait for an explanation. Followed by his aides he spurred his horse forward until he reached the ring of light from the vanguard's burning torches. As he slowed, he noticed the damp ground before him was rent and churned with the deep rutted marks of many hoof prints. A dead horse lay to one side of the track. Fearing the worst Varus dismounted and hurried into the light to the centurion commanding the vanguard.

'Well Centurion, why have you stopped?'

In the flickering light of the men's torches, the general could see a lingering look of shock and horror on the man's dirt streaked face. The centurion shook his head. Silently he lifted his torch up towards the surrounding trees.

Varus gasped with horror. Nailed to the trees above them, with arms stretched wide were the bodies of Decurion Vala's men. Every one of them had died in agony, eviscerated by the rebels as they hung from the trees. Entrails hung down from the open bellies of the dead men, glistening red and blue in the flickering torchlight. Blood still dripped in dark puddles beneath each crucified body. In the silent forest, one of Varus's aides' suddenly looked away and vomited noisily onto the churned ground beneath him.

His face reflecting the horror, Varus tore his eyes from the ghastly sight of his mutilated cavalrymen and stared at the centurion again.

'Where is the Decurion's body?' He demanded.

The vanguard commander pointed further up the track.

'He's there sir, at the base of the tree.'

Varus kicked his horse forward. At the very edge of the vanguard's light, Roman Decurion Numonias Vala hung from a massive tree trunk, nailed in the same fashion as his men. He hadn't been gutted like the others; instead, his throat had been cut, sliced deeply from ear to ear.

Splattered with the Decurion's blood, the vital scroll which Varus had entrusted to him dangled unrolled. Someone must have read it, and then tied it firmly around the gash of the dead officer's neck.

But something else caught the General's eye.

Resting against Vala's limp body, secured at the bottom of the scroll something small glittered in the torchlight. Curious, Varus climbed down from his horse and approached the body. He reached out and grasped the object. Snapping it away from the thin strip of hide which held it in place, Varus opened his fist and held it up to the torchlight. It was a ring which could only belong to a Roman citizen and member of the noble Equestrian Order. It certainly didn't belong to the dead Decurion and obviously hadn't been overlooked as a trophy of war.

Suddenly painful realisation dawned as recognition came to him, as he stood surrounded by the dark Teutoburg.

The ring was a silent messenger, taunting the commander of the mauled Legions. Varus had seen the ring and its wearer many times before...His heart sank as he accepted the truth. There was only one man under his command who wore such a ring. *It belonged to Arminius!*

The General staggered back, overpowered with sudden shock. His chest heaved as blood pounded and roared in his ears. Varus shook his head in the semi-darkness as he tried to comprehend the magnitude of what he had discovered. Frantic, his mind churned in turmoil as he tried to make sense of it all.

So it *was* true. Segestes had been telling the truth after all. It had to be Arminius who was leading the Germanic tribes so expertly against him. After all, had he not been trained in the art of war by Rome? Varus thrust his palm against his forehead. How could he have been so grossly and completely deceived, he wondered? Why in Jupiter's name had a man he had treated as a son turned against him so? He stared into the black forest around him but found no answers in the night. As a dark cloud of growing acceptance enveloped him, Varus reluctantly admitted to himself that he had been completely fooled; unknowingly he had nurtured a poisonous viper filled with the deadliest of venom at the very heart of his Legions. He knew it was his responsibility. The Emperor would hold him absolutely accountable.

Shoulders slumped, his anguish mixed with a deep sense of betrayal, he turned back towards the horses. Misery eddied through his mind as Varus walked back to the waiting vanguard commander. He knew that ultimately, he would have to pay for his mistakes.

The awful truth made two other facts painfully clear. The treacherous Cherusci weren't coming to his aid, and glancing back at Vala's body for a moment, neither he thought sadly was the two reserve Legions stationed on the Rhine.

His adjutant stood beside the vanguard centurion.

Dalious watched the General walk towards him. Even in the semi-darkness he could see by the General's gait that something was very wrong. The general walked with shoulders slumped, like a broken man. When Varus was just a few paces from him Dalious said.

'What is it sir, what have you found?'

Varus passed the Prefect the ring. Despair filled his voice. He said quietly.

'We have our traitor Dalious. We have been betrayed...'

Varus climbed wearily into his saddle. With a sigh he looked down and said softly to the centurion.

'Cut these bodies down and conceal them in the forest.'

The General's sad eyes glittered in the torchlight. 'I will not bring the column forward through the darkness until you signal it is done. I don't want the men to see this, they are frightened enough and their courage hangs by a thread. Is that clear centurion?'

Grim faced, his vanguard commander nodded.

'Yes Sir. Perfectly clear.'

Chapter 34

As the head of the column broke out of the forest, the first light of dawn lit their way. Exhausted men cheered and wept when they felt the sun's warmth on their faces for the first time in days. Some knelt down and kissed the earth in their unbridled joy at having survived the terrors which still lurked behind them.

The route they must take if they were to join the main supply route would force them to turn right and head north along the slope of a wide flat valley. Before them lay several miles of low-lying scrubland dotted with trees which rose sharply to their right along the very edge of the Teutoburg. Once the column was fully out of the forest, the land behind would be closed to them. It was nothing more than a broad expanse of flooded marshland. To their left a ridgeline rose up sharply and ran parallel with their projected route beneath a dense mat of covering trees.

Prefect Dalious turned with concern to his General who rode morosely beside him. He had hoped Varus would recover from the shock of finding out that Arminius was a traitor, but looking at him, it didn't appear to be so. The last few days and in particular last night's events had clearly shaken the old man to his very core.

An uncomfortable silence had existed between the two men for the last hour. Varus had muttered softly to himself as they rode through the darkness, but had not uttered a single word to anyone around him since they left the cavalry ambush site. His eyes remained downcast and he showed no acknowledgement or emotion of any kind as they finally rode clear of the forest into the glow of the early morning's watery sunlight.

Dalious could feel the turmoil and doubt which raged through the General's mind. He wished with all his heart he could just leave the old man to his despair but the Prefect had more important matters concerning him. He urgently needed to know the general's plan to advance up the valley. The barbarians could launch their first attacks of the day at any moment, and the men must be deployed into defensive battle formations if the surviving legionaries were to stand any chance in the fighting Dalious knew was sure to come soon. Was a strong rear-guard to be left behind to slow the rebels who were certainly following even now not far behind them in the forest? How were they to protect their flanks and should he order scouts to be sent on ahead to spy out the land? Reluctantly clearing his throat Dalious broke the silence.

'General Varus Sir. What are your orders of the day....?'

Almost dreamily Varus lifted his head and replied.

'Orders, what orders?'

Worried by the reply, Dalious stared at his General for a moment.

'Yes General. What are your orders for the men's formation? I must know your plan to move them up the valley sir.'

Varus inclined his head slightly to one side as he stared at the ragtag line of desperately fatigued legionaries staggering almost drunkenly from the dark forest. The general's gaze drifted to the horizon. Staring into the distance, suddenly he nodded to himself and announced.

'I wish to speak in private with my adjutant.'

Catching Dalious's eye Varus nodded towards a patch of scrub close by which was clear of both officers and men. When Varus and his adjutant were out of earshot the General brought his horse to a stop and waited until Dalious was beside him. With a sigh Varus said.

'I didn't want this commission you know. I was content and happily retired to my villa outside Rome when the Emperor's dispatch reached me... It's funny really. Augustus didn't order me; he simply requested that I took command and became his General in the north.'

Varus looked at his Prefect. Dalious had the distinct impression that the old man was looking straight through him, as if he wasn't there at all. The general's tone worried the Prefect; it had the distinct ring of a man who had lost everything.

'But how do you say no to the absolute ruler of such a vast Empire?'

Varus smiled a sad smile as he looked about him.

'I'm ruined I'm afraid. Our situation is hopeless you see? If I were to survive this debacle and return to Rome there would be no forgiveness for me from the Emperor.' With a deep sigh he added. 'Alas, my entire family are also finished if I let things remain as they are.'

The Prefect's eyes narrowed with suspicion. His mouth was suddenly dry. What was Varus suggesting? Dalious had a nasty feeling that he knew. Locking eyes with the General he shook his head.

'No Sir, you can't mean? Not now, we need you!'

With the sad smile still playing on his lips, resigned to his fate Varus shrugged and shook his head slowly.

'It's the only way I can save my personal honour, and the lives of my family. It is time to die like a noble born Roman officer...I have no other choice Dalious my old friend. Like my father before me who took his own life after his defeat at Philippi I must atone for my mistakes and die by my own hand.'

Straightening slightly Varus continued.

'Such an act will be accepted in Rome. If there were another way, believe me I'd take it but alas, there isn't. No...I must fall on my sword to wipe out the stain of such a defeat as this....It is the only way to protect the name of Varus.'

The Prefect recoiled in shock. He would have argued and protested more but knew in his heart that the tired old man before him was speaking the truth. His command had been decimated and if he returned to Rome without either his Legion's or their Eagles the immeasurable disgrace would rock the Empire and shake it to its very foundations. Varus might even have to face execution for such abject failure. A noble born Senator and Patrician publicly strangled before the baying mob of Rome. It was...unthinkable.

With a resigned sign Dalious nodded his understanding.

'Is there nothing I can say that might dissuade you Sir?'

His rheumy eyes searching the horizon Varus shook his head.

'No Dalious, it is what I must do, and do quickly before my resolve crumbles to dust.'

Nodding sadly Dalious enquired.

'Where shall you do it Sir?'

Varus pointed to a small stand of trees nearby. Dalious noticed that somewhere in the conversation the colour had drained from his general's strained face.

'There. I shall do it quietly over there. My servant will assist me. Please ensure my body is burned afterwards, and my ashes are buried. I don't want my grave desecrated by those Godless barbarians.'

Varus smiled suddenly as a thought occurred to him.

'It is a great shame I won't live to see the look on that dog Arminius's face when he learns that I have cheated him from the pleasure of torturing me to death.'

Dalious saluted. He knew there was nothing more he could say that could change what had to be. His face grim the Prefect nodded.

'I shall see that your instructions are carried out General. It's...it's been an honour Sir.'

Varus lifted his hand from his saddle's pommel in acknowledgement.

'Thank you my friend. You are to take command. Keep pushing the men towards the main supply route; it is all you can do; it is your last hope.'

Varus turned his horse towards the trees. He said quietly over his shoulder.

'Farewell my friend, I will see you again in the afterlife.'

With those last words, General Varus kicked his heels against his horse's flanks and calling to his servant cantered over to the lonely copse to die like a Roman and save his family honour.

Like the others, Rufus was exhausted by the journey through the mist shrouded forest. They were dragging themselves towards the top of yet another densely wooded ridgeline. There had been so many in the last few miles. He hoped it was the last.

Rufus had felt the energy sapping effects of utter exhaustion before in his career. It had been bad years before when he was just another young legionary marching behind his eagle during mile after mile of gruelling forced marches across the arid wastes of the Syrian Desert, but this was way beyond that.

Determined to keep them alive, Rufus had chosen to lead his men through the most difficult terrain. The rebels would be moving fast and wouldn't choose the arduous route he had used to get his men to the end of the Teutoburg.

They had eaten nothing for two days and not one of them had slept a wink of sleep. Every bone ached and every muscle in their bodies was screaming for the chance to lie down, just for a few blissful minutes. They had reached the stage where there was no alternative. His men were utterly spent and completely finished. Rufus had to stop soon before they fell down and lost the will to continue.

It was obvious to their centurion that not one amongst them had the energy to lift a sword, let alone defend themselves if they were attacked. If they were bumped now he thought grimly, they would all die. He knew he must find them a place to hide and allow them time to rest.

Rufus was first to reach the top of the ridge. He fell to his knees and lent against the rough bark of an ancient oak. What he saw ahead momentarily cut through his exhaustion and for just the most fleeting of moments filled him with equal measures of relief and triumph. Instead of more endless green canopy, the panorama of a broad valley filled with low-lying scrub spread out before him. Turning to the nearest men behind him who had almost reached the top he whispered softly.

'We've done it lads, we're out. We're reached the end of the forest.'

When the officers heard the news of Varus's suicide, they were filled with foreboding and poorly concealed anger.

Prefect Dalious had done what he could to offer his officers hope, but to little affect. After the terrible days of crossing the Teutoburg, which had seen the once proud army of the North reduced to less than five thousand exhausted, hungry and frightened men, morale was at rock bottom

As two of the surviving veteran centurions rode back to their hastily reorganised fighting units, both men's mood was black with despair.

'The old bastard has left us in the lurch Dmitri. He's taken the coward's way out. Where does that leave us now? I'll tell you where. No bloody General to lead us and no bloody plan to get us out of this shit.'

Grinding his jaw, Dmitri's friend nodded in silence as he mumbled a curse on all the Roman nobility, and in particular the House of Varus.

He was about to reply when from the tree line to their right, the silence was suddenly rent by the mournful baritone blasts of barbarian war horns.

Dmitri and his companion frantically spurred their horses forward as in their thousands a howling seething carpet of warriors brandishing their weapons in the bright sunlight swept down from the trees only one hundred paces above them.

Rufus had taken the first watch. Sleepily he guessed he had been on guard for at least an hour. As he lay on sentry duty, the minutes ticked slowly by as the warmth of the sun burnt off the last traces of mist. Visibility was excellent; the air around him was now crystal clear.

His little knot of men lay sound asleep, concealed in the middle of a dense thicket just behind him. He was struggling against his own desire to sleep; he dared not allow himself to succumb. There had been no sign of the enemy but Rufus was convinced they were close by.

Suddenly he stiffened and his heart began to race. On the valley floor below, he spied movement among the scrub. He recognised the troops clad in red cloaks instantly. Relief flooded through him; it drove away his fatigue. Rufus exhaled deeply. They hadn't overshot and missed the column after all. His joy was short lived. From his left, only a few hundred paces away great blasts of Germanic war horns suddenly shattered the peaceful silence which until that moment had filled the valley below. To his dismay, he saw many hundreds, perhaps thousands of barbarians running helter-skelter down the slope, whooping and waving their swords and spears as they dashed towards the Roman formations.

With a great clash and roar, the human tidal wave of warriors broke on the nearest extended shield wall.

In seconds, a pitched battle was waging fiercely on the valley floor. Rufus could hear the ringing clash of steel, and hear the agonised cries of men as they were wounded. Causalities quickly began to mount on both sides. A horseman galloped down the slope from the trees. He reined in hard and blew a series of short rapid blast on the horn he carried.

Almost instantly the warriors stopped fighting, disengaged and withdrew back up the slope. Rufus was dismayed at the large numbers of fallen Romans who lay scattered on the ground at their comrades' feet. A few were helped up, but most stayed where they were because they had taken a mortal wound during the savage hand to hand fighting.

Almost as the last warrior disappeared back into the forest, groups of slingers and archers appeared from the tree line. They made their way down to within fifty paces of the mauled Roman formation, just out of range of any javelin which may be left. With impunity they began to lay down a deadly barrage of lead shot, stones and arrows. More legionaries' fell, struck by their deadly missiles, unable to avoid them within the densely packed ranks of the diminished phalanx into which they were now crammed.

Rufus cursed. He cursed the damned hit and run tactics of the enemy, and he cursed his own impotency. There was nothing he could do to help his comrades. All he could do was lay where he was and watch as the pitiless slaughter continued below.

The Romans were down to two fighting formations manned by the survivors of all three Legions.

Dalious had planned that one formation would offer mutual support to the other as they both moved slowly up the valley. The forward phalanx had taken the first attack, but now, after more blasts on the hidden war horns another great throng of warriors attacked the rear ranks of the second formation, while the first remained pinned down under the merciless bombardment of the slingers and archers.

It was clear to Rufus what the enemy were doing. They were launching unrelenting attacks designed to grind down and bleed the formations of their manpower. The trail of bodies dressed in red which lay scattered on the ground behind the slow moving formations bore silent witness to the effectiveness of the enemy's battle plan.

The pitiless attacks continued all through the morning. As one phalanx was attacked and bled the other was bombarded. After numerous short but savage attacks, the roles of the warriors were reversed and the formation which had just beaten off the last attack would come under accurate and deadly fire from the slingers. The formations had managed to move less than one quarter of a mile.

Watching the battle from a nearby hill, Arminius committed warriors to the battle from fresh tribes who had finally joined the rebellion. Greatly encouraged by the thousands of dead Romans in the woods, they had at last joined the revolt, hungry to enrich their lives by grasping a share of booty.

As the fighting continued and the bloody hours wore on, both greatly weakened Roman formations ground to a complete stop when news from his forward scouts reached Dalious. To his consternation and dismay the centurion in charge reported that the way ahead was blocked.

'The barbarians have thrown up an earth rampart across the valley floor sir. They have built a low wicker wall on top of it. It's held by hundreds of the enemy.'

Having absorbed the dire news from within the lower phalanx, acting General Dalious conferred with his surviving staff officers. After the heavy losses sustained already, the casualty rate was becoming critical. Lacking artillery support, his appreciation was stark and brutally frank.

'We must breach this barbarian wall and keep moving Gentlemen, or we are finished.'

No one argued the point. These were desperate times and even the most junior officer present knew it was the painful truth.

To the background din of men fighting for their lives which raged all around the small huddle of officers, with the loud clang a stone hit a shield nearby. Dalious ducked involuntarily as he turned to the 17th's 1st Centurion who commanded the upper phalanx. The centurion was the highest ranking field officer still alive, who Dalious had left to command it.

'I want you to make a direct attack on the wall. I don't care how you do it but you must force a breach somehow. I will bring the second phalanx up behind you to protect your rear while you make the assault... Casualties are immaterial. I don't care how many men you lose, you simply must bludgeon your way through. Have you any questions?'

The centurion shook his head. Everything he needed to know had been in his brief orders. It was clear that the survival of what little was left of three once mighty Legions rested squarely on his armoured shoulders. It was a heavy burden.

From his vantage point, Rufus watched the attack go in.

The phalanx marched to the base of the earth wall, and immediately came under attack from showers of rocks and spears hurled down on the legionaries' heads by the defenders. Stepping over those already hit the front five ranks closest to the rampart quickly formed a tortoise to protect themselves from the constant rain of heavy missiles which smashed onto their upturned shields like blows from a giant's hammer.

Urged on by desperate shouts from their few surviving officers, legionaries struggled valiantly to fight their way up the earth ramp which fronted the wall and establish a foothold beside the tightly interwoven wicker wall which surmounted it.

Try as they might, the flexible wall, which stood no higher than a man's shoulders resisted their efforts to break it down. The barbarians behind the wall thrust a forest of long spears at the Romans and arrows hissed back and forth all along the wall as men fell back dead or gravely wounded onto the carpet of shields beneath them. Legionaries wielding pickaxes hacked furiously at the wall to breach it but there was too much give. Even the most determined rain of blows merely bent the wicker and the legionaries' heavy tools rebounded without effect. Despite fighting hard, and probing all along the wall, no breach was forced.

Seeing that his attack was wavering, the phalanx commander gathered some men from his reserve to him. Drawing his sword he ordered them to follow him towards the thickest of the fighting.

Beneath a roof of raised shields which bore the emblems of all three Legions the 1st Centurion rallied his soldiers at the foot of the earth ramp.

'We must cut through men. Without a breach we will all die!'

He turned and nodded towards the legionaries who held their shields above him. He counted.

'Three, two one...*NOW!*'

The shields swung back, clearing the centurion's way forward. Filling his lungs the centurion roared.

'For Rome and the Empire...Charge!'

Followed by a dozen men, the centurion scrambled his way up the ramp. At the top, there was just enough room to stand against the wicker palisade, but no more. The centurion frantically swung his blade slashing and hacking at the yelling warriors before him, as his men rushed up and joined him, standing and fighting shoulder to shoulder on either side. For precious moments it appeared that the centurion and his men's sudden and ferocious attack was working. A small gap appeared in the defenders as tribesmen began to fall back, stabbed and slashed by the Roman's swinging blades.

Roaring at his men to keep fighting the centurion turned and called for pickaxes to be brought up, but he spent a heartbeat too long shouting down at his men behind their raised shields. Suddenly cut off in mid-sentence, the centurion felt a powerful blow in his back. He froze for a split second and gasped as his eyes bulged. Stabbed from behind, his glazed eyes closed. The last thing he saw was the bloodied head of a Mattaci spear sticking out of his chest. With a roar of victory the Mattaci tribesman pushed the impaled centurion off the rampart. Still skewered by the long spear, his limp body landed with a crash on the shields below, to the horror of the men holding them.

It was too much, the last straw. Somewhere, someone in the front rank screamed in despair.

'Fall back!'

With minds fuddled with exhaustion and fear the attack broke apart. While a few isolated men still fought hopelessly on at the wall, the rest of the armoured phalanx broke and fell back in panic and disarray.

Rufus watched helplessly and with growing dread as the attack failed. Without any means of escape, he could see that what was left of the three Legions was surrounded, outnumbered and absolutely trapped.

It was the moment Arminius had been waiting for. He raised himself up in his saddle and ordered waiting reserves to launch a concerted attack from three sides of the phalanx which stood just a few hundred paces behind the fleeing remnants of those who had attacked the wall. At the same time, he ordered the defenders to charge down after the fleeing men, whose attack they had so easily blunted.

Heavily outnumbered by the charging warriors, many of the exhausted legionaries were brutally cut down in the running skirmish that followed. Too tired to run anymore some, like Prefect Dalious and his staff rallied to each other and fought on in small groups until they were simply overwhelmed by the enemy's vastly superior numbers. A few survivors had had enough. They dropped both sword and shield and invited a quick death from the enemy. The last Eagle was taken amid the savage chaotic fighting.

The 17th's Eagle had been brought forward to encourage the attack but now the few men of the 1st cohort who had survived so far were crushed by superior enemy numbers, while valiantly trying to protect it.

The remaining phalanx was beginning to crumble. As warriors fell to the Roman swords, the dead were instantly replaced by fresh tribesmen who were focused solely on killing the legionary before them. The barbarians could easily afford the losses, but the Romans could not. The shield wall buckled somewhere in its middle under the unrelenting attack and a wedge of howling warriors cut into the men behind it, splitting the wavering phalanx in two.

Torn from the massacre unfolding before him, Rufus tensed as he heard sudden movement behind him. He grasped the handle of his sword. It was half drawn as he rolled over. Instantly, he relaxed. It was Severus, come to relieve him from sentry duty.

Blinking away the sleep Severus rubbed his tired eyes and yawned, unaware of the tragedy and fate of his comrades below the ridge. In a voice barely audible Severus whispered.

'Get some sleep sir. I'll take the next watch... Is there any sign of the column yet?'

Ashen faced Rufus remained strangely silent. Severus noticed there were tear streaks running down his centurion's dirty face. Startled Severus enquired.

'What's the matter sir...what's happened?'

Rufus said nothing. He shook his head and silently jerked his thumb over his shoulder.

Confused, Severus crawled forward and cautiously raised his head above the parapet of the slope to see what was happening below.

Rufus stayed where he was, he'd seen enough, he couldn't look anymore. His whole life was being torn to shreds on the valley floor below.

Just above him, he heard Severus gasp softly with revulsion and horror as he desperately tried to comprehend and absorb the full meaning of what had transpired amid the slaughter and carnage down in the valley. Unblinking, he stared mesmerised at the carpet of Roman bodies, unable to look away even as the last of the legionaries fell.

A sudden and terrible roar of victory erupted from the throats of thousands of wild tribesmen. It echoed across the valley, as a lone horseman broke cover and rode slowly into their midst, waving his acceptance of their cheering adulation, and his victory over the Romans.

His face white with shock, Severus slid back from the cover offered by the wooded tree line. Sliding down beside his centurion, still trembling in a faltering voice, he said softly.

'They're gone sir. They're dead...all of them!'

Pain and utter confusion showed in Severus's face. How could this be?

'What are we going to do now sir?'

Rufus stared at the young man lying beside him as he considered the question carefully. Softly clearing his throat he replied.

'Best stay here until dark lad. We'll slip away, head west and somehow find our way back to the Rhine; it's our only hope now. I have a duty to our dead to make a full report and tell what really happened.'

Severus nodded sadly at the thought of the lost Legions. He had been their prisoner but it didn't seem to matter anymore, they had been his family. There was a long silence between the two men then awkwardly, almost reluctantly Severus enquired.

'What will happen to me when we get back sir?'

Rufus shook his head and sighed.

'They're all dead Severus. As far as I'm concerned the charge against you died with them.' He shrugged. 'I know Crastus is dead so who else will know who or what you really are, or where you came from? The lads still asleep are all mates of yours; they won't say anything.'

Suddenly feeling older than his years Rufus wiped away the damp marks from his mud streaked face.

'I owe you the debt of my life son, and I promised you I would never forget. On the shades of our dead comrades down in the valley, I swear I will never betray you...'

-THE END -

Epilogue:

It is believed that like Crastus, captured Roman officers were separated, tortured and sacrificed not only as part of the Germanic tribes' religious ceremonies, but also to celebrate their victory over the hated invaders.

Emperor Augustus considered the three Legions had failed in their duty to Rome. He had them struck permanently from the army list as collective punishment.

Rome's Legions crossed the River Rhine and returned some six years later in a series of punitive raids, where one of the captured Eagles was recovered. A year later, in AD 15 under Germanicus, Rome launched a two pronged attack which devastated the area between the Ems and the River Lippe. Here, they forced the return of a second Eagle.

Germanicus crossed Varus' earlier route as he returned. More than half a decade had passed but the forest remained strewn with the wreckage and bones of the fallen army. He commanded his men to collect and bury the remains as best they could. He also ordered a monument erected, honouring the memory of Varus' lost army.

Arminius fought a series of subsequent battles against the Romans. Although he never again inflicted a crushing defeat on Rome, the victories he won convinced the Imperial High Command that the potential cost in manpower and materiel far outweighed any gains which might be gained by reinvading the territories east of the River Rhine. The river and a chain of reinforced forts became a solid bulwark; the official northern border of the Imperial Empire.

Rome never again sought to expand eastwards beyond the mighty Rhine.

Beyond the new border, Arminius continued to build on his vision of a united Germany, but he died over a decade later under mysterious circumstances. It was rumoured he was poisoned by members of his own family during bitter internal feuding over power and Arminius' future as a nation builder. There was deep suspicion as to his ultimate goal; it was believed Arminius wanted to weld the wild tribes of Greater Germany together, and become their all-powerful king. - DB

Also by David Black

The Great Satan

In The Great Satan, the first of his compelling new Shadow Squadron series, author David Black has produced his own fictional nightmare scenario: What if the Iraqi weapons that were said to be dismantled in the late 1990s included the ultimate WMD? And what if the deposing of Saddam Hussein left one of his most ruthless military leaders still at large, and actively seeking a customer for Iraq's only nuclear bomb? . . .

Can the newly formed SAS Shadow Squadron find the bomb, and stop the terrorists from detonating it?

Published on Amazon in Kindle Format & Paperback.

http://www.david-black.co.uk

Also by David Black

Playing for England

What makes a man want to join the reserve SAS? - The famous British Special Forces Regiment whose selection process boasts more than a 90% failure rate during its gruelling selection process..

David Black's third book - Playing for England gives the reader a fascinating first-hand insight into the rigours of the selection and training process of those few men who earn the privilege of wearing the sandy beret and winged dagger cap badge of the SAS.

Published on Amazon in Kindle Format & Paperback.

Also by David Black

Siege of Faith

The Chronicles of Sir Richard Starkey #1

Far to the East across the sparkling waters of the great Mediterranean Sea, the formidable Ottoman Empire was secretly planning to add to centuries of expansion. Soon, they would begin the invasion and conquest of Christian Europe.

But first, their all-powerful Sultan, Suleiman the Magnificent knew he must destroy the last Christian bastion which stood in the way of his glorious destiny of conquest. The Maltese stronghold... garrisoned and defended by the noble and devout warrior monks of the Knights of St. John of Jerusalem...

A powerful story of heroism, love and betrayal set against the backdrop of the cruel and terrible siege of Malta which raged through the long hot summer of 1565. The great Caliph unleashed a massive invasion force of 40,000 fanatical Muslim troops, intent on conquering Malta before invading poorly defended Christian Europe. A heretic English Knight - Sir Richard Starkey becomes embroiled in the bloody five month siege which ensued; Europe's elite nobility cast chivalry aside, no quarter asked or mercy given as rivers of Muslim and Christian blood flowed...

Published on Amazon in Kindle Format & Paperback.

http://www.david-black.co.uk

Also by David Black

OUT SOON!

Dark Empire

Shadow Squadron #2

Sgt. Pat Farrell and Two Troop are back in action!

Sgt. Pat Farrell and his reserve SAS troop are on a training exercise in Kenya when they are suddenly ordered into the primitive jungle of the Congo on what should be nothing more than a straightforward and simple humanitarian rescue mission.

Unfortunately, *nothing* is straightforward in Africa. Pat and his men find themselves trapped and facing the disastrous prospect of no escape from the war ravaged blood-stained country. Hunted by a feral legion of savage, drug-crazed guerrillas, things don't always go to plan...*even for the SAS!*

http://www.david-black.co.uk

ALSO COMING SOON !

Inca Sun
Chronicles of Sir Richard Starkey #2

Sir Richard and his giant servant Quinn begin their next great adventure, aboard the Privateer '*The Intrepid*', in the treacherous waters off the Caribbean and South America coastline. Their heretic English Queen Elizabeth I has secretly commanded Sir Richard to prowl the high seas in search of King Phillip II of Spain's fabulously wealthy treasure convoys. They sail from the New World for Spain laden with gold and silver ripped from the Conquistador's mines in Peru and Mexico; dug from the dark earth by their cruelly treated Inca and Mayan slaves.

What Richard doesn't know when he accepts his latest Royal commission is that his arch nemesis - Don Rodrigo Salvador Torrez has become Governor of King Phillip's Mexican province of Veracruz.

One thing is certain, mere gold cannot pay the debt of honour that exists between the two men, since their first encounter on Malta during the great siege. The only currency which will settle the terrible debt will be the loser's noble lifeblood....

http://www.david-black.co.uk

Printed in Great Britain
by Amazon.co.uk, Ltd.,
Marston Gate.